Over the Rusty Gate

Also by Maureen Mitson and published by Ginninderra Press

Paper Chase

Jumping the Cracks

Take Time… (Pocket Poets)

Insulae (Pocket Places)

Beatrice's Commonsensical Approach

Rupe (Pocket People)

Esther's Wars

Maureen Mitson

Over the Rusty Gate

Over the Rusty Gate
ISBN 978 1 76041 417 7
Copyright © Maureen Mitson 2017
Cover photo: Maureen Mitson

First published 2017 by
GINNINDERRA PRESS
PO Box 3461 Port Adelaide 5015
www.ginninderrapress.com.au

1

Day Twelve since leaving Australia and Andy was sitting on a branch high up a giant English horse chestnut tree.

He'd left his mother in their holiday rental – called the Barn – organising their link to the internet. Andy reckoned a quick walk and look around the place would be good after all the travelling then the big London city smells.

So this is the Singleton Park that Gran's always on about. It's all trees and birds. Couldn't walk on London's grass, signs everywhere saying KEEP OFF. Houses were all squeezed upwards to fit together, like the people. Thousands. Here, houses are kilometres apart but Mum says I don't need a mountain bike to get around. Walking's too slow to get anywhere.

'Exercise those long legs of yours, Andy, for now. I've put some lunch in your pack, all ready. We'll see about a bike later, when we're into a routine, okay?'

'What routine? Just get us on the 'net, Mum. In touch and connecting, and all that stuff. So I can talk to Tom – and Dad.'

He knew he had to keep fit for cricket when he got back, and with a bike he could explore more, get around better. All his mum wanted was to get on with her freakin' book.

Then he saw the tree. *Well, it's not the gym, but it is exercise. Massive big horse chestnut tree, so it's called. Dunno if we have 'em in Aussie.*

He didn't time himself climbing up but by the time he reached his present perch he was stuffed. He was way up high; the sheep below looked like little dots.

Good for the biceps, Ando. The tree branch he'd reached was narrower than the ones below but still too fat to sit astride and lock his ankles together. He leant back to feel more steady. He tried to remember when he last climbed a tree. *Never seen one big as this anyway. It's a freakin' monster. Bigger than the Moreton Bay figs near the zoo – ones me and Tom were climbing when we got told off by that gardens bloke.*

He leaned forward to peer through the leaves ahead. *Ahah, there's the Big House our Mrs Reeves talks about.*

Whoa…what the heck? Jet engines. A distant rumble – an overhead roar – a retreating boom. The air seemed to tremble, the branches around him quivered. Sound waves caused the leaves around him to tremble then fall. Andy's ears popped and opened up again. He gripped the branch tighter between his knees to keep his balance. *Wow.*

It was a flight, a trio of swept-wing jet fighters shooting over the Tree. Craning upwards, he caught a flash of silvery green, a streak of red, white and blue. He blinked and as he opened his eyes, they'd already gone.

Woohooo. Jets. Combat, action fighters. He leaned forward and thrust a branch aside, just in time to watch their glowing after-burners disappearing into the distance. *Crikey. Their air force uses this quiet place for training flights. Great.*

He grinned. *Hope to see more of those jets. Could be a flight path. Who cares about noise – not this Ando. And gotta admit, some view from here. Over there's a line of sea meeting the sky an' turn round, Ando…*

Up behind him, the hill continued sweeping upwards till it met a long stone wall. He reckoned there was a road on the other side of it. Using the little compass on his mobile, he saw that where the sea seemed to meet the sky in that distant place was due west. Another direction, peering down the meadow, he could see their rental – the Barn – standing at the bottom of the long tree-lined drive.

He looked again at the Big House. It must be the one that their landlady, Mrs Reeves, talked about. She said it was lots of flats; he called them apartments. Its massive roof simply bristled with antennae and discs. *Have to be kids living there.*

He switched his mobile to record. 'So all this is Singleton Park. So bloomin' quiet. Lot o' space an' nobody in it. S'pose it's sort of interesting seeing where Gran used to live as a kid. And from all her old photos, this has to be the tree she used to climb. Yeh, over an' out.'

'Okay, Tree, Mr Horse Chestnut, she told me to talk to the trees so are you listening, Mr Tree? Keep your branches steady, please.' He grasped the next branch above and swung his long leg over to sit astride.

This branch was narrower than the one down below. This one he *could* straddle and lock his ankles together underneath. *Cool. Now where's my drink? Wow – I'm higher than I thought. This tree is massive.*

'Crikey, Mr Tree – this is nearly like being up in a chopper. All those sheep down there are like little black and white beetles from up 'ere. 'S just like that chopper flight I had for my birthday over London. Decent ride, that was. Blast.' He lost his pop top, couldn't catch it and down it bounced, off one and then another bough, bounce, roll, bounce…heading for the ground below.

Stupid sheep'll get a shock. 'Hoi, sheep. Get outta the way.'

He sat back on his bough. 'Okay, Tree. Beaut planes, but I was promised other kids around here to hang out with. Real kids who I'd talk to and they'd talk back. Tree? So where are they? Indoors watching TV or on the Play Station?'

He pulled a leaf from his hair. *That's a thought. They might have the PSVR here already – top o' the range and with virtual reality. England's sometimes quicker than Aussie. Wow! What wouldn't I give for one of those… Okay, back to the* real *world, Ando. That Big House roof is flamin' massive. Lookit those chimneys. TV aerials and satellite discs, at least twenty. Must get shows from all over the world. Sure, certain and f'r a fact, as Mrs Reeves says. But that garden's not so friendly, I'm thinking. It's a bit like that London park telling us to 'keep off the grass'.* 'D'you agree, Tree? Whaddya reckon? All big pots and statues, can't set up a wicket on that lawn. There's a blue four-wheel drive parked up at one end on gravel, looks like a Hilux. And that big gate, a long white one like the one at the bottom of the drive next to us. Ours stays wide open as well.'

He sat back. 'Okay, Mr Tree, that's the Big House. Pr'aps I'll go there tomorrow and look for some new faces.'

2

His lonely voice was answered only by the wind rustling the leaves around him. Even the sheep's baaing from below was faint.

'If this keeps on, Tree. You'll be all I have to talk to. How am I going to last out three months in this place without going somewhere, meeting other kids? Imagine being BORED for all the time. But other kids here are all on the summer holidays. So that could be good for hanging out if they aren't going away… Wonder if those RAF aircraft come back? Looked like our FA18s. Shake this place up a bit, be good. You know, Mr Tree, it's not like London.' He mumbled with his mouth full of crisps, 'All those cars, trucks, big red buses and planes – helluva noisy place. Smells too. Worse 'n Sydney. Old buildings and palaces, big white swans on lakes in parks, enough's enough o' them. An' that old King Henry's suit of armour – he was some obese guy – in fact, that massive Tower wasn't bad for a visit. It's a thousand years old – nothing as old as that at home. Bet you're not that old, Mr Tree.'

A gust of wind rustled the leaves around his head and blew his hair over his face. Some leaves and a twig fell down onto his pack. He heard a harsh 'caw, caw.' Crows? They were causing the twigs and leaves to fall on him, big wings in landing mode.

He opened his sandwiches. *Peanut paste sarnies – yeah, okay, a banana and a bottle of water at the bottom, yay good one, Ma. All this nosh, hah… I know: she wants to make sure I stay out as long as poss. Wants to get on with her book. Hope that IT bloke's been…*

He leaned back against the tree trunk. Through the branches he saw a big crow fly away from the tree up a bit higher. London. *Big birds like that at the Tower. That red-coated guard in the skirt, he reckoned it was a legend that a massive disaster will happen if they fly away. No mistake – it was an awesome place, London. Better than on TV. Specially when Mum booked me that chopper flight on my birthday. Fan-bloody-tastic.* 'Sorry, Tree.'

He wriggled around to escape from a knot of wood under his backside. He stuffed the last of a sandwich into his mouth as he remembered the last days in London.

'You know, Mr Tree, most people there looked just the same as people do in Aussie, same clothes – well, mostly. Those kids walking round in patchwork gear held together with big baby nappy pins, though – called it fashion. Some had cracked boots on their feet and odd socks under old camo-cargoes. Girls had weird black tops and holey tights up their legs looking like they ran outta money, an' black paint, heavy, round their eyes, and bright red lips. Looked like pandas with their throats cut. Others had black lipstick and real white faces. Mum called 'em Goths an' Punks. I called 'em free to choose – *they* didn't get dragged to where trees and grass grow an' nobody else…'

That was the day he'd texted his dad to try out the setting in his new mobile and had an answer back, pronto. From the Top End half a world away.

AWESOME. ENJOY. Luv, Dad. X

'Can you hear me, Tree? This is just plain boring sitting here and you not talkin' back. At least London was NOT BORING.'

He peeled the banana, remembering one he ate while he was looking at old King Henry's armour. They saw the place on Tower Green where kings and queens and other folk who got fat King Henry angry had their heads chopped off.

Take note: Andrew wishes capital punishment to be restored – I know a few likely candidates, effin' Rezzo and his mob at school for a start. And how about ol' Potts?

Andy grinned widely at the mental vision of the principal

kneeling by the block and waiting for the axe to fall and his ugly old head to roll. He laughed out loud, spraying banana mush all over the leaves in front of him.

Yes, they'd been busy days in London. He remembered the London Eye – a big wheel – that went high over the River Thames; even higher than where he was perched up this bloomin' horse chestnut tree. It was an awesome ride.

Then on his birthday his mother took him to the Lords' Cricket Ground. Day to remember, that was – credit where due, Mother. Awesome. Andy closed his eyes imagining Ponting, Clarke, Warne – all the famous Aussie players running over the pitch to score the runs. He was actually allowed to walk on the green at one end and watch a practice game for a while. Hallowed turf, Mum called it. Cadet teams were the players that day. He'd decided to look it up on Google. A guy could wish.

Then as a special present his mother bought him that flight in the blue chopper. From up high he saw the Emirates Stadium, the Arsenal soccer team's home ground, as well. Awesome stuff.

At dinner that night, Mum said that day had been their last in London. Okay by Andy. Back in his hotel room, he pushed the plugs of his MP3 into each ear and stretched flat on his back, letting the raw energy of the music revive him. His mother did her reviving under the shower. He was supposed to start packing for an early start in the morning so he reckoned he'd do his planning listening to some decent music.

Stretched out on that bed, tapping his fingers to the rhythm and sound of one of his favourite tracks from One Direction's *Steal My Girl* album he decided he needed some new stuff to play. Get a few downloads soon as we're online. Let's get up there to this place and get connected, Mother.

Next morning they collected their hire car and headed off to Singleton Park, checked into their rental and got settled, as Mum put it.

3

Perched up the tree and remembering, Andy grimaced. *London's a different world to this place. Okay, Ando, head home to that computer and send some emails.*

A big ugly black crow suddenly flew in through the branches, squawked at Andy and took off again without perching but it gave Andy a shock.

'Nick off, bird. Come back, did yer?'

He started to clamber down, wishing he'd worn gloves. His hands were getting sore from grasping and gripping on the rough bark. Then his fingers touched a smooth, flat area on the trunk, just above the next branch he was going to stand on. *Huh? Different.* He sat astride, facing the flat bit.

It was a smooth ring in the bark. Like polished. Big as a dinner plate. Magic.

'Un-be-lieve-abubble. Mother, you'd want to see this. Probably some abnormality. Maybe got damaged hundreds of years ago when it was young.'

He rubbed his palm over and around the shape, feeling the difference where the smooth edges of the pattern melded with the rough bark. His finger traced over a split.

He breathed out, noisily. 'Oy, Mr Tree – someone's carved something.' He traced the cuts with his finger. *Like an M. Okay, next comes a circle – an O and down and across – that's the letter L. No more, so that's M O L. Wonder who Mol… Crikey – it's Gran's initials. My Gran musta been here. Yonks, aeons ago. That's why it's not too sharp on the edges. Reckon she knew about this, that's why she kept on talking about this tree. I'll get a pic and send it to her.*

This is real evidence. This is where she was. More 'n that, she did it half a century ago an' it's still here. Weird.

He pulled his mobile from his safely zipped pocket, checked for the signal, and took a pic of the shiny dinner plate thing. He thought his Gran would like that.

Rain had started plopping from the leaves above onto him and onto the branches. 'Mr Tree, your English rain sure is wet stuff – every drop goes plop 'n' sinks in. Have you enjoyed my company? The birds can have you back now.'

Dunno what the other kids back home would say – me, hero of the cricket scoreboard, basher of sleazy knicker-pickers – talking to a tree. Laughing to himself, he gingerly descended, growing wetter as the foliage seemed to lessen and the rain increased.

It was good to get on the ground again. All the sheep panicked and scattered as he landed. He spotted his pop top bottle down the slope. It'd lost the top and most of its contents. He looked for the pull-top and then the rain started bucketing down. *Forget it, Ando.*

He ran across the meadow towards Mrs Reeves's back fence, his backpack bobbing and his backside wet and stained from the wet climb down on the branches. In all the time he'd been away, he hadn't seen a single person to talk to. Pickles ran over woofing and wagging in welcome. Andy grinned. *Who needs kids when there's a dog around?*

***

Mum was full of questions.

'Climbed a massive horse chestnut tree, Mum. Must be the one in Gran's old photo. Great view from up top.' He waited for her eyebrows to shoot upwards. Sure enough.

'Andy, I hope you were careful.'

'Can't get to a gym here, Mum. At least it's exercise.'

'Mmm. Looks like Mrs Reeves is right, lots of flats. Usually means lots of people, Andy. Should be other kids up there to hang out with. That would be great. I really hope so, son. I don't want you to be lonely or bored while we're here.'

Course she doesn't. She just wants to get on with her book and not have to think too much about me. Mother, motherrrr. I don't care – means I'll be free to do more of my own thing. Let me get a bike…

His mum was telling him all about the computer technician. They were now connected to an Internet service provider.

'Cool. So we're on the Internet? Double cool.'

'Andy, what's happened to wicked or weird? They at least I know.'

He laughed and got up from the table. 'Okay, Mum, get the message. They're only words. Hey look at this pic. Gran's been doin' graffiti.'

Mum laughed but was as thrilled about it as he was. 'She'll be chuffed to see the initials, Andy. Do send it off to her. Nice thought, that. But do give her plenty of time to get back to you. Not everybody checks emails every day, you know. And Andy, I'm sorry to be a bore but Potts'll want to see that journal when you get back if we want you to be reinstated for Term 4. Do get some writing done.'

Later that evening, Andy dutifully sat on his bed, thinking what to add to his journal if Potts were to see it. He wasn't really in the mood for writing but he could write about the Tree. He grinned at the idea of his old Gran – who came on strong about vandalism and graffiti and stuff – carving chunks out of a tree to leave her initials. Right or wrong, it gave him a good feeling to find them.

His newly washed gear was on his bed to put away so he knew his mum must've tried out the washing machine. On top of the pile was that funny little green marble Gran had given him; must've fallen out his pocket.

Mum says it's agate, and worn to a sphere with age. Like who played marbles in history? An' it's more wobble than roll. Sure isn't spherical. Gives me a funny feeling in my hand. P'raps it's really ancient, from Egyptian sands or Biblical times. Like that Rosetta Stone… Oh yeah.

He put it in the pocket of his camouflage pants, thinking he'd wear those next day when he investigated the Big House.

Good to get that pic off to Gran; good to be in touch with the world again.

His Mum was pleased too. All her files and research books were in place by the computer, ready for some serious work.

'I'll be able to get going with my book again, son, meet those deadlines.' Then, yet again, 'You'll not get bored and lonely while we're here, will you, Andy?'

Andy had no intention of getting bored. Failing all else, he had a couple of DVDs to watch and the Call of Duty game, *Modern Warfare 3. Update coming out soon, they said. Great. Should be able to get it here quicker than in Oz. Mum says it looks brutal. She would.*

Kneeling up on his bed, his head almost on the beams above, he stretched out of the little window. Although it was nearly eight-thirty at night, it was still daylight – and raining. Dog Pickles didn't care. He was lying in the wet, totally engrossed in gnawing on a bone next to the downpipe.

***

Andy grinned and settled back, his journal on his knee. *Okay, Ando – new page – First Impressions of Singleton Park. Bloomin' Potts…get it over with.*

He thought back to their arrival. Pickles had come bouncing and barking around the side of the house as they pulled into the parking space, his black and white doggy coat shimmering and a bushy tail flicking from side to side in welcome. Then Mrs Reeves opened the red-painted front door and waved. She was about his mum's age, which surprised Andy, who'd expected an older woman.

'I see Pickles has introduced himself,' smiled Mrs Reeves. 'I've got the kettle on, then we'll get you settled round the back. You must be shattered after travelling all that way, and then driving.' She quickly produced a hot cup of tea for Mum, a cold Coke for Andy, and the key to their rental in the back garden. A wooden plaque proclaimed it 'The Barn'.

Mrs Reeves smiled. 'It started out as a barn, way back. Stored a tractor or two later. We modernised it inside, thinking It'd be good for my husband's mother to live in, but she's gone now, so it's good to have it put to use.'

Andy reckoned that must be the 'old' Mrs Reeves who Gran knew before.

Okay, is that all I've got to write about? Written about London, now this place, but it's not what I'd call EXCITING.

He clicked his pen top again, in and out, in and out, looking round his little bedroom. Leaning over to switch on the light, he started a new page in the journal for his Discovery of Gran's Tree – and its secret places and carvings.

Tongue in the corner of his mouth, he soon completed his entries. *Great, all done an' dusted. Mum'll keep off my back now for a while. Wonder if Potts'll read this? Bet he won't.*

4

Next morning, his mother was eager to get to work on her book. She practically chased him out the house. 'Do keep your mobile switched on, Andy.'

'Promise, Mum. I can't wait to see if kids actually live at that Big House. And who drives the big Prado, Hilux – or whatever… Thanks for the snacks. Oh yeah, got Gran's old marble this time, 'case I find her stables like she wanted.'

He patted his pocket and fancied he felt it warm on his skin through the fabric. Whatever ancient quartz it was made of, it wasn't cold like glass. Almost as if it was pleased to be back where it came from, like Gran had said. He had to laugh. *So Gran calls it a lucky marble. Whatever. Who plays marbles?*

The air outdoors was warm and filled with smells. *Maybe the warm sun brings 'em out. Not smelly traffic ones, though.* He sniffed and rated fruity whiffs, sheep pongs and, in one place where hundreds of yellowy wasps clustered around a tree trunk, a waft of sugary honey. *Crikey – best steer clear.*

The long driveway was lined on both sides with huge trees. Their thick canopies meeting each other made him feel he was in a tunnel. He spun round and round, looking up through the tunnel roof. *Don't remember this from yesterday. Well, not so many of 'em. Didn't Gran call them copper beeches? Deep red coloured leaves.*

He laughed and called out to the wind and the birds. 'Hey, world. This city boy's looking at trees. I'm free an' can do what I want an' I'm gonna see who's at that Big House. Gotta problem wi' that?'

His Mum had rattled on about this place over a cup of cocoa last night. 'I was so pleased, Andy, to find this flat on the Internet. It was such a happy coincidence and it's so quiet and peaceful after London, isn't it? I sometimes feel we're in a different world, one where time stands still.' She drained her cocoa. 'I might even get my book finished earlier than I thought.'

Andy thought of this as he hopped and strolled up the drive. *Mum had said three months we'd be here. Originally. But it's much too soon to think of going back. Here in England the schools are still on holiday for the summer. At home they're already back. What school would I have had to go to if I hadn't come here? Dad moves around too much for me to go to him at the mo. Maybe next year…*

He broke into a run. He could feel the little green marble bumping against the front of his leg from the zip pocket in his camos. It was quite heavy for its size.

Andy began to whistle – it was a 'good feeling' sort of a day.

Soon he came to the end of the tunnel of trees, revealing a big patch of sky. *Okay, here's the big gate. Or is it?* He frowned. 'Hey. This is weird, mega… This isn't the gate I saw yesterday from the Tree. That one was big, yeah, painted white and wide open. Like ours at the bottom of the drive. This gate's shut tight, closed. An' it's lopsided an'…well it looks not used. Hasn't been for *yonks*.'

A rabbit, startled by the sound of his voice, ran out of a clump of grass and took off over the field. Andy watched it head towards the Tree where he'd climbed only yesterday.

He moved nearer to check out the gate. It was the same solid sort he'd expected but this was not the same one he'd seen from the Tree only yesterday. *Can't be. No way.*

A heavy chain, coated in peeling rust, tied it to a concrete post. And that was set square into the ground. The paint on the gate's crossbars had been white. Once. Now it was greyish and peeling. Moss and lichen covered much of the timber and the bottom crossbar at the other end sloped out from the wall like a hinge had given way. The metal drop-latch looked as if it was rusted into place. Andy tried to knock it upwards but it wouldn't move.

This is weird. I know it opens, I saw it yesterday – from just over there. He waved his hand towards the tree halfway up the meadow. *Makes sense. Or does it? Must be another way in, near here.*

A faded wooden plaque had slipped from one of the struts and he tilted his head to read it aloud. '"TRESPASSERS WILL BE PROSECUTED". Huh. Is that so? We'll see.'

He tossed his pack over the gate, and with a heave and a roll fell headlong onto gravel on the other side.

5

'Oy. Who are you?'

Andy got to his feet. He brushed down his pants and looked at the speaker. The boy looked about his own age and was standing feet apart, knuckled hands on his hips and with a fierce expression on his face. He wore a short-sleeved checked shirt with a couple of buttons undone on the front and some muddy streaks down the side. His knee-length grey shorts were stained with blotches of ink or paint, and on his feet were old canvas sandshoes, no socks. His hair was shaved short around his ears and up the back of his head but it bobbed thick and blondy-brown above his eyebrows.

'I saw your rucksack first. Then you. You're trespassing. I live 'ere.'

Andy raised his hands in mock surrender. 'So do I. We're staying with Mrs Reeves.'

'Whaddya mean, stying? You talk a bit odd you do. You American?' As he spoke, the boy held out a grubby hand, took Andy's and shook it. 'How d'ya do'.

'American? No way. I'm Australian but my grandparents came from England.'

'Got an aunty in Melbourne. Do you live near there?'

Andy started to explain just as another boy in a go -cart whizzed from the side of the house and came to a screeching halt nearby.

The first boy pointed at Andy. 'This lad's just come over t' gate from the Reeveses and 'e's from Australia.' He turned back to Andy. 'I'm Jimmy and this is Billy on his dinky.'

Billy was just a bit taller than Jimmy, though not as tall as Andy. His eyes were so blue they sparkled and he had the beginnings of a dark moustache below his sunburnt nose. He too wore shorts above the knee that exposed suntanned muscular legs. His hair was chopped off in the same fashion as his brother but was very black.

'G'day, mate. Name's Andy. Do you live here as well?'

'Yes, I'm 'is big brother. You talk funny, you do. Is that the way all Australians talk?' Billy let the dinky fall on its side then came over to shake Andy's hand. Blue eyes assessed blue eyes; almost on the same level. 'How do, Andy.'

Andy was indignant. 'Me talk funny! You don't? Listen to you. Don't you ever watch *Neighbours*? It's high in the ratings, and they all talk like me.' He laughed and shook his head. 'not me. I'm into *Dr Who*.'

Billy turned to catch his cart before it ran too far.

Jimmy frowned at Andy. 'Why should we watch neighbours? It's enough hard work keepin' out of their way. And what's ratings?'

'Hey, you serious? Television – rating which programmes are best.'

Billy spoke up from the seat of his wooden cart. 'We saw Coronation on television at Uncle Colin's. He made it. It had a little screen nearly six inches long and we could watch it happening from cameras in the abbey. Just like newsreels at the pictures but this was while it happened. Smashing, it was.'

Andy's thoughts were rampant. *Six inches? About fifteen centimetres. Like my old DS. No TV? Bummer. Should have realised – Jimmy's haircut and old clothes – this is maybe an orphanage. Or something. Better be careful what I say.*

He gave a nervous cough. 'Wow, not bad to make your own TV. My mum always says how she wished she could've seen the moon landings in colour instead of black an' white. I've seen 'em a few times since, repeated and digitalised. 'Course I wasn't born when it happened either.'

Billy looked at Jimmy with his eyebrows raised.

Not very talkative, this pair. Oh, I know… Pulling out a pack of Smith's Crisps, he offered them around. 'Have a chip – they're chicken and chives, hope that's okay.'

'Crisps. Bags I the salt.' Billy grabbed the bag and fossicked through.

'Silly duffer, they're already flavoured,' cried Andy. These boys sure were the oddest he'd met in years. 'Mum an' me went shopping coupla days ago.'

Billy and Jimmy looked at each other, their mouths full of chicken and chives, and Billy nodded. 'Come on up to our house and Mam'll give us all a drink. Save what you've got left, Andy, and you can tell her where you got them.' He laughed. 'I thought you meant chips – you know, hot ones. These we call crisps, like on the packet. But hey, these are smashers and a lot better than what my mam gets.'

It was Andy's turn to look puzzled. Mum always got him the Smiths assorted packs. He chose the flavours when he was with her; the supermarket shelves were full of them.

He followed the boys up the stony drive, round the end of the Big House and through a tall gate into a cobbled backyard. A green door was open above a pair of steps. A black and white dog ran out to meet them.

'Hey, you look just like Pickles.'

'Huh? This is Panty – see his back legs, black with white socks? Collie he is, good stock.'

Andy was led into a hallway and then a warm kitchen. A woman dressed in a wrap-around flowery apron like his gran's was putting black barbecue coals onto a fire behind a high grate. Bits were falling and sparking onto some bricks below as she prodded it into huge glow of flame. Looked like hot, hard work. Andy had seen nothing like it before and reckoned his own mother wouldn't be pleased if they had one like that in The Barn. Finally, placing the poker onto a hook on a stand, the woman turned to them with a smile, rubbing her hands on her apron.

'Jimmy, I was calling you. I asked you ages ago to bring some coke in from the little shed.' She gave Andy a quick look up and down, her smile widening. 'Who's this tall lad in the army keks?'

Billy was teasing the dog and Jimmy answered. 'This is Andy. He's from Australia and he's staying with the Reeveses, Mam.'

'That's nice. I didn't know they had visitors. You're from Australia for the holidays, are you, Andrew?'

'Just Andy, please. Yes, my mum's writing a book and we're here so she can see her publisher. And what's army keks?'

Jimmy grinned. 'Mam, Andy speaks different from us.' He turned to Andy to explain. 'Keks is what we call slacks sometimes, or kekkies for shorts.' He looked at Andy's camo-cargoes. 'Yours are long kekkies or mebbe short keks.'

Both boys laughed.

'Andy gets some great comics, too, Mum. Better 'n Dan Dare he is. Seen men walking on moon, he has.'

Andy stared at Jimmy. *Weird kid.*

'Has he now? Well, I'm sure you know to keep your stories not too frightening for the smaller children, Andy. My lads know the rules.'

Andy reckoned she said it like you wouldn't answer back. He nodded quickly. 'Er, are you a real family then? I mean, is this Big House all yours?'

Their mother laughed as she put three glasses on the table. 'Bless you, lad, no. We live in this middle bit and we've neighbours both sides.' She poured what looked like Coke into the glasses. 'Here you are then, Andy. Now, what sort of book is your mother writing?'

Andy took a big sip. 'Ooh,' he grimaced, and then remembered his manners. 'Sorry, but this Coke's lost its fizz.'

'Coke?' Jimmy laughed. 'Coke is what Mam burns on t' fire. This is dandelion and burdock. Hasta never 'ad it afore?'

Jimmy was growing more curious about this stranger and Andy was finding Jimmy harder to understand. Who burned Coke on a fire? He finished his drink, not sure whether he'd enjoyed it or not.

'Thank you, Mrs…Missus. Er, Mum's book, she calls it a social commentary, fiction based on fact. Thanks again for the drink.'

The boys beckoned Andy back outside. The black and white dog chased after Billy, who was quickest out of the tall gate.

'Panty. Come on, Panty,' yelled Billy. 'Rabbits.'

Jimmy stayed behind. He was curious about this Australian. He took Andy up to a couple of huge tractor tyres swinging on ropes from tall, thickset trees. 'Tip rain out first, Andy, an' jump in. Let's have a smashing swing an' you can tell us all about where you come from. First things first: what else you got in that rucksack?'

Jimmy marvelled at the pop top of green lime cordial. 'By heck. You pull the drink thing out with your teeth and then push it back in not to spill.'

Billy joined them to swig from the pop top. 'Forget the rabbits.'

Andy was stuck for words. *They don't know chips and they don't know pop tops.*

'Okay. Well, I live in Adelaide with my mum. It's the capital of South Australia, sort of near the middle bottom of the map. My dad's gone to live in Darwin in the Top End – that's like eleven o'clock on the map.

Billy nodded. 'I know how you mean and I know what the Australia map looks like. Your dad lives a long way away from you. Why's that? His work?'

'Yer, he's a mining engineer. Goes where the job is.'

Billy patted him on the back in sympathy. 'Long way between yer. Bet you miss your dad, dontcha?'

Andy didn't want to talk about it and changed the subject. 'My gran knows this part of the country. She told me lots of stories about this place, and the farms near here.'

He stopped suddenly. Hadn't Gran talked of a Billy? *I'd better learn what's what here before I say too much.*

'Hey, Jimbo. How old are you? I'm fourteen. Two weeks ago.'

'Hey, Andy – I like being called Jimbo. I'll be thirteen in October. Billy was fourteen last month. He goes into Lower Fourth form next year an' only two more after that maybe, lucky beggar. You an' him's about same age. I'm half an inch bigger 'n him – that gets him hoppin' mad. You're bigger 'n both of us. Are all Australians tall like you?'

Andy laughed. 'My mate Tom gets pissed off because I'm taller 'n him. And I have another three years at school after this one if I wanna go to university.'

Jimmy put both feet through the middle of his tyre and pushed off. 'Biggest push gets biggest swing. And, Andy, don't let our Molly, that's my sister, hear you swear like that, even outside. She'd tell. My dad hates swearing anywhere.'

Whatever. 'Okay.'

6

'What's that you keep saying?' asked Jimmy as he banged into Andy's tyre and they bounced off each other.

Billy ran back to the house, whistling Panty to follow.

'Your brother doesn't say much, does he?'

Jimmy defended his brother to this new lad. 'Billy's got a lot on. And a project for school to finish off.'

'Erm… Well, okay means just like, you know, all right,' replied Andy, swinging deliberately into Jimmy's tyre. 'Wowie. Gotcha.'

Andy soon got the hang of bouncing off the tree trunks and spinning. Going backwards he could get really high then swing forwards over the bank. He just hoped the ropes would hold – they looked a bit green and battered and the tyres were huge and heavy. But soon he was kicking off higher than Jimmy. They slowed down for a while and Jimmy explained about the birds above in the treetops.

'Them's rooks.' He pronounced it 'rewks'. 'They're territorial birds, don't like us trespassing on their patch.'

That was language Andy understood. He pointed over to a tall building with nearly all one side of it open and with what looked like a big glass and metal roof. 'What's that over there? Is it a garage for your car?'

'Nah, that's where Russell keeps his old car. Used to be old stables…'

'The stables? Wow. I nearly forgot.'

The aggie. Andy slipped down the middle of his tyre to stand on the worn grass. He took the agate marble from his pocket and rolled it around in his hand. Funny old thing – felt warmish and hummed on his palm like a fresh egg feels when you take it from under the chook.

Jimmy was curious and came to see what Andy had taken from his pocket. 'By 'eck, it's an aggie, a prize big un at that. Did yer win it?'

Andy explained about Gran and Jimmy looked at him with a grin on his face.

'My grandma bakes us little loaves of bread but I've never seen 'er on t' floor playin' marbles. Your Gran must be somethin' special.' He held out his hand for the green marble and rolled it around on his palm. He was careful with it, gentle and almost respectful. 'I useter 'ave a smaller one made of summat like this but I lost it to a lad with a steely.'

Andy listened carefully, trying to catch every word. It wasn't hard to understand Jimmy if he listened carefully. He remembered Mum explaining about steelies and alleys and other marbles. Is all this why Gran wanted him to bring this aggie back here? *'Cos it belongs here?*

Then Jimmy dragged a couple of big white marbles from the pocket in his shorts. He rattled others still pocketed. 'Gi' yer a game,' he grinned. 'Come on, Australia. I'll use these potties first, though. Steelies could be too heavy for your aggie.'

'Jimbo, I've not played marbles for yonks. I'm as rusty as that old gate down there. Still, I'll have a go, see how the aggie goes,' replied Andy. He hoped he'd remember how to play. *Flick with m' big finger off m' thumb, that's it.*

Jimmy winked at him and took off towards the stables. 'Ohhhhkaaaay, Andy. We've both got shooters an' I've got a big glassie for target, eh? We'll play a chase game, shall us? Stable floors are smooth for lying on.'

Andy clenched his fists in a victory salute 'Yes.' He knelt down near Jimmy. *This was Gran's stables. This is the right place. Wow.*

Floor wasn't the best. Lots of old flagstones joined together. Big ones but not very flat. *Okay, so it's only a fun game…*

It turned out to be more fun than Andy expected, though he soon realised every game of marbles was a serious one for this Jimmy. As raindrops plopped onto the mouldy green glass roof above them, Andy realised he needed to forget all about little kids' games back in primary school. *This marble game is not just a game for this kid.* Jimmy was very solemn and technical; spanned his fingers to measure distances and squinted at angles. He laughed that Andy was 'rusty'. He positively chortled when Andy carefully dusted off the knees of his camos. Hearing the word 'rusty' again, reminded Andy about the big white gate mystery.

'Huh? It's never open, not that gate. Supposed to keep fell ramblers out. Our dad uses top drive gate onto Paddy Lane. In fact, everyone does. There's only one gate, Ando. Can't yer count?'

What are fell ramblers? Andy had no time to ask or retort, Jimmy was on with the game. *He's hot, this kid. Gotta watch him. He's all technical an' wanting to win, an' I've gotta win some of his if I'm to keep playin'.*

He took note of Jimmy's careful calculating, his shooting techniques, and was well pleased to win one of Jimmy's potties and then an alley. *This game has rules.* He resolved to look it up online when he got home. He was pleased not to lose Aggie. He hadn't brought her back to the stables to lose her. That reminded him about the time, and he checked his mobile. It had gone flat. Dead as a dodo. Must be a dud battery…had it on charge overnight.

'Come back tomorrer, Andy, if yer can. Yer ohkay for an Aussie.' Jimmy sang it again and tossed his biggest alley up in the air. 'Ohkay, okey dokey.' He grinned. 'We'll play again, eh? Boss or Holey…?'

Andy waved assent and ran back over the gravel. He flung himself over the top bar of the gate and ran off down the drive. His mobile chirped. Signal back. Wasn't the battery then. Black spot, that's why…but Mum had texted to ask where he was. Oops.

He strolled in the door of the Barn still reading the message.

His mum was sitting at the table drinking a coffee. 'Andy, you look filthy. What have you…?'

'It's only dust from the stables floor, Mum. Had a good game of marbles with a kid called Jimmy.'

'Marbles, Andy? Marbles. You do surprise me. How many times recently have you told me marbles is a kids' game and you aren't a kid any more?' She raised her eyebrows. 'Guess that old aggie started this off. Well, what's this Jimmy like?'

Andy took a coke from the little fridge. 'He's nearly thirteen, in October I think he said. He's okay in that he acts older some times and at other times he's a typical kid.'

She couldn't resist it… 'Oh, right. You who are only just fourteen can remember what a typical kid acts like?'

'Moth-er. But it is a bit weird. They call Coke what they burn on the fire. It's a fuel. They've no TV an' they don't know what a tumble drier is for clothes.

'Andy, however did that come into the conversation?'

'Well, we were swinging on the tyres and Jimmy said it was near his mum's washing line. Oh, Mum, it just started us talking, you know? They called my backpack a rucksack and yer know what? They don't say "the" in front of things. They just miss it out, the whole word. They talk really different, that's for sure. And their mum's a real greenie like you. They call her Mam.'

Mum laughed. 'Andy, I'm not a greenie. It's just that I'm environmentally aware.'

'Okay…and there's Billy, who says he plays cricket at school but only because he has to, whatever that means. He's not real interested in it. You know what? He's never heard of the twenty-twenty series. How about that, eh?'

'How old is this Billy then?'

'Billy? Few weeks older 'n me. He was fourteen in June, and when he goes back to school he's in the Lower Fourth form – whatever that means. I think that's what he said. An' you know, he told me when I talked of the moon landings that I've got more of an imagination than Dan Dare – that's a guy in a comic he gets. Honest, Mum, like Armstrong never walked on it.'

'Just having you on, son. Do they look alike, these brothers?'

'Billy's got black hair, Jimmy's more like me an' Jimmy's taller than Billy.'

'Well, that can happen. And this Billy might be due for a growth spurt, like you had when your hands stuck out of your school blazer's sleeves. Does Billy play marbles too?'

'Dunno if he's as keen, Mum. He really likes school and science and things like that. That's a bit funny too. I told him about Tom and his robotronics at school and he didn't know robots. When I said one group was making a model of the first Sputnik – no, Sputnik 2, because they did a Lego dog to go in it – I had to explain about Sputnik and when I said it was one of the first satellites, he said I was getting mixed up with radio waves going round the earth and stuff like that. What with the moon an' that, I think he's suspicious of me, Mum. Not called me a liar, not quite, anyway. I just don't think he wanted to admit he didn't know about it, Mum.'

'Well, Sputnik was a heck of a while ago, son, before I was born even. I think you should look it up on Wikipedia or something.'

'Yeah, good idea. But from what he said I don't think he's learnt anything about satellites, not for radio transmission or anything. Anyway, back to Jimmy. He'd rather go to another school where he can learn to be a motor engineer but has to wait for another year an' his dad says they'll think about it then. He likes making things, not books, he says.'

'What does their mum do?'

'Funny, that. When I asked, Billy said her job is them and the house. He sounded sort of shocked I'd even thought different.'

'Ahah. That used to be the norm, Andy. That was a woman's role and many women still like to do things that way. If they have the income support and, well, with five or six children, she might be quite content to do that. Good on her.'

'Yeh, but Billy went on to say she's on some committees in the town and she chairs one of 'em and uses a typewriter a lot in the evenings. He said she's always busy. Like you, I reckon.' He grinned.

'A typewriter? You mean a keyboard, computer?'

Andy though for a moment. 'No, he said typewriter and I didn't ask about a computer. They didn't mention one. You know, I don't get it, Mum. They aren't short of money, well, I don't think so, but their mother hasn't got a washing machine and they don't even have a fridge. I said something about keeping drinks cold and Billy said yes, their cellar's cold enough to make ice at times. Their dad has his own business, they have a lovely old car – well, it's one of those old models done up like new – and the boys go to a private school. Well, Mo said it's called a miner public but called it awfully expensive and they have to talk properly there and no local dialect, says Mo. Which is funny. But their dad's not a miner, so…'

'Andy, slow down, son, you're prattling. She means *minor*, I think. It means not so well known…'

'Aw, right. I shoulda got that. But some things they don't seem to know about – things we all know about. Makes it awkward because I feel I can't talk about some things, you know? And I was asked not to swear.' *Wait for it, Ando.*

Right on cue. 'Andy, I hope you didn't.'

He chuckled. 'Oh, Mother. Well, only once. Billy said "bloody", I heard him, and Jimmy said "damnation" when one of his alleys went down a drain. That's as strong as it gets, as they dare.' He stopped, as Mum was laughing her head off.

'Sound like serious greenies, that family, and with good standards. And who's this Mo? If she makes the lads talk properly, well, I wholeheartedly approve, Andy. Words are my interest, as you know, and my business. Are you going there again soon?'

'They asked me for tomorrow. I think I'll go. You know, they're different and seem young in a lot of ways, but Billy is actually older than me. Then they do something or say something that seems responsible in an odd way. Not like kids, I mean.'

'Andy, you seem to have learnt a lot for just a first day's acquaintance. You like them, though, the boys?'

'So far they're okay, Mum. Ah, Mo? She's their sister. She has to be older than me but, you know, she doesn't look it, or dress up in fashion like Rosalie does at home, in Aussie, I mean. They say she's bossy, orders them around. I don't know much about her but she's nice enough to me.' He stopped and looked in the fridge again. 'How about these sausages for tea? I'll peel some spuds if you like. I'm ravenous.

His mother grinned and went to check out the vegetables.

He continued. 'Hey, yeah, that's another thing. Jimmy didn't know what okay meant. And their mother called my camos army keks. They're not easy to understand at times – not only funny words but they pronounce things quite different from us. Yet Jimmy told me I talk funny. He runs all his words together and I have to think what he's saying.'

Mum looked thoughtful. 'Keks is a new word to me, love, must be the local dialect.' It was her turn to grin. 'But it's like when I talk to Mrs Reeves. I have to listen hard sometimes to understand everything she's on about. Interesting, though, isn't it, how people can speak the same language in so many different ways?'

'Sure is. And what's "fells", Mum? Is that the local name for the hills?'

'Just that, Andy. Good thinking.' However, his tale about the crisps had her puzzled. 'Maybe there's a cheap shop around here, Andy. The sort where they sell seconds or stock nearly out of use-by dates. But I've not seen any plain packets with twists of salt inside.' She turned back to him. 'You know, they could be ex-military stock from the Iraq war perhaps. With all those kids, I'm not surprised she shops around. As for whatever they're called, chips or crisps, does it really matter? It's the magic of words, Andy, but in this instance, just call them what's on the packet. Tell you what, next time you go, take a packet for this Billy and Jimmy as well, okay?'

'Cool, thanks. Oh yeah, their mother invited me to stay for tea but I said I had to get home. If they ask me tomorrow, can I be a bit later?'

'Tea? Bet they call their lunch "dinner", like Mrs Reeves does. Well, why not? Okay, Andy, but be back well before dark, okay? That gives you plenty of time.'

Andy explained about his mobile going dead.

'Hmm. You're probably right, Andy. Could be a signal black spot. With all these hills around,' she grinned, 'fells, I mean, it's hardly surprising. Perhaps if you go up that drive often, I'd better buy you one of those cheap watches.'

'Another thing, Mum. It was the Big House where I've been today but when I was up the tree I saw all the TV masts on the roof, too many for three houses, Mum. Can't work that out.'

'Hmm, Andy. I don't know, unless they're old ones and they have new ones put up regularly, but I don't know why they would. I'm sure the explanation will be simple when you find it. Why not mention it to this Billy? Andy, I'll get started on those potatoes, so how about getting on the computer? There's an email from your Gran and she's sent a map of her favourite hidey holes. Hasn't mentioned your pic, though. Give her time.' She shook her head, smiling. 'Whatever do you two chat on about?'

Still smiling, she started the tea as Andy checked Wikipedia before his emails.

He yelled out to his mother, 'Sputnik 1 was launched in 1957, and on Jimbo's birthday, 4 October. He has to know of that, Mum. And how many rockets have there been since then?'

'I must say, Andy, they sound interesting, these new mates of yours.

7

Jimmy really starred at marbles, all the games – Boss, Holey and others. Playing the games was a challenge Andy really enjoyed, to his surprise. Jimmy was really technical in his way of calculating drift, size and weight of the various marbles – all against the lie of the floor – which was something that had never interested Andy.

'Y'know, Jimbo mate, in the marble games I used to play, we usually had coloured glassies. I bought 'em by the bag from K-Mart or somewhere. You look out special marbles for certain moves, pot, glass, steel or agates. I guess my way of playing was like snakes an' ladders to your chess.'

'Aargh, I'm not into chess, myte,' Jimmy grinned. 'Billy goes to school chess club – not my thing, y'know? I have a game of draughts with my dad sometimes, though.'

'Just that your way of playing marbles reminds me of my dad's table war-gaming. You plan strategies 'n' all that – it's just not only whacking a marble with another, is it? You really play serious, an' that makes it more of a challenge, eh? But still good fun.'

Over the next couple of days, Andy improved his game no end – had to or he'd lose the few marbles he'd won. He liked playing Holey best. Jimmy was still quicker to score when they played Boss. However, the little green aggie was a real good luck mascot. She always seemed to find the target even though she looked to be wobbling along. Andy really liked the satisfying 'clunk' she made when she hit a bigger marble. He fancied that her 'clink' when she hit a glassy or a potty sounded just like a big grin.

Then one afternoon, Jimmy asked him to help fix up a little nesting box for a broody hen they had. 'You're winning all me best steelies, myte, an' I've to use me time more usefully, me dad says. Nesting boxes for hens are more important. D'ya want ter give us a hand?'

'We call 'em all chooks,' laughed Andy, 'but yeah, great.'

Jimmy asked him to saw some boards all the same size. 'Twenty-one inches square, Dad wants it. Well, that's three sides and a base.'

'What's that in millimetres? Or centimetres, if you like,' called Andy.

Jimmy was engrossed in looking over a pile of wood offcuts. He didn't hear. *Ahah, the tape's in inches anyway. No worries.*

The saw had a wooden handle and a short blade with big, widely spaced teeth that made quick work of the old timber. Andy was pretty pleased with himself when he'd finished the job, though his arm muscles ached.

Then Jimmy's brother David came out with two small bottles of ginger beer. 'It's from our Mam an' it's for Andy as well. Yer gotta tek bottles in again, Jim.'

It was good stuff and Andy smacked his lips at Jimmy.

'Aye. Mam makes it herself. Got a piece of root and sugar and stuff bubbling in the cellar nearly all the time.'

Something else to tell Mum. Andy put it safely at the back of his mind to interest her later.

Jim had rescued some old nails from his dad's box and while Andy held the boards, Jim hammered them in place.

'Dad never wastes good nails, Ando. He allus uses these cleaned-up ones for jobs like this. They go in straight enough.'

They did too. The nesting box was 'dead level' according to Jimmy and balanced steady enough after he set it up on a couple of bricks.

'I'll show Dad when he comes home. Thanks, Ando. I'd not've

finished it on me own. If Dad likes the work, he'll prob'ly ask me ter mek some more.' He held out his hand to shake Andy's.

Andy had enjoyed sharing the task. 'Good stuff, Jimbo.'

They both laughed and Andy felt good that he'd helped to make something useful. He resolved that if they did make some more, he might suggest they increase the height of the sides at the front edge to enable the roof piece to go on at a slant. Best for when it rains. *This shaking hands is good, too, now I'm getting used to it. It's a feel-good thing.*

On his way down the drive back home that evening, Andy had a lot to think about. *Still no answers about the TV aerials. And if the lads' father is an engineer, how come he doesn't have more modern tools to make up a little chook house in minutes instead of taking longer 'n about an hour for one?*

He really had enjoyed sharing that job with Jimmy… Hey. That explains the tools – they're carbon neutral, o' course. Jimmy said it was all recycled stuff.

It was a good feeling to make something useful and he must remember to tell Mum about their recycled stuff. But there was a bit of a mystery about Billy that Andy was determined to get to the bottom of it. He asked Jimmy, who'd been muttering about how he'd had to do his chores for him these last two days.

'Huh? Billy? He's up in t' attic at top of house doing a holiday project for school – it's a crystal set.'

Andy said no more. He'd never heard of boys making things with crystals. *Could be old rocks and stuff, even like my agate marble. Won't ask. I'll find out sometime.* He didn't like to show his ignorance. Jimbo would only laugh, but Billy got that superior tone in his voice at times when he was talking to Andy. Andy sensed Billy was suspicious of him, maybe didn't really like him. He shrugged. *See if Mum knows anything about crystal sets – might be earth science or something.*

His mother was surprised he was home for tea. 'Thought you

were staying up at the Big House later. No worries. Good to share tea here with you. I'll do some pasta…'

'Great. I'm just in the mood for some spag bog, Mum. I'll do the meat, shall I? Good smell that, mince and onions sizzling in the pan.'

She laughed. 'Go your hardest, chef.'

Later, while winding up the spaghetti onto his fork, he asked her about crystal sets.

'Hmm. Some kind of primitive radio, I think. Your dad made one once, at school.' As a thought struck her she nearly choked, chuckling with a mouthful of pasta, 'Oh Bloke, you didn't think he'd be threading beads, did you?' She grinned at her own joke. 'Probably an elective at his school. Why not check online?' She was fascinated by the home-made ginger beer story and said she might ask Mrs Reeves about it.

Andy was himself quite intrigued when he Googled 'crystal set'. Mum was right, it was also called a crystal radio set and would actually pick up radio station signals. *Is that why Billy went on about radio waves around earth when I was talking about Sputnik? He made some connection and didn't want me to know more 'n him. Huh.* Jimmy had said Billy had got into trouble for pinching a saucepan lid for it. Something Andy couldn't work out. An example online said a capacitor could be fashioned from discs of aluminium. Maybe that's what the saucepan lid was for. Now he'd learned something about crystal sets, he could pick a good time to ask Billy for a look-see.

***

Next day, Billy wasn't around. Jimmy said he did 'some jobs' for ol' Capper sometimes and got paid for it. Jimmy had to do Billy's chores. Jimmy grizzled about this quite a lot, in Andy's opinion. The jobs included sweeping out the generator room from where the big machine generated the electric power for the whole house – or so Jimmy described it. Andy had to wait outside while Jimmy was in that area, as Jimmy explained it was one of his dad's rules.

'On'y one at a time in here, Ando. Too crowded, else…'

So it was. Most of the room seemed to filled with glass containers holding water that had to be kept topped up.

'Battery acid's the risky stuff, Ando. We 'ave to wear gloves and that big apron.'

Seemed a responsible job to Andy. At home they'd be calling in Occ Health and Safety to check on all this. *But Jimmy's very careful and, what's the word, 'precise' in measuring levels of whatever that liquid is. I'll ask him later; interesting.*

However, after Jimmy'd shed his apron and come out, locking the door carefully behind him, he was more intent on getting a drink from their house and then tackling some more nesting boxes.

'Then us'll have a few shots at Boss or Holey after, eh, Andy? Your turn to choose.'

Andy was still weighing up the responsibility shown by Jimmy doing that generator room job – with acid – with the fact he was really only a kid.

Sure enough, Jimmy's dad was pleased with the nesting box and asked if they could fix up another two or three. Andy thought their dad was okay. He looked about the same age as Andy's, but he had black hair, cut short at the back like the lads' and he was about Andy's height. *He's muscly, though. Must be his job does that…* Jimmy said he worked in the family business.

Later, at home, Andy complained to his mother that he still hadn't heard from his gran about his climb up the tree. 'Okay, so climbing a tree isn't exactly exciting, but finding her initials was and she hasn't answered yet.'

'Andy, it definitely went, but you have to be patient. Your

gran doesn't check her emails every day. She might have received it only as she was sending the other one to you, Andy. Give her time. Check tomorrow.'

However, Andy didn't have too much spare time next day to worry about whether Gran had his message or not because he was kept busy at the Big House. He and Jimmy set out to make another four nesting boxes. As before, they shared the tasks but this time changed the side panel measurements as Andy suggested.

'Dunno why I didn't think of that before, Ando,' chortled Jimmy.

Andy also had a thought about roofing them, too, and rescued a large galvo empty paint container from a heap of rubbish. Big thing, must've held at least twenty litres or more. Its handle and rim were gone and the base rusted away, but the curved sides were in good nick, and he had an idea for them…

'Jimbo, got any metal cutters, shears, like?'

'Yeh, somewhere. Why?'

Andy explained his idea. It involved cutting the container in two from rim to base. It took some effort, and both had stiff fingers from gripping and snipping but they had two curved panels when they finished. They flattened the cut edges and then fitted the curved metal as roofs to the nesting boxes, trimming the timber sides to fit.

Jimmy was dancing in delight. 'By 'eck, Ando, that's a bloody good idea. Wait till Dad sees 'em finished.'

Jimmy's dad inspected them that same night and then next day drove home in the middle of the day to bring Andy and Jimmy each a big bar of Cadbury chocolate.

'Smashing job, lads. Real Aussie initiative too, Andy. Thanks. Now instead of tucking into that chocolate already, why don't you both shoot inside and enjoy a good hot dinner?'

'Wow. Cool,' exulted Andy. He was always ready to eat thick

soup and homemade bread rolls with butter. Topped off with chocolate afterwards of course.

Jimmy was excused further chores so he and Andy played a few games of Boss in the stables until it was time for Andy to go home.

Wonder if that initiative I have extends to padding my knees with something. Getting a bit hammered on that stable floor. I'll check with Mum.

He practically ran down the drive home, he was feeling so good about his day. Then his mum said Gran had sent him an email.

'About time.'

She was chuffed with the picture. Said it really 'took her back'. Mum said she had probably gone 'all nostalgic' and had to think carefully about things before answering. Gran called the pattern in the tree trunk a 'deformed bole'. Andy thought that even if it was the right wording, he preferred his own description. She wrote, 'I had quite forgotten about carving my name up there. It was the very last day I was there before we left for Australia.'

He was glad he'd thought to take the pic for her.

'You really struck a chord, Andy,' smiled Mum.

8

Andy went up to see the Singleton Park lads most days. Once or twice, the rain fell so heavily there was no sense venturing out. Andy quite enjoyed a session or two on his DS or PS2; he even brought his journal up to date, at his mother's urging.

'It seems wrong for you to go up there in such bad weather and trailing rain and muddy shoe prints indoors at their place. Why not catch up on your journal, Andy?'

One wet day, Mrs Reeves asked Andy if he'd watch little Jacynta for her for about an hour and a half. 'I have ter go into t' town ter collect a parcel from t' post office, Andy, and she'll mebbes sleep for most of that anyway. An' with it raining cats an' dogs like…'

Andy quite enjoyed the task. He spent about an hour on the carpet playing wooden trains and building houses with big wooden blocks for her to knock down again. *Not a bad kid; don't mind now and again. Keeps Mum off my back.*

His mother was going well with her book. She was pleased when Andy agreed to help Mrs Reeves that day, meaning that she didn't need to offer.

'I would have offered, Andy, but I have to say, when you said yes to Mrs Reeves I was quite surprised – and chuffed. I think if you'd been asked to do something like that for anyone over home, you'd have been quite scathing about even being asked – let alone agreeing. This family up the drive must be having a good influence on you, I think.'

'Huh. Not making a habit of it, Mum, but yeah, the boys' little brothers are okay as kids go. They're cool as long as they

keep out of the way and don't try and nick stuff when Jimbo an'
I are busy.'

'Okay, Bloke. I think I'll arrange a meet with their mother
sometime soon.'

She quizzed Mrs Reeves about the family at the Big House
but Mrs Reeves didn't know them, though she admitted some
kids she didn't recognise had occasionally come down the drive
to 'the bottom gate'.

'If families are going up to t' other end of town, they'd take
the Top Drive and turn left along that part of top road.'

Andy's mum was happy with that. 'I really must walk up and
meet them, especially their mother. She's so good to Andy. She
seems a dedicated greenie. I like that.'

Mrs Reeves nodded. 'Be good to meet her that would. And
tha' can let me in on t'secret about ginger beer, an' all. I've never
done it but I know me mam useter…'

Billy and Jimmy sometimes laughed at the way Andy talked,
but usually gave him a hearty welcome. He teased them about
their accent sometimes, and Jimmy would laugh but Billy didn't
like an Aussie kid criticising his natural language.

'Enough, Aussie. That's our own language, not yours. I speak
it with an accent or without one. You have an Aussie accent all
the time and sound more American than English. I have cousins
in Suffolk down south, and I'd challenge you to criticise the way
they speak it an' I can tell you they *are* hard to understand. The
point is, Aussie Ando, my language is my own.'

'Crikey, our Billy. We've got Aunty whatsername in
Melbourne and those cousins'll talk like Andy as well, so don't
be so hard on him.'

Billy wasn't always as friendly as Jimmy and once even
counselled Jimmy when they were alone not to believe
everything Andy said. 'He tells fibs, our Jim, does Andy. He
invents things just for effect. Look at how he was talking about

that man Armstrong walking on moon. He reads comics and then gets sucked in to believe what's in 'em. Does he think we're gormless, is that what it is? An' if that'd really happened, then o' course we'd know.'

Otherwise, Billy had to admit he liked the way Andy played marbles with Jimmy and stopped Jimmy heckling. He was hoping Andy could keep Jimmy off his back for all the rest of the holidays, so he could really get his attic project completed.

Andy liked Molly. Her brothers called her Mo but she didn't really mind. She would be starting Lower Sixth at school after the holidays.

Then one day he knocked on the door and it was the lads who were not at home.

'They're over at the farm helping Mr Capper wash his pigs.' Molly looked serious. 'Best not to go over, Andy. It's a messy job and you have to know how to handle big pigs. I expect them back about three o'clock or later.'

He nodded and went to turn away, but she tapped his arm.

'No, don't go. Come on in if you like. I've made rock buns and you can meet our cousin Joan.'

Andy liked rock buns; he didn't know about Joan.

'Joan, this is Andy from Australia. We've told you of him, I know.'

He put out his hand to shake Joan's. Like they all did here.

'Hello, Joan. Nice to meet you.' *Not a bad-looker; my age or Molly's? No make-up, though.*

She sat down in front of a big jigsaw that was only about half completed, then looked up at him, smiling. 'I've heard of you, Andy. Look, do sit down and help me with this – I'm stuck.'

Lovely smiley eyes. Doesn't daub eyeshadow on, or that thick black gunk on her lashes. Not like those London girls.

Andy sat down next to her. The jigsaw was a picture of Buckingham Palace in London – loads of same-coloured brickwork needed completing on the puzzle. Andy didn't mind helping Joan one little bit and he could feel the warmth of her leg through his camos.

'Wow – bit of a complicated subject, Joan. Masses of bits the same colour.' He matched the corner of a window. 'I saw the Palace when Mum and I were in London a few weeks ago. And the guards in their high black furry hats.'

Joan was envious. 'I haven't been to London but Molly has, haven't you, Mo?'

'Yep. I waited outside Clarence House with my aunty for the Queen's baby to be born. Princess Anne it was. What did you enjoy seeing most, Andy?'

'I liked the Tower with all its history, but best of all was the Eye – that huge wheel. I saw the roof of the House of Parliament and right up and down the river from the top, awesome.'

Molly looked at him puzzled. 'You'll mean the big ferris wheel? The one they built for the Festival of Britain?'

'I dunno when they built it but it was fantastic.'

Both girls were looking at him in that funny way Billy sometimes did. Just briefly, he flashed in quiet anger. These Singleton Parkers needn't blame me for their ignorance...'

Then Molly smiled, wiping that frowny look off her face that reminded him of his mother; the 'I'm not sure about what you're telling me' expression. 'I thought they were going to take it down. Andy, you've been really lucky to ride it before they do.'

Andy didn't understand. He thought the Eye was only quite new. Safer to change the subject. 'Hey, did you offer me a rock bun, Molly?'

She laughed. Munching rock buns and trying to avoid spilling crumbs on the jigsaw, the three of them persisted with the intricate front façade of Buckingham Palace.

A door banged. A lad's voice, Billy's deepening one. 'Bags me first.'

In they burst onto the peaceful scene.

'Rock buns. Hey, Aussie Ando. Didn't know you wus coming.'

Andy wasn't sorry to leave the jigsaw. Not the most exciting way to pass some time. He liked Joan, though. *What bloody lovely eyes, that terrific greeny deep sea sort of colour. Tom, you dunno what you're missin'.*

Molly laughed at her brothers. 'You and your rock buns. Off to clean yourselves up, lads. Poo – you pong. And Jimmy, the word is not "wus". It's "were".'

Billy grinned at Andy. 'Dad says a dialect locks folks into their comeuppances.'

Andy knew his mum would not agree. She worked with words and once told him that local dialects in speech showed individualism. But that was Mum – words and sounds were her business. Nor did he want an argument with Billy.

He managed some more pieces of the jigsaw, earning a lovely smile from Joan before the lads came back downstairs, smelling a bit sweeter.

'Bit late, Ando,' said Jimbo, 'but how about a game of Holey in stables. Got your aggie?'

Happy to leave the jigsaw behind, he waved Cheers to the two girls and ran out with Jimmy. He admired Joan again; decent body too under that old-fashioned cotton dress, nice legs when she'd got up to look for that piece that fell on the floor.

Competing at Holey quite took up all his thinking. *This Jimbo may be younger than me, and I'm taller, but by Jupiter, he's got technique.*

Two hours later and Andy still hadn't lost a game. He even won another of Jimmy's prize steelies and performed a victory dance around Jimmy's recumbent form.

'Silly beggar, Ando. Yer look like one of them Scottish soldiers dancing over t' swords. I let yer win, yer know.'

Andy thumbed his nose at his mate, then laughed and gave a high five. He ran home, well pleased. He knew Mum would want to know about Joan, this cousin. Every day she had questions about almost everything up at the Big House and more than once Andy had suggested she walk up and meet everyone for herself.

Today she wanted to know all about Joan as well as what Mrs O had been doing. She was cross that Andy still hadn't noticed the colour of Mrs O's hair; she had asked him enough times. He told her it was a sort of brown. That did not please his mum.

She also asked persistently what their name was. 'You can't call people by an initial, Andy. It's plain rude.'

However, when he explained that was what she had said her name was, as the full name was a long one, Mum cheered up.

'Seems a local habit, Andy. Mrs Reeves invited me to call her Mrs R as she doesn't like her other name. Okay by me.'

'I'll try to remember to look at her hair, Mum. It's just that being with the lads is all doing, Mum, not looking.'

He did tell her about Joan's green eyes. And that she didn't paint her face like some of those London girls, or use mascara on her eyes. That made Mum's eyebrows shoot upwards.

9

Next morning over breakfast, Andy knew he was trapped. His mother had that 'I want to talk' look on her face. He took another piece of toast.

'You know, Andy, I've been thinking. I know we've talked about the Os at the Big House being short of money, but I've been thinking that may not be. I know you find it hard to imagine that someone may prefer not to have TV, DVDs and other mod cons, but I just think she's a sensible parent, Andy. A dedicated greenie. Mrs Reeves recycles most things but she uses electricity like it'll never let her down. But this Mrs O seems a woman after my own heart. Who cares if they wear old clothes? Sensible, with what you all seem to get up to. But the way your clothes get dirty, Andy, I don't know how she copes without a washing machine. Being back to nature like she is sure reduces their carbon footprint. I really admire her strength of mind, Andy. Not that I'm ready to relinquish my washing machine. Yes, I really must arrange to meet her. You're up there just about every day.'

She snapped her used tea bag from her mug. 'As for you playing marbles and getting all technical about it like it's chess or something, well, that certainly is a change. What about taking your DS up there one day and have a game electronically?'

'Yeah, s'pose, Mum, could do. But you know, I really like this competitive marbles. It's got rules, takes some concentration. Like I have to plot my moves. And Aggie really is a lucky keepsake – or whatever Gran called it. And I'm winning. It, she, whatever, really is a lucky mascot.'

'Y' know, Andy. You never used to be without your DS or your MP3. Now it's like you've gone back to nature. And you know what? I like this new version of you.'

He smirked at her. He still liked his DS, and his PS, but he was usually so tired after eating his tea he couldn't be bothered playing tactician on *Call of Duty*. And in the mornings he liked to go up to the Big House straight after breakfast but if he played *Duty* then, he'd forget the time. *An' if I wanna play games on the PS3 after tea, that's when Mum likes to watch her TV, so I can't. But okay, no big deal.*

Mum continued, 'I'll get you that cheap watch tomorrow in the town. Sorry I keep forgetting. Actually, Andy, why not come with me tomorrow? We'll get you those gumboots. Let the lads know, will you?'

'No worries, Mum,' and he ran out, wearing Mr Reeves's clumpy rubber boots.' The lads had mentioned a mushy barn and said to wear his wellies. He'd gone online for that word and found out that wellies' name came from the long-dead Duke of Wellington. Mum said she knew that – of course. He'd need them if the mushy barn was still a goer, didn't want to muck up his sneakers.

His pack bobbed on his back. *Even Mum's calling them lads now.* He thought about Billy and Jimmy as he jogged up the drive. *What is it with 'em that they act like kids some of the time and then suddenly come out with real thinking stuff? Like Billy and all that about submarines in World War Two and even in World War One. He's really into the wars. And okay, they've got their own words like rucksack and keks, but Billy thought it was disrespectful of me to copy army uniform. He meant my camo cargoes. He thinks camos is a silly word. Anybody knows it's only short for camouflage. And this business about wearing jeans. Billy didn't even know what jeans were and went on and on again about me making it up.*

Mo had defended Andy, saying that Americans wore jeans,

she'd seen them at the pictures, and with turn-ups. Almost like a new language, all this, but Andy thought he was learning fast enough, and teaching them some of his. Like 'okay' – Jimmy now sang it non-stop.

He climbed the mossy, bit-wobbly gate and sat astride its top. It was jammed shut as usual and that was still a mystery. He hadn't seen another gate that opened like the one he'd seen from the tree. *Even if everybody in the Big House does use the Top Drive to get on the road, I know I definitely saw a big white gate, open wide. Somewhere around here.*

He slid down to the gravel. *Ow. Yoicks. A bloody big splinter. Like having a flaming injection.*

Billy was sitting astride the dinky only a few metres away. 'Helloooooo, Andy. What's with the swearing again?'

'And g'day mate to you too,' Andy yelled back. 'Got a splinter – a cracker. Here y'are – crisps.'

At least Billy approved of them. 'Thanks, Ando.'

Andy was carefully teasing the wooden splinter out of his hand. He managed, but it didn't bleed.

Billy peered at it curiously. 'Phew. That's not okay. Not all out. Better come and see Mam.'

Jimmy ran to meet him. He banged into the gate and promptly sat down next to Andy's pack. Andy threw him a bag of crisps.

Jimmy fell on them ravenously. 'These are really smashing, Ando.'

'They're chicken flavour, this time. Is that okay?' Andy was preoccupied with the splinter under his thumb.

Billy finished his crisps and carefully folded the packet and put it in his pants pocket. Neat. No litter. Andy knew his mum would approve of that.

As they made their way to the house, Andy asked Billy about Mr Capper's farm and the mushy barn. Most of the fields round about belonged to him. Andy now knew they were Capper's sheep in the field with the Tree. He also kept cows for milking and had a big Friesian bull that was usually kept locked up.

'It's 'orrible,' chomped Jimmy.

Billy agreed. 'Bloomin' bad-tempered my dad says. Hey, our Jimmy, fetch dinky back up, will yer?'

Jimmy pulled a face but obliged.

***

At the house, Mrs O washed Andy's hand then pulled a tiny bit of wood out with some tweezers. 'I don't think I've got it all, Andrew. We'll need to draw the rest out.'

That sounded gruesome but Andy was no coward. He stood quite still waiting for a Band-Aid. However, she took a bit of gauze bandage from a cupboard, sliced a little sliver of laundry soap onto it and then a sprinkle of sugar.

She winked at Andy. 'Just pass me your hand.' She poured a spurt of hot water onto the gauze from the kettle. She waved it to cool it a little then quickly slapped it onto Andy's wound.

Surprisingly, it wasn't as hot as he expected.

Then she spiralled another strip of gauze bandage around his hand and thumb and fastened it with a little safety pin. 'Now keep it on till tonight, Andy, and that'll fix it. Your hand might be a bit sore for a few days, though. Is it your useful hand, Andy?'

He shook his head. 'No, I'm right handed, thanks.'

Why can't she use a Band-Aid? Much less fuss. Then he wondered how he'd known instinctively not to make so much of differences with this mother. *Get with it, Andrew – you know from Billy, you duffer.*

Mrs O held up her hand. 'Wait a minute, lads. I've got something in the pantry.' She came out with a plate of sticky gingerbread. 'Take a big slice each and then be off with you. And be good, our Billy and Jimmy.'

51

Jimmy led the way. 'Just gotta get my big bag from stables. It's only paper but I saved it because it's got like a tarry lining, be good for mushies.'

But by the main entrance to the stables, a group of men were standing around a large, beautiful car, its hood folded down by varnished spokes.

'Oh heck. Old Russell,' moaned Jimmy. 'He's the one with the big handlebar tash, Ando. Useter be a flyer in the war. And our mushy bag's in t' other stall, next to his. Go talk to him Billy, eh, while I get bag.'

His moustache does look like the flamin' handlebars on a bike. But oho, lookit that car. Andy walked up to the shining brass trim on the vehicle's nose and stroked it reverently as he introduced himself.

'It's a bullnose Morris Cowley, isn't it? A 1925 tourer, right? She's a beaut vehicle. My dad would be so green with envy.'

Mr Russell smiled so widely his moustache bounced. It bobbed as he spoke. 'Nice to meet you, m' boy. From New Zealand are you?'

Andy introduced himself and Mr Russell smiled.

'It's a Morris Oxford, to be accurate.'

'Sorry, sir, I should have remembered. They changed the engine to an 1802cc as well, didn't they? My dad loves vintage cars and he'd be over the moon to see this one now. You know, somewhere he's got one of these radiator ornaments.'

'Vintage, you say. Yes, I suppose she qualifies if she's a '25 model. Well done, m' boy. You know your stuff. Anything else?'

Andy started to move away.

'No, boy, tell me, what else do you know about this model?'

Andy looked sideways at Billy, noting his stormy expression. *Oops — oh heck, why not?*

'I think they gave it a longer wheelbase, too, sir. And leather seats.'

'You're spot on, m' boy. Such knowledge needs a reward. Ever sat in one?'

'No, sir, never been so close. She's in beautiful nick. Silver grey and a maroon bonnet cover, awesome.'

Mr Russell had the driver's door open and waved Andy towards it.' 'Jump in, lad. Just take your wellies off first, eh?'

'Oh, oh hey…' Andy climbed in, couldn't find the words. His tall frame and long legs felt just the right fit as he dipped the clutch, toed the accelerator and gripped the wheel. *Oh, could I ever take this lovely vehicle around these curly English roads? Billy, stop frowning, just handle it, mate.*

He checked the timber instrument panel, and wriggled around on the grey leather seat. Then he heard the men laughing, and of all things found himself blushing. He went to get down.

'No, you're all right, m' boy. It's good to see someone your age admiring such craftsmanship. And knowing some of the specs.'

Andy shrugged, lost for words and feeling a bit self-conscious.

Billy was standing over to the front, now with a definitely black look on his face. Jimmy, his mushy bag over his arm, just looked envious.

Mr Russell spoke again. 'Andrew, right? Well, Andrew, like to give the horn a blast?'

Oh cool. It's an actual honker. He gave it an eager squeeze. Its deep echoing note set the rooks cawing and Panty running up, barking madly until he saw the lads.

Andy climbed down and Mr Russell handed him the wellies.

'Thanks a million, Mr Russell. That was fabulous.'

They shook hands, then Andy rejoined Jimmy and Billy.

Jimmy was awestruck. 'Cor. He never invites us into the car, does 'e, Billy?'

Billy didn't answer, fuming that the Aussie was getting all the treats yet it was he himself who had grown up with engines, not him. He stalked off, his heavy industrial gumboots clumping.

Andy followed with Jimmy, turning to walk backwards and staring at the lovely old car.

Billy turned back. 'Are you coming, Aussie? We've got to get over this wall. You don't look where yer going, yer'll walk into it head first.'

'Sorry, mate. Just love cars, you know? Right, with you now.'

10

They scrambled over the rough stone wall into a small field and Jimmy explained.

'This is old Capper's lambing paddock but lambing's over for this year so he won't be using t' field. Come on, lads. Ando, we're heading for that old barn over there.' He pointed across the field and over another stone wall.

Andy broke into a clumsy run, Mr Reeves's rubber boots clumping loosely despite his thick sports socks. *And Mum thinks no one can have bigger feet than me.*

Billy seemed to have recovered his good temper now they were out of sight of the old car and its admirers. He whooped repeatedly, just enjoying the exploit. Every now and again, he performed a perfect cartwheel on the lush grass.

'Tha big show-off,' yelled his brother and he trialled a couple of handsprings on the sun-warmed grass.

Andy, not to be outdone, did a reasonable backflip. He lost a wellie and landed across a pat of cow poo.

'Lucky for you it's a dry one,' laughed Billy.

Jimmy reached the barn. He checked the door. It was bolted.

Andy thought it looked more like an old stone house. Its main door wasn't big enough to fit animals or carts through.

Jimmy grumbled, 'By 'eck. It's all padlocked. Mingy ol' Farmer Capper, tight as a duck's…'

'Jimbo,' yelled his brother, 'you watch that language, or I'll tell Mam and she'll skelp your backside. When Andy swore before, you threatened him wi' Dad's belt, so just think on, eh? Let's go round t' back.'

Andy stood, grinning as he listened to the lads. 'Skelp' – another new word to tell Mum.

Andy grabbed one of Billy's mucky wellies and bunked him up to the bottom window frame. He tore at a corner of loose netting. Tore it right across the bottom. Another shove, and Billy tipped head first into the barn. They heard him drop into something squelchy.

He yelled out, 'Bloody 'ell. it's the jackpot. Give us paper bag, Jimbo. 'Urry up.'

Jimmy was posted on lookout but came over, pulling the big, coarse paper bag from under his jumper, which he thrust into Andy's hand. 'You're bigger 'n me, put it through window to our Billy, eh,' and he darted back to peek around the corner of the barn.

Andy was still grinning at Billy's swearing when he'd threatened his younger brother with a skelpin' but he scrambled up to the window and thrust the bag through. Billy yanked it in.

'Billy, what's in there?' he called, scrambling to get a grip on the bricks.

It was nearly dark inside and with a garden-mulchy kind of smell. There was a bank of sacks over the floor area with straw and soil breaking out of the sides and hundreds of big white round things like… Mushrooms. *We're nickin' mushrooms.* Why hadn't he recognised the smell before? It was like the pong in Mr Rapsoulas's vegie shop back home.

'Bewdy Billy.'

Billy called back. 'Ando, grab this and I'll try and get up and out.'

As Andy reached in to grab the heavy paper bag in his hand, Jimmy sprinted round the corner, panic all over his face.

'Ol' Capper's coming. He sneaked up on that ol' bike with a basket on t' front. And his big brown dog's trotting behind. It'll smell us any minute.'

'Bugger,' came the loud whisper from his brother inside the

barn. 'You two head off across t' field while he's in here. I'll duck down and try to sneak out while he's picking his mushies.'

Andy looked at Jimmy.

Jimmy stole a peek around the corner of the building. In a hoarse whisper, he reported over his shoulder. 'He's parking 'is bike. Now padlock's clunking… Let's go, Andy.'

Off they ran, bending low like soldiers escaping enemy fire. Andy got too low and fell over the mushroom bag, the mushies scattering everywhere. He froze; not a muscle dared quiver. Jimmy elbowed over and helped him stuff mushrooms back into the bag. They put them up their jumpers and in their pockets till every single one was accounted for. They hadn't gone through all this to lose them.

Back on their feet and bent over to maintain a low profile, they made it to the wall and scrambled over. Andy lost one of his over-sized wellies at the bottom of the wall.

'Heck.' A hoarse whisper into Jimmy's ear. 'They're Mrs Reeves's husband's boots. I'll have to get it.'

Jimmy sneaked a look. 'It's okey-dokey. No wurries, myte. Billy's runnin' and Ol' Capper's still in t' barn. 'Ow the 'eck did Billy sneak out? Stupid dog musta got a rabbit smell up its nose. Oh 'eck, hurry up, Billy.'

Suddenly a liver-coloured streak headed from the barn towards Billy.

'Oh no, it's got us, Capper's dog. Oh 'eck.'

Billy scrambled over the wall just as the dog ploughed to a halt. It stood on its hind legs, panting and dribbling, its long tongue lolling over its evil-looking teeth. Its yellow eyes looked straight into Andy's. It growled, from deep down in its belly. Then it started barking. Billy was still crouching on all fours trying to catch his breath, mushrooms falling out from under his woolly jumper. His sweaty face gleamed under the stinky straw still caught in his hair from the mushroom beds.

'Ol' Capper can't 'ave 'eard us,' he gasped. ''E's still in t' barn.

We'll get your welly, Ando. Later.' He straightened up, just a little. 'Let's keep our 'eads down and dog'll give up. Capper might not suss us out.'

Suddenly an ear-splitting whistle reached across the paddock. They stared open-mouthed at each other. What now? But the yellow-eyed dog stopped its woofing and hared back to its master.

Billy counted to twenty, then checked. Capper wasn't in sight so he scrambled up and over to rescue Andy's boot. 'Phew.'

Andy was looking at the mushrooms. He loved mushrooms with a passion – fried or grilled and chopped with butter dripping over them. 'Cor, there's more 'n two kilos, in the bag and our pockets and Billy's jumper. How many in there, Billy?' He sniffed loudly. 'Billy you don't 'alf stink. It's 'orrible.'

Jimmy grinned. 'You think you don't? You got all that cow pat on your back. And what's kilos? Oh never mind, you gotta face your mum. Our mam, at most, will give Billy a whack on t' legs, send him upstairs till teatime. Then we'll all have mushies and bacon.' Jimmy laughed at Andy's face. 'Mam and ol' Capper are fierce enemies ever since he put his geese in our orchard last summer. You've 'eard what's good for the goose is good for the gander, 'aven't yer?'

The two brothers laughed loudly and winked at Andy. He grinned and soon all three boys were laughing together and rolling around in the grass.

'Ay, lads. I've some mushies up my front, they'll be squashed.' He rescued a few flat ones and stuffed them into the bag. 'And hey, I'm staying for tea today.'

'That's smashing, Ando, but that changes t' plans a bit,' pondered Jimmy. 'Mam can think we picked 'em. Well, we sort of did.'

'Worth a try,' cautioned his brother. 'I heard Mam and Mo talking about making a cake because Andy's staying again, so we'll have to change tactics.'

They reached the back door to be greeted by Molly. 'I heard

that, you lot.' She smiled. 'Some field mushies will be nice for breakfast. Tea's all ready, anyway, lads. Andy, you've plenty of the mushrooms for your mum?'

He nodded rapidly and she grinned.

'Get yourselves off for a proper wash, you two, and Andy, you come and let us check that splinter.' She took off the filthy bandage, but didn't ask Andy how it had become so mucky, for which he was thankful.

The brothers were already running to the bathroom. Mrs O came over to examine Andy's arm and he hoped she wouldn't ask him about the mushrooms as he wasn't sure how much to say. Molly gave him a sly wink to signal there was no need to worry. True, Mrs O was more concerned about his splinter.

'A little bit of it's still in there, Andy. Down deep. I'll check it again when it's really clean, when you've had a wash.'

Andy tore up the polished wooden stairs to the big bathroom. *Wow, Mum'd like that heritage toilet. It's got all blue patterns on the pottery, and inside. An' check that chain to pull for a flush. What a massive big bath, more blue flowers, and brass feet. Eat your heart out, Mum. But no shower? Huh.* He wiped his finger around the edge of the bath, it was cold and so smooth.

Downstairs, they all found a spot at the table. Tea was a riotous meal. Jimbo cracked jokes and had everyone laughing until Molly pulled them all into line.

'No talking with your mouths full please, and Billy, use your fork properly, or Andy'll think you're not fit to eat with.'

However, Andy was more interested in the food on the table than watching for good manners. Heck, he had enough reminders about manners from his own mother. Talking of mothers, where was Mrs O? He asked Molly.

'Mam likes to eat with Dad when he's home, later. He likes a bit of peace and quiet when he eats after a busy day and this lot – well…'

Andy tucked in. It wasn't cooked stuff, meat and veg and that. There was Spam, and tomatoes and brown bread to make their own special sandwiches, as many as they liked, and lettuce and cucumber and hard-boiled eggs. The butter on the table was nearly white not yellow.

'Comes from the farm,' whispered Jimmy, 'but Mam buys it, it's not nicked.'

Andy and Billy couldn't stop laughing.

Big sister Molly shook her head. 'You lot behave in front of the younger ones, all right?' She cut slices from a huge yellow cake layered with fresh strawberries and cream.

David and little Chris ate as much as their bigger brothers, Andy noticed. Andy ate till he could eat no more. That coincided with Molly reminding him of the time.

'You said you'd to get home, Andy. Let Mam see to your splinter first'.

Mrs O smiled at Andy, who felt a bit of a sook. It was only a splinter. But he stood politely while she washed it carefully, again, then applied a little dob of yellow ointment and secured it under a thinner layer of gauze. A Band-Aid or that other sticking plaster would've been quicker and easier, but…

'That'll get you home, Andrew. Can't have your mum thinking we don't look after you. Lads, see Andy down and help him over the gate.'

Andy was glad to escape all the ministrations. 'And this is just great,' he sang loudly, holding out his backpack, containing an extra paper bag of mushrooms. 'Mum'll love these.'

At the gate, he turned around. 'Oh heck. I nearly forgot. I can't come tomorrow. Mum wants me to go shopping.'

'Poor you,' chorused the two lads and waved at him.

He grinned and climbed up – warily – and over the big old gate.

At home, Mum was sharing a cuppa with Mrs Reeves while

little Jacynta made a tea party picnic on the carpet with toy cups. The women exclaimed at the state he was in.

'You're a mucky lad and no mistake,' laughed Mrs Reeves.

'What's wrong with your hand? Let's have a look,' said Mum. She went to unwind the strip of gauze.

'It's okay, Mum. Mrs O put soap and sugar on when I did it and just before I came home she put this on.' He told her all about the splinter and the lovely cake.

Mrs Reeves leaned over to have a look at his bandage. 'Did you say soap and sugar? Haven't seen that old poultice since I was a girl. And I remember the smell of that ointment – Dettol, isn't it? I haven't used it for ages. I like the disinfectant sprays.' She supped her tea. 'You're right, you know. That mam up at the Big House is a real old-fashioned greenie type by t' looks of it. But this'll have done its job. All clean.' She laughed. 'Cleanest part of you, I think, Andy.'

Mum laughed with her. 'Keep your hands still Andy. Okay, it's still got a bit of wood in there, working its way out. Just take that stinky jumper off, please, and nip up for a shower. Oh yes, there are emails for you from your gran, and Dad and Tom.'

'Aaaaaaand da-dah,' sang Andy as he emptied the mushrooms from the bag and his backpack onto the table. Both women whooped in pleasure. There were plenty for everybody so he made his escape. With a bit of luck, they'd think he'd picked them in a field. Tomorrow was another day.

11

Next day, Mum and Andy drove into the town.

'Worse things to do in such weather, Andy. We've had a few showers lately, haven't we? More of a nuisance than anything else. They keep you home…'

Yeah, Mum, under your feet, do you mean?

She was continuing. 'However, this weather looks like it's come to stay. It's late-night shopping today in the town, so after the shopping we should have plenty of time to fit in a movie – if there's a cinema, if there's a decent movie showing. I need a short break from the computer and anyway, it'd be nice to share some time with my son and heir to my future fortune.' She hugged him. 'Or we could maybe hire a DVD or two. Make a change, hey?'

'Sounds good, Mum. How about the new *Lord of the Rings* series?'

'Oh, you and your magic stuff, Andy. You're as bad as your gran. Parallel worlds, magic, time travel, they're all products of someone's imagination. Haven't you grown out of all that yet? Still, it makes for a good story, I suppose. Aah – here's a parking space.'

She gathered up the shopping bags and locked the car.

Andy grinned. 'C'mon, Mum. Isn't it time travel of a sort to fly over here – day when it's night at home, summer when it's winter?'

'Okay, mate, you've made your point. Now, do these new mates of yours talk about a cinema at all?'

'Well, Billy likes the Palladium. It's on Sandy Avenue, or

something like that. But Mum, they haven't even heard of the Harry Potter movies, nor the *Lord of the Rings*.'

'That surprises me, Andy. When you were younger you badgered me incessantly for those Hogwarts stories. As for the movies, they're award-winners worldwide. We'll have a squiz later at the Palladium and see what's showing. I'll drive slowly and you can read the boards and lights. Right now, we need to stock our cupboards.'

In the supermarket, Mum pointed out to Andy a whole aisle bursting both sides with different varieties of crisps. 'You know, Andy, you said the lads' mother couldn't get any of these. Just look at them all on the shelves.' She waved her arm in a wide semicircle. 'Those lads are having you on, Andy, big time. They must know about these, but I'll buy some extra. Put some of those big packs in the trolley, please. You know what flavours you all like.'

Later, when everything was safely packed into the car, they drove off to find a cinema.

Mum stopped on one street and hailed a postman.

'Palladium, madam? Nay, no more. Palladium's been gone now, oh, more 'n twenty, even thirty year. There's one o' them bijou places where the Roxy used to be, I believe. Not sure, off my route. It's all DVDs and videos and stuff now, isn't it?'

He moved on, and Mum looked at Andy. 'What's going on, Andy?'

Andy was as puzzled as his mother. 'Dunno, Mum. The lads go most Saturdays to a matinee at the Palladium. I'm sure that's the name. Their latest was some movie about swimming. A swimmer called Esther Something-or-other.' He rolled his eyes. 'Their Mo said it was a smashing picture – smashing means "cool" – and all in colour too.'

Mum looked surprised but quickly looked back to the traffic ahead. 'Oh, Andy, that star's been dead for years. I know that old movie because it was one of your gran's favourites and she loved it. This Palladium is probably one of those bijou cinemas the postman mentioned. Perhaps they show all the ancient ones digitalised or something. If so, not our cuppa tea, son.'

Andy grinned. 'You sound like Mrs Reeves, Mum. But I'll check next time with Molly, not the lads.'

'Anyway, no matter. Hop out. That bakery smells delicious, Andy. Hey, I really fancy biting into something really chocolatey or jammy and creamy. And I can have a cuppa and you, well… whatever…'

Andy was happy to agree.

Later on, while sipping his Coke, Andy was reminded about the lads' home-made ginger beer and told his mum all about it, as much as he knew. She said she really would enjoy meeting this greenie mam.

Sure enough, she was on his wavelength. 'Andy, if we perhaps hire some DVDs, we could invite the Singleton Park lads to watch them. Ask them any time, Andy. Maybe I can ask their mother for a cuppa one day soon, even if she doesn't watch the movies. She does so much that interests me, your Mrs O. I really must meet her, talk with her. It's odd that Mrs Reeves doesn't know her. In fact, it seems to me the Big House people never come down to this end of the drive at all, bit odd.'

She pursed her lips into her usual thinking expression. 'Mrs O may have to live economically but she's obviously very cluey about saving the environment. I mean, cleaning windows with vinegar and newspaper, like you told me last week, and using soap and sugar as poultices instead of all the CO_2-emitting chemicals, great stuff. I'm really impressed.'

Later, at the hire shop, Andy chose the Star Wars DVDs. 'Cool. The lads would like these. Booked 'em for a week, Mum. The Os don't have a TV so they won't have seen them.'

Mum found the newsagent she wanted. 'I need a couple reams of A4 paper. I'd like a newspaper, too. I wonder if they sell any Australian papers here. Like your dad gets that English football paper in Darwin. If you want a Phantom or some other graphic novel – or whatever you call those fat comic books you like – see if you can find one.'

Great. She was in a really good mood – more DVDs and good stories. He wandered off to browse the shelves while his mother scrutinised her list to make sure nothing was forgotten.

Walking back to the car, they reached a pet shop where they were allowed to cuddle some little pups.

'Cute, Mum, like Pickles and like Panty, too. Not at all like that horrible hound of ol' Capper's. Him with the yellow eyes.'

She stopped and looked him in the eye. 'I know of Panty, but who's this Capper and why's his dog horrible? Andy, c'mon, do tell…'

So there, standing in the entrance of the pet shop, with Mum cuddling a wriggly pup, Andy told his mother about nicking the mushrooms. And about Capper the farmer. She looked at him, very seriously, as he told the tale. When he got to the cow pat, she raised her eyebrows. By the time he got to Capper's ugly old dog, her mouth was twitching. She carefully replaced the little pup in the window, her smile getting wider all the time. As Andy finished, and tried to pull her out of the shop, she laughed out loud. The lady in the pet shop looked up from her counter and Mum just gave her a little wave and a shake of the head.

'Oh, Andy, these lads you've met are incorrigible. You know, I really must meet their mother. No more putting it off. Tell you what,' she continued as they made their way back to the car, 'why don't I ask Mrs Reeves if she'll take a note up to Mrs O tomorrow, inviting the lads to come and watch the Potter movie with you one day next week? Mrs Reeves is going to walk up tomorrow to the farm, she always gets her eggs from there, and she might perhaps pop it in their letter box if they aren't home.'

'Great, Mum. That'd be good. So we're off on another visit on Saturday, are we?'

Mum just nodded and set off towards the car park. Andy trailed after her, swinging his carry bag of DVDs, and muttering to himself about the Saturday visits. *It's okay if other kids are there but that doesn't happen often.*

'All those oldies' houses smell the same, like they never open windows. It's okay for you to say, Mum, that it's because of the cold. And why can't they use decent mugs instead of cups with silly saucers underneath to catch the drips? They wobble and they always give me one and I don't even like drinking tea. If they know we're coming to their house, why don't they get a Coke or something ready?'

Mum was unlocking the car. 'Come on, Andy. Stop grumbling and climb in.' As they drove off, she turned to him. 'I know it's a bit boring for you, Andy. It is even for me sometimes, but I do get some interesting snippets of information for my book. That's one reason your gran wrote to just about everyone in the district who she remembered and told them we were coming to England.'

Andy settled back in his seat, looking out of the window as his mother continued.

'Remember, mate, my book is a social commentary. That means some of the stuff they tell me I can look up online and maybe use it. Tell you what, if you take your DS, I won't mind if, after you've said hello and chatted a bit, you take it into the garden or somewhere quiet and you can probably get going on your game. You usually get asked if you want to see the garden, don't you?'

Andy grinned, that was better. He usually had to leave his DS in the car. 'Who tomorrow, then, Mum?'

'Mr Scott. He's an old friend of Gran's parents so he's really old, in his nineties. He's in a nursing home, so it'll be a bit different. What's more, he knew your Gran when she was just a girl. Might have some stories to tell.' She laughed.

'Wow, Mum. That's ancient.'

'Well, by my reckoning, if my grandmother were alive, she'd be ninety-two or three. Mr Scott must be about the same age if not older. He's only in the home, Andy, because he has no living family who can look after him.'

'Oh, Mum, that's sad.' Andy felt quite contrite. *That's why some of these old guys make such a fuss of me. They don't see many younger people. That's gross. P'raps I should try to be more talkative with them, 'specially if I can't escape with my DS. But DS is old now. Wish I had an iPad. But like Mum's always saying, 'Try to make proper conversation.'*

Then he thought of something, something he wanted to get straight before they met up with this oldie. 'What about you and Dad, Mum?

She looked sideways at him as he continued.

'Nobody's asked me yet, but what if they do ask me about you and Dad? What do you expect me to say?' He looked out of the window again. 'I know things, Mum. I'm not a kid any longer. I heard you argue and stuff, and two and two make four, Mum. Now Dad's gone up north and you're over here because you're having a trial separation. So what do I say if they ask me about him and things? Mum, I don't really want to think that you and Dad are going to split.'

His mum was quiet for a few minutes and he thought she wasn't going to answer. *Like she usually doesn't when I ask her questions about her and Dad.*

'Andy, your dad and are really good friends. Honest. But yes, your dad needs some space away from me always writing and researching and such, because he can't share in it and it's boring to him. Yet I need to do it. And yes, being apart like this isn't altogether bad. What happens in the next few months –

well, we'll see when you and I get back to Australia and home. You know, love, parents do need space at times to do their own thing. That's all we're doing right now, your dad and I. You have no need to imagine we're going to separate permanently.' She smacked her hands on the steering wheel.

'I know what incompatible means, Mum.'

Mum reached over and gave his hand a squeeze. 'Well, if this ancient Mr Scott asks tomorrow, Andy, just leave it to me. Don't you worry about things like that. I can tell you, though, that your dad and I are better friends apart than together. Does that make sense to you?'

They pulled up in front of the Barn.

'Tell you what, why not email Dad tonight all about Capper's dog? That's if you haven't told him already.'

12

That night, Andy lay on his bed, thinking and remembering. *The way Mum explains everything, and Dad texts her as well as me, things can't be too bad. Anyway it's the other thing that bothers me more. That Star Wars movie started me remembering about Armstrong and the moon walk. Mum said she watched it – live – when she was in primary school an' I've seen it replayed lots of times since. But both lads laughed when I talked of it an' Billy said I was telling fibs and even Jimmy said I was having 'em on.*

He buried his face in the pillow and muttered into its stuffing so Mum couldn't hear. 'They had to know about it, they couldn't not. And the Apollo missions, the *Challenger* and *Discovery* and all those terrific shots sent back by the Hubble telescope – they're *huge*. No way can they pretend they don't know.'

He turned onto his back, chewing his lip in anger. *Billy even made me promise I was telling the truth and still looked at me like he didn't believe me. He said it was from the Dan Dare comic and I can't separate truth from fiction. When I got fed up and told 'im 'is head was buried in the sand, he called me a liar and walked off indoors. I do not tell lies. Weird, but it's all true. What's wrong with these people. Is it 'cos they live in the countryside and don't have TV?*

He tossed over onto his side, pulling his doona cover with him. Something else was nagging at him too, from the back of his mind. Joan's jigsaw. It was Buckingham Palace and London… it was when Joan was talking of London. *What the heck was it?* He screwed up his eyes tight to think.

Something was really niggling. *Okay, so the Big House lot don't have a busy city life around them, they don't have a TV, but they get newsreels when they go to the movies and they have a radio. Even if they do call it a wireless, it's a radio and it works. Funny old thing, though; kept in a cupboard and you have to open the doors and turn the switch to pick up the station. Talk of ancient. An' when I mentioned satellite transmission, Billy went right off. But the lads go to school in term time – they must all talk there of NASA an' all that, mustn't they?*

Andy kicked his doona straight, arguments hammering in his head. So many things didn't add up. And when he'd emailed his dad about their car, the Standard Vanguard, Dad answered they were classic vintage and worth a mint if well maintained. The lads' dad's car wasn't just maintained, it was new. Which was weird. No, the Singleton Park lads weren't short of money.

Okay, Mrs O is a dedicated greenie. But what's funny is the lads don't talk about any other friends and I think lots of kids would like to come up here. It's a great place, this Singleton Park. Sure, the lads are good friends with each other, but they're different. Billy's nearly the same age as me but I get on a lot better with Jimmy. But where are all their mates? Gotta admit, I miss Tom like crazy – not that I'd tell him. He managed a smile and tried to settle to sleep. No way could he shut down his brain. It was too busy pumping out questions he couldn't answer.

He mentally changed the subject. Whispering, he counted on his fingers, 'How long have we been here now? London first, then the Tree, then next week has to be our fourth here – no, fifth, won't it? I'll check my journal, it's nearly up to date.'

Most weekdays he'd gone up to the Big House. He'd only missed going there on really wet days and there hadn't been many like that. Or weekends. Then Mum liked to go to town for the markets. On those days he didn't mind having a go on *Call of Duty.* His mum was usually on the computer but she had this thing about him getting exercise and fresh air when the weather was good. He knew it was all part of her plan for him to 'sort himself out', as she said more than once.

The thought that he was missing some clue that could fit it all together was really adding to his niggles. He pummelled his pillow, feeling peeved. *Have I put anything into my journal that'd give me a clue?* He'd managed to keep up reasonably well with it, but he knew he hadn't put all his thoughts in its pages. Mum mustn't read it. She'd go bananas. He knew she didn't pry and peek at stuff. It was tucked under his mattress anyway. It was just that if she *did* read it, she wouldn't believe some of what he had written anyway, she'd call it 'imagination'. He pummelled the pillow.

Mum deals only in facts. Comes from doing lots of research, she says. Everything has a logical explanation, she's said time and time again. So how can I ask her about all these contradictions that keep bobbing up? Well, how do I know what is puzzling me? It's all a bloody big puzzle on its own.

He sat up. 'That's *it*. The puzzle.' *Sshh…mustn't let Mum hear me.* He put his arms up in the air, fists clenched and mouthed, 'Yes. Mo-Molly had said she was in London on holiday when Princess Anne was born. Couldn't have – she's crazy. The princess is a grown-up woman and her daughter's grown-up as well. She rides horses in competitions. I've seen her in the papers.'

He exhaled deeply and lay back. *It's a time warp, dunno how, it just is an' that explains…*

As Andy finally drifted into sleep, his Mum was sitting on the sofa doing some thinking of her own. She was feeling guilty because she'd been so glad Andy was happily occupied with his new friends and she hadn't yet bothered to go up the drive and introduce herself to the lads' mother. 'I could do it easily now that Manchester's got my draft. I must plan to make that visit and *not* forget.' She moved back to her keyboard to write in her journal, typing as she spoke, 'This Mrs O (full name?) sounds as if she's a total greenie. I've made such good time with the writing and research, I'll make definite plans to get to know her because, not least, she's been so good to Andy. And all the back-to-basics lifestyle Andy tells me predominates at No. 2 Big House – can't be that they're short of money, because Andy says the boys go to private school at secondary level and that's not cheap.'

She stopped, closed down the system and sighed. 'It's late. Time for a Milo…help me to sleep. Need a clear head for tomorrow.'

***

Old Mr Scott was so pleased to have visitors Mum felt really glad they had made the effort. She thought him a 'dear old soul' and smartly dressed, though he'd shrunk a bit inside his clothes. He was so eager to talk about the old days, about Singleton Park and her mother. As for Andy, well any talk of the Big House interested him.

Andy thought him a decent old bloke; a bit old-fashioned because he even tried to stand up from his wheelchair to shake his Mum's hand. Like when you stand up in church when the procession comes down the aisle. He was quite tall, not fat, and rather bent. Andy considered his wrinkled neck too small for the collar of his shirt. *Is this what you look like when you get into your nineties? Yuk. Looks like a tortoise…*

'Nice to see yer, young man. I miss seein' all the young 'uns I used to see in me shop. That's a few years ago now, though. How are they doin', the Singleton Park lads?'

His accent was strong but his voice a bit wobbly – Andy had at first to listen really hard to understand. However, the old man understood Andy well enough and smiled from ear to ear. Then his top dentures dropped onto his lower ones. Andy hadn't ever seen such a thing before and had to stop himself from staring. He quickly spoke of Billy and Jimmy and some of the things they'd all done together.

Mr Scott chuckled and his teeth dropped down again but he pushed them up with his tongue as if nothing had happened.

'I remember them lads well. They were young tinkers, that pair, always trying to pinch sweeties off my counter.'

Andy's Mum felt that big imaginary question mark sizzle in her brain. 'When did you retire from your shop, Mr Scott?'

He grinned again and pushed his top dentures back into place with his thumb. 'I couldn't wait, lass. Spot on sixty-five and due for my pension I was.'

'Why, I sort of thought, Mr Scott, you'd worked until quite a great age. Andy's new mates have mentioned you and your shop.' Mum was rapidly trying to calculate. No way could this old man have left his shop twenty-five or thirty years ago; that made no sense. Andy's new friends were only Andy's age now. 'You had family take over from you, did you? So you could visit now and again – down memory lane and all that?'

He didn't answer. Deaf, poor old thing. Her mind was buzzing. In family businesses, the old ones often stay working to help the young ones, but lads of Andy's age? He must mean the previous generation. This dear old fellow must be getting confused. However, he has that right, being ninety something.

Andy was oblivious to his mother's anxious reckoning. *The old guy's talking non-stop and he's a comic an' a half.*

Then he winked at Andy, saying how lucky he was to travel from one side of the world to the other. He would have loved to go on a modern plane like the Airbus. 'Not flown since the war, young feller-me-lad. They sent me to Egypt an' I found meself called a Desert Rat.'

Andy thought that awesome. He listened carefully.

'A fair few of my friends were killed by Rommel. Yer know, I still remember how they looked when they was young men like me. I'm looking forward to meeting them again, God willing. But I've grown into a miserable old sod and if they're upstairs,' and he smiled, signalling beyond and above the bedroom ceiling, 'they'll still be young and handsome. They'll not reckernise me…'

Andy laughed so much his eyes watered then noticed Mum was looking a bit upset. *What's spooked her now?*

'Andy, do tell Mr Scott about your carpentry up at the Big House.'

Andy grimaced. Just when things were getting interesting. Typical of his mother to call woodwork 'carpentry'.

'It's great fun, Mr Scott. I help with some of their jobs, like making the nesting boxes. They're different jobs from at home, y'know, and their mam says it's good to be busy. She says idle hands make idle minds.'

The old man chuckled and put his knobbly hand on Mum's arm. 'She was a one, that woman. She tried to give me a geography lesson on your country.'

Andy's mother sat up straight, her eyes fixed on Mr Scott.

'I well remember she set off quite a kerfuffle in my shop one day when she come in and wanted some crisps. She showed me a funny, crinkly paper packet. "Like them, please, Mr Scott," she said. It had what I s'posed was a date, like a line of number ones, or summat. I said that musta meant they'd come from the war and the funny packet was to keep them going off. She tossed 'er 'ead in the air and said they'd come from Australia and were quite fresh. She showed all the other women in the shop and, eh bah gum, it was quite a kerfuffle.' He chuckled, his dentures click-clacked together and his head dropped onto his chest.

Andy's mum got to her feet. This was too much. She shook her head and whispered, 'Whatever is he on about, Andy? How could he have seen your crisp packet in his shop? Oh, he's waking up again…'

Andy spoke about the crisps, mentioning Mrs O, but Mum was too engrossed in her own puzzlement to catch every word. In a hoarse whisper, she asked, 'What *is* he on about, Andy? Wartime surplus? He's dreadfully confused about past and present – is he ever.' She sat down again, thinking it'd be best if she just smiled at whatever he said.

Andy realised his mum looked a bit pale. 'Mum, are you okay?'

She just shook her head but Mr Scott was alert again and spoke out, loudly. 'I useter go up to Singleton Park quite a lot, tha' knows. They 'ad a grand old car, a bullnosed Morris Cowley – one that'd done a London to Brighton run.'

'Mr Scott, it's still there. It belongs to the Russells,' exclaimed Andy.

'Eh, it's never. Must be as old as I am, that car. I thought it was smashing.'

Andy thought that too. It was a big and powerful machine, kept clean and shiny for its age. He said so.

The old man chuckled and said, 'So am I, Andrew, so am I. The father and me was great pals, tha knows. We were at school t'gither. Then at fourteen I left to workin' in t' family's shop and he left to get apprenticed to his dad in their business.'

It was Andy's turn to be puzzled. 'You went to school with their dad? He's only as old as my dad, Mr Scott. He's not an old man like you.' Then he realised what he'd said. 'Oh sorry, I didn't mean…'

Mum hadn't noticed. She was remembering Mrs Reeves's warning that the old man was losing his marbles a bit. Mum had thought it was a bit of a cruel thing to say. But he really did mix all his yesterdays with his todays. At his age, of course, he was entitled to be confused.

Mr Scott gave a sleepy chuckle and slipped down in his chair. Andy and Mum sat still and Mum raised her eyebrows, thinking maybe it was time to go. Andy was ready to go home anyway. He was peckish. He wondered what the lads were up to and if they really were at the pictures. Mum leaned over to him and beckoned. They left and said goodbye to the lady at reception.

'I'm so glad you came to see Mr Scott today. Do come again when you can. He gets very few visitors and, as you would know, he has no family left now.'

Mum was startled. 'He was talking about his shop. I thought, perhaps, a son or someone must have taken over and, you know, let him stay on in an advisory capacity?'

'Oh no. His shop was in a row of buildings that were bulldozed for the new bypass. That's, oh, must be twenty-something years ago.' She smiled and turned to answer the telephone. 'Hope to see you again.'

They walked over to the car park. Andy looked at his mum. Her mouth was open; looked a bit shocked. Stunned, that was the word. He felt a bit the same.

'Mum, I don't get it. Jimmy and Billy's dad's about as old as my dad. It's weird.' He noticed her puzzled expression. 'Poor old Mr Scott's a bit muddled. Not much fun getting really, really old, is it?'

'Sure isn't, Andy. C'mon. Let's find that nice sticky bun place. I need a sugar fix.'

The puzzle of Mr Scott pushed aside for a while, they made for the café on the High Street. While Mum sipped her cup of tea, Andy bit into his big iced bun oozing with jam. He wondered if the lads ever came to this café. He must ask them. He looked out of the window.

Today was Saturday and the lads were here in town. Somewhere. At the pictures, as Jimmy said. So where was their cinema? Yesterday they hadn't been able to find it and Jimmy had definitely said it was in the town. Another puzzle.

Lots of kids were running past the café window and one speeding on a RipStik looked a bit like Billy from the back but was wearing cargoes. Andy finished his bun. He wasn't in his cargoes today; they were still at home, thrown on his bed with Aggie safely in the pocket. And it hadn't been a bad day, for a

Saturday. Not lots of rellies, just an old, old man – and he was an interesting old bloke, no denying.

Andy was very thoughtful as they drove home. His mother was quiet too.

13

Monday was a mizzly day, or so Mrs Reeves cheerfully commented. Mum translated that as misty-drizzly. Mrs Reeves wanted to apologise for not taking Mum's note to the Big House and for not being around yesterday. The Reeveses had driven to visit her husband's cousin in Sedbergh and stayed over because the men went to the pub.

'That's okay, Mrs Reeves. No problem. I'm sure if the weather improves Andy'll want to go up to the Big House. He can tell the lads then.'

Andy nodded. 'Yep, no worries, Mum.' *Want to tell the lads what old Scott said about them nicking lollies. An' the stables are always dry. I've got those new marbles games from America off the Net; be good to try with Jimbo. Maybe even clever enough for Mr Billy.*

Mum smiled. 'You've got your rainbird jacket, haven't you? However, before you go, did you manage to answer your emails last night?

He shook his head. 'They can wait till tonight Mum. Okay?'

She nodded. 'You know, Andy, you really surprise me lately. You've always been a real techno-rat. A real button presser – DS, PS, not to mention DVDs and stuff. Yet you hardly pick up even your DS now. I really find it strange. And you don't rush on to the computer whenever I'm not there.'

'Mum, you're always complaining. My DS isn't wasted, but it is getting old. I do play a game on it sometimes. I'd rather have an iPad but I have to wait till Christmas, you said. You used to say I was on it too much and you're still grumbling when I'm not.' He checked his backpack. 'Look, it's good fun with Billy and Jimmy, okay? And I do like to play with my gear when I'm home. I did play *Duty* on my DS yesterday on my bed. It's good to have. When it's bad weather. But with the lads there's marbles, the trees, watching Billy with his crystal set – hey, Mum, he's got sound now, bit crackly, but no battery. And he's a really clever lateral thinker, Mum. His capacitor top is made out of half a saucepan…'

'Whoa, mate. Capacitor top? Who's teaching who – I mean *whom*?'

'Okaaaay, Mum. Your turn to look something up online. Jimmy was gonna fix a new steering mechanism for the dinky out of an old broom handle – I hope he hasn't done it yet – and then put a seat on the other one to tow young Chris. It's different stuff, Mum, okay? But stuff I can do as well – it feels good to make something that's useful…like the chooks' nesting boxes.'

'I like this new Andy. You don't swear like you used to. You don't crack a fruity any more if something's slow to download on the laptop. This greenie life of making and mending stuff with the lads has a lot to recommend it, Andy.'

She turned to make another coffee while Andy gathered his things together, his mind working overtime.

Greenies. How can I tell her, as a f'rinstance, I've been thinking time warp stuff? More and more when I'm at the Big House I get this funny feeling I'm living in another time. I know now that Molly went to London when their Princess Anne was just born and it was just a couple of years ago to her and to me about sixty and before rockets and robots and DVDs and DSs… An' if I'd taken them the newspaper the other day, the one with the archive photos of the Discovery shuttle getting ready for its last launch 'cos they're saving the money now – I just know I can't do that. But why not? How come I just know, really really know, they just don't know about all that? What I want to know is why *they don't know. They don't even know about computers. Nor do the lads believe there's ever been a man on the moon yet. There's only one way they can* not *know about all this – and it's just plain bonkers to even think it – is they're in the past; they're living in some other time. They're real to me, anyway. And if they are in another time, well, so am I when I go there. How can it happen?*

I wish I could talk to Mum about it, have a proper talk. But I know she'd either tell me I'm overtired and need a good night's sleep, or talk, on and on and on, about rational explanations. Best way to go when she asks is 'no comment'. Like in the TV cop shop programmes. For now, anyway.

Oops, good job she's not expecting an answer.

She took a sip of coffee and looked at Andy, a question creasing her eyebrows. He gave her a grin and quick wave, threw his jacket over his shoulders and made out of the door and off up the drive, his backpack full of crisps and whatever other stuff his Mum had packed.

***

Meanwhile, in the Big House, Jimmy was escaping his chores and arguing with himself that Billy could be yelled at to do the fire for Mum today. It was his turn anyway. Just because his stupid old crystal set was a school project, Billy got out of his jobs. Not fair. Quietly he slipped into the scullery for his wellies and his old mac with no top button. It was his favourite – it had two great big pockets in the front with flaps to keep the rain out of whatever he'd hidden inside. Nor did his mam flap if it got dirty because it was only an old one.

He ran out of the house before anyone spotted him and almost bumped into Andy, who was running through the yard gate.

'Hi, Jimbo.'

'I'm bloomin' glad to see you, Ando. Come up to the swings. They're not too wet.'

Ensconced on one of the massive tyres, Andy threw a pack of crisps to Jimmy, who caught them mid-swing.

'Yer know, Ando. Me mam started a row in Scott's grocery shop on Saturday.'

Andy nearly choked on his crisps. 'Howd'ya mean, Jimbo?' he managed to croak out.

'Ol' Scott said there weren't no flavoured crisps. Then Mam handed him one of your crinkly packs. She'd carefully flattened it 'cos me and Billy wanted some of the same sort.' He shoved another few into his mouth. 'Scott got real mad when Mum kept on about yours.'

Andy sat quietly on his tyre, feet just dangling. Goosebumps crept up his arms. *It was me gonna talk to the lads about ol' Scott. This is mega-weird he's tellin' me. Scott's an ancient ol' bloke and he only told me and Mum about it day before yesterday. And it happened years an' years ago when he still worked in his shop.*

Jimmy was chatting on happily, his mouth stuffed with the last of his packet of cheese and onion. Andy couldn't think what to say, so he just crunched his salt and vinegar – the crisps that apparently didn't exist. His thoughts were tied up in knots. It got worse as Jimmy continued – even a mouthful of crisps didn't shut him up.

'Mam grumbled that Mr Scott said them crisps were leftovers from the war years when the Americans had special rations. Me and Billy told 'er they didn't taste old and stale, Ando. Ol' Scott had never seen the crinkly paper stuff of the packet before. He really gave Mam a hard time over the mysterious code near the bottom of the pack. Look, like this one: "Best by 101118".'

Mrs O was up behind the swings hanging some washing on the line to blow in the wind. She'd overheard some of what Jimmy had said. 'Andrew,' she called, 'can you clear up a wee problem for me?'

Andy was rapidly trying to work things out in his head. *What Jimmy just said had happened to his mam, happened only two days ago. And it was that same day, the very Saturday as me and Mum visited old Mr Scott. He told us about the crisp packet kerfuffle and said it happened years and years ago. So at the same time as Mrs O was arguing with Mr Scott about the crisps, the ancient Mr Scott, long time retired from his shop, was telling me an' Mum all about it.*

It was all too much to think about and Andy felt sick. Frustrated and angry he spoke out, loudly, 'This is something like an action replay on the TV but oh, *weird.*

'Oh, Andrew, please…' Mrs O was determined to know about the crisps.

Andy couldn't give her an answer. *This is me, gobsmacked, really gobsmacked, a total dork, acting like a kid.* He pretended his mouth was too full to talk.

She pursed her lips and continued. 'Mr Scott told me they were dated 101118 or something like that. That is way before even I was born, so I'm really puzzled. He told me they were probably leftovers – you know, rations made for the troops in the war.'

Then she went on to describe to the lads the same occasion, almost word for word, as Old Mr Scott had told Andy, the day before yesterday. Andy listened but couldn't concentrate on what she was saying. His mind was playing word tricks with him, repeating to him the words his mother said he should use instead of gobsmacked – words like nonplussed, flabbergasted, flummoxed. 'Discombobulated.'

He realised he'd spoken that last one out loud when Jimmy turned to him with a questioning look on his face. Andy just couldn't think straight. He certainly couldn't say anything Mrs O would want to hear.

This is a brainteaser to end all brainteasers. If I told all this to Mum, I can imagine what she'd say. I'd get all that guff about coincidence and rationality again. But this Mr Scott and the crisps thing is just too much.

Mrs O was persistent. Her laundry all now pegged on the line, she turned to face the lads, one hand holding the end of the laundry basket, the other waving to emphasise her point. 'I told Mr Scott the crisps were fresh, perfectly fresh, because I'd tasted them. I told him you'd come from Australia, Andrew, and before I could explain – a second time – that your mother had bought them in our town, he actually accused me of black-marketeering.'

Jimmy was listening wide-eyed and then, to Andy's relief, he interrupted. 'Mam, why don't you go down to Mrs Reeves, and talk to Andy's mum and find out? P'raps you can go into the town together and…whatever.'

Thankfully to Andy, that seemed to satisfy Mrs O.

'Well…yes. Now that's a good idea. I'll send a note home with you, Andrew. Mebbes your mum would like to come here or I'll pop down there.' She hitched the empty wash basket on her hip and turned to go. 'Come to think of it, Andrew, I'd really like to meet your mother anyway. Haven't met a writer before.'

Andy's brain was still in a kerfuffle, using Old Mr Scott's word, so he just nodded.

14

The two lads kicked their swings into motion again. Andy decided to put something to the test while Jimmy was obviously curious about things.

'You and your mam told me about this Mr Scott in his shop, yeah? Well, Mum and me went on Saturday to visit this nice old geezer whose name was Scott. Mum knew he useter have a grocery shop years ago. Yet your mam had an argument with him on the same day. In his shop.'

Jimmy shrugged. He was not at all fazed. 'So what, Ando? You prob'ly talked to Mr Scott's grandfather or summat. I know they've had the grocery shop for years and years and years. Mam likes to support what she calls family businesses because our business is one. Goes back before the First World War.'

Andy wasn't finished. 'Yeah, okay, but how could Old Scott tell me on Saturday what he told your mother on Saturday, that he told us happened years and years ago and I've only just been here a few weeks?'

Jimmy laughed so much he fell through the middle of the tyre. 'You've been on the strawberry bubblegum, Andy. Now look what you've made me do – tip the rain out of the bloomin' thing all over me feet. Oh, Ando, let's clear off into the orchard. Mebbes do some early scrumpin'.'

Andy laughed in spite of himself. This was new. 'Speak English, mate.'

Jimmy thought it hilarious that an Australian should tell him, a *real* Englishman, how to speak his own language. He gave Andy a friendly thump. 'Come on lad. Scrumpin' it is.'

They made their way through the kitchen gardens into the orchard where Jimmy's dad kept the hens.

'Noisy things, chooks,' ventured Andy.

That set Jimmy off cackling. 'You and yer chooks. Not chicks, they're layers, you clot.'

'All chooks to me. That includes all types, roosters and hens. Fewer words to remember.'

'By rooster do you mean cockerels?'

'Yeah, like that one there,' and Andy pointed at a huge white leghorn rooster that started strutting its comb in full colour around the edges of the pen. It was watching the lads approach.

'That's Nebuchadnezzar. I hate 'im. He's a vicious ol' beggar. Worth a lot of money, though, 'cos his chicks, when Dad sells 'em, get a good price. Billy and me have to feed him in the afternoons when we get the eggs and he attacks us if we get too close. He fought off a fox one time.'

The big white bird ran right over towards them, making loud crowing noses, his wings outstretched in warning. Jimmy pulled his catapult out of his pocket and pretended to aim it at Nebby. He wished he dared fire it at the horrible bird.

Andy said how he had a slingshot at home but it was illegal to fire anything from it so it got put away.

'What's a slingshot? You mean a catapult? Heck, you sound so American sometimes, like at the pictures. Do you copy America a lot in your country?'

Andy reckoned Jimmy was in the mood for an argument. Well, he could argue all he liked.

This time, though, Jimmy didn't wait for an answer. He tried to pull an apple off its tree and then turned to Andy. 'Apples are still too green and hard, give us bellyache. Let's see if old Russell's redcurrants are ready yet. 'E won't know. Come on, Ando.'

Andy didn't know redcurrants, but he was happy to leave the chooks behind, noisy birds. The redcurrants looked tempting enough, little orangey-pink bunches hanging in clusters on tall canes. They reminded him of grapes. 'Not bad, Jimbo.'

The two of them pulled them off by the handful. They stuffed them into their mouths almost as fast as they put them in their pockets.

Then Andy heard the noise. It was a strange, pitter-pattering-on-wet-grass noise.

He turned, half expecting to see Panty, Billy's dog, coming to find him. It was old Russell's goat.

Jimmy couldn't care less about the goat. He was used to it. It didn't scare him. Andy wasn't too sure. It wasn't very big, about the size of a medium-sized dog, but with a bony head and bad tempered-looking stripey eyes. It wasn't very fat; its bones stuck out all over.

'Scraggy ol' no-good-to-anyone, that ol' goat. Dad says neither use nor ornament.'

'It sure isn't an ornament, Jimbo – ugly old thing and doesn't look too friendly. At least it has no horns. Sure, certain and f'ra fact, it doesn't even have much hair.'

'Mr Russell told Dad it earned its living by keeping down the grass. Dad telt me that's so ol' Russell needn't mow it. Says Russell thinks mowing's not a gentleman's job.'

Jimmy was still munching mouthfuls of berries even as he told Andy about how his mam had chased it away from her washing line once. He was spitting juice as he laughed about how she had caught it snatching down a towel and chewing it. 'She was MAD, Ando. The goat charged at her and butted her. Its bony head really gives yer a bruise, watch it.'

Andy *was* watching it. Tall as he was, strong as he felt, he wasn't taking any risks.

'Mam got it by its collar and dragged round to the Russell's back door. She were *furious*. Mrs Russell promised it would be locked in the orchard.'

This was the orchard. The goat trotted over to Jimmy and butted him quite gently. It seemed to be in a good mood, so he put his hand out to it and rubbed the hard bony lump in the middle of its face. The goat smelled the berries and started to lick the juice from his fingers.

'Gerroff, you chump.' growled Jimmy, but it didn't like being shouted at.

It butted him seriously hard, right against the pocket full of redcurrants.

'Oh 'eck,' swore Jimmy. He put his hand in his pocket and brought it out full of squashed fruit. The juice dripped through his fingers and down onto the toes of his wellies. 'You might as well have the lot,' he muttered, and threw the rest of the sticky pink mess on the grass.

The goat snuffled and snorted around its unexpected bounty, its big white eye with the black stripe turned towards Jimmy all the while.

Jimmy grizzled to Andy about its horrid eyes. 'See its eyes, Ando? They look sort of like dead ones, not friendly and there's no expression in them, no talk. Not like dogs' eyes do, or even horses.'

Andy agreed.

Jimmy picked up his catapult and shoved it into the other, not sticky, pocket and found a roll of old leather rein. 'Yeh. Lookit this. Bit mucky, but it's dried out a bit. Hey, Ando, what can us do wi' this?'

It was all mucky from the puddle he'd found it in some weeks back. He'd thought it worth saving, and at least it was all dry now. He looked at the goat eating the berries. He looked at the long leather rein in his hand and flicked it around a bit. Andy looked at Jimmy, watching his mind work. This was one of the days when Jimbo seemed more like a kid and the year and a half between them showed up.

'It'd make a good whip, Jimbo, a stock whip that cracks,' he offered.

Jimbo was undoing his coat to hang it on a tree branch out of the goat's reach.

Andy swung himself up and over an adjacent to the one above and rolled onto it, lying full length.

Casually picking another clump of berries and thrusting them into his mouth, Jimmy wandered idly over towards the hen pen.

Andy stayed up the apple tree, gazing through its branches at clouds blowing over; grey clouds in different layers, black ones up higher. *Whatever year you think of, clouds would have behaved the same way; there's always been weather, and seasons, though politicians tell us we're killing the planet. This sky's grey and greyer. Not a glimpse of blue sky.*

A rush of homesickness swept over him. *What's Tom up to? Be in bed right now but I bet there'll be plenty of blue sky around when he does wake, usually is as winter comes to an end. Bet Gran's been tending to her garden; her word, 'tending'. Wonder if she ever grows these redcurrant berries? I've never looked before; guess I always thought gardens were boring. I like these apple trees, wish we could have massive horse chestnut trees. That other one is monstrous, terrific. I'll have to climb up it again…*

Suddenly there was a furious cackling from Jim's direction. Andy turned to see. Silly kid. It was the chooks around the rooster. Old Nebuchadnezzar was squawking to challenge Jimmy, his wings outstretched as if he was going to fly over the top.

'Yah yah ye yah yah,' chanted Jimmy and danced up and down, waving the leather rein at the cockerel.

It cackled and squawked and threw itself at the wire netting, tangling its floppy red comb in the mesh.

As Andy watched, Jimmy seemed to decide not to encourage the silly bird to hurt itself.

He came back towards Andy. 'Are yer birdwatching up there, Ando?'

'Watching you is watching birds, you dill. Why tease the bloody things?'

'Why not? Animals, birds, got no brains.'

Jimmy looked around the orchard for inspiration. The old billy goat was over by the fence. It was munching the long luscious grass under one of the fruit trees; all calm and content it was. He decided it was time it was back with Mrs Russell but had to catch it first, mebbes a lasso… He'd tell her it was eating her redcurrants. What if he said it got out into the field? He liked the idea. She might give him a reward. But where was Andy? He'd need Andy's help.

Andy had jumped from the apple tree and was now climbing onto the high orchard wall. He reached the top – it was all rounded off with ancient tarry, bitumen stuff with shafts of glass sticking out of it. Not at all friendly.

'Hey, Andy. Watch you don't fall. I've got an idea. Wanna be in on it?'

Okay with Andy – the wall was slippery from the rain. He jumped down and yelled to his mate, 'This wall's deadly.'

'Yeah, I know. Supposed to stop raiders or summat. Been there since it was built.'

Andy smiled at the funny logic and jumped down, landing on soft soil. Soft, but he still jerked his knees. *Wonder if Billy's finished his crystal set yet.* Half of him wanted to find a quiet place without weird moody kids and noisy chooks, so he could think about old Mr Scott and a younger Mr Scott and crisps and parallel times and all the other weird things. His other half just didn't want to know about it. He still hadn't talked to Mo-Molly again about the cinemas, nor about the Lord of the Rings books. He felt she'd give him some straight answers.

But first, he had to know what to ask.

15

Jimmy was knotting the long leather rein to form a lasso. Swinging it slowly and casually, he walked over towards the grazing billy goat. Its eyes flickered a little towards Jimmy as it watched him get nearer, but it kept on munching. Suddenly, Jimmy tossed the length of rein in a high loop towards the goat.

Andy had been sitting on one of the new, still empty, nesting boxes. He stood up, staring at Jimmy. 'Whatever you planning to do, you crazy mutt?'

The lasso fell neatly over the goat's nose and around its neck.

'Yahoo,' yelled Jimmy, elated. First time lucky.

Old Billy Goat was not impressed. He danced up off the ground, all four feet at once, tossing his head up and down and from side to side. The loop flicked off the animal's neck and lay on the grass, with Jimmy still gripping the other end. Jimmy got ready to try again but the goat charged, head down, straight at Jimmy.

Andy laughed. 'Serves you right, you duffer.'

The goat sped past Jimmy. He certainly wasn't going to look scared, not with this Aussie lad watching. He dropped the lasso and rushed towards the goat, waving his arms and yelling. The goat dropped its head down and trotted towards him; it passed him, then wheeled and came to a stop by the red currant canes. Its stripy eyes suddenly looked very lively indeed as they fixed on Jimmy. Jimmy bent over, with his arms outstretched to catch it at its next trot. But it snorted, pawed the ground with one whiskery hoof and charged. Goats can move when they want to. Its anger bristled up the hair along its spine.

'Ooer,' cried Jimmy. 'Discretion… And all that.'

He raced to catch up with Andy, who was now curled up on the grass at the other side of the gate. He was laughing so hard at Jimmy's antics that his sides ached.

Jimmy couldn't sprint on two legs as fast as the goat on four and it butted its bony head into Jimmy's bottom.

'Ow. You rotten, stupid animal.' He didn't even swear.

For each step Jimmy took, the goat butted him again in his bottom. He was going to be bruised all over. The goat headed him off and they ended up going round in circles. Andy was laughing so much he cried real tears. The goat wouldn't give up and Jimmy couldn't escape the goat. Now Andy had the hiccups.

Jimmy was angry. 'Oweeeeee. Help,' he yelled, at the top of his voice. 'You bloody old good-for-nowt.'

Suddenly, a gap. He ran over to the chook pen, flicked open the gate and darted inside. Safe. The old goat snorted, but stood there, its sides heaving, just watching. It even lifted a lip in a sly grin.

Jimmy rubbed his backside, hard. He was going to be black and blue.

What the goat knew very well, what Andy was just realising and what Jimmy hadn't reckoned with, was Nebuchadnezzar. The King of the Cockerels and Master Guardian of the chooks and chicks had watched the whole performance with his beady eyes.

While Jimmy was rubbing his bruises and congratulating himself at getting away from the goat, Nebuchadnezzar was running, wings outstretched, from the far side of the hen pen. He was determined this time to get him, the hated lad who'd earlier teased him at the fence and now dared to enter his territory. Jimmy was too busy pulling a face at the old goat to see him, but Andy did…

'Jimmy, watch out!' But his warning came too late.

'Yeeow,' yelped Jimmy in anguish, as a sharp red beak jabbed into the back of his leg. 'Ow, I'm stabbed. Yeeow.'

The huge, angry bird scrambled up his back, wings whirring, onto his shoulders. Jimmy could hardly see for feathers. He put up his hands to protect his eyes as the bird jabbed ferociously at his bare head with its beak. Its claws were frantic on his shoulders through his shirt.

Tears of fright and pain rolled down Jimbo's face. 'Help! Help! Gerritoff!'

Not funny any more. Andy had seen enough. He was a bloomin' idiot kid sometimes but he was his mate. And now he was in *real* trouble. Vicious bloody rooster. He grabbed a broken bough off the ground and ran up to the chook pen, swinging it madly above his head and yelling at the top of his voice, 'Get off him! Get *off* him!'

The old billy goat realised he was in the line of attack. He trotted off out of the way.

Andy reached the chook pen, flung the gate wide open and ran inside. Now he swung his stick madly from side to side, swiping wildly at the big white bird. Its eyes glittered red like blood.

Andy felt like the knights of old in the Tower of London. This was a charge and his mate was in real trouble. His stick was Excalibur in his grip, sharp and deadly. It hit the big bird again and again as it squawked and swiped with its wings. Still squawking, it fell back to the ground. Jimmy by now was on his knees and Nebuchadnezzar really had his dander up. He backed off a little and then charged again, beak open and head extended, at Jimmy. The skin of his eye flicked open and closed, his little tongue protruded beyond its beak. This was a bird burning with the thrill of a fight.

Jimmy was staggering a bit, blood running down from around his ears. Andy gave a two-handed chop to the big bird's outstretched neck and it collapsed onto the gravel.

'Time to get up Jimbo, c'mon.' Andy grabbed his now sobbing mate by his arm and yanked him out of the gate. He snecked the gate tight. A couple of chooks had wobbled out – too bad. Jimmy was his priority.

They plonked down on the wet grass, together, one sobbing, one panting and snorting.

Jim was in a mess and trying to dry his tears. His nose was running and he wiped it on his shirt. 'By 'eck, Ando. You saved my life in there. Ooh, I'm sore.'

'He's a rotten old bird, Jimbo. Bloomin' dangerous, I reckon.'

'Hope the 'orrible thing isn't dead, though.' Jimmy looked back at his dad's big white cockerel. He was pleased to see it was upright again, if a bit wobbly on its legs. He knew the bird was worth a lot of money, horrible creature though it was.

Andy was inspecting his mate's scratches. 'You're a heck of a mess, mate. One big un on your shoulder and your shirt's ripped on your shoulders and down your back. Took a bite outta your ear, by the looks – quite a bit of bleeding. Good job you had your wellies on, though, or you'd have had a huge slice out of your leg when it was scrambling up.' Andy tried to sound reassuring. 'You'll feel better when you're cleaned up. Get under the shower – oh, you can't… Must wash everywhere, though, and do that quick, mate. The old rooster has filthy feet. You don't want to get infected.'

Jimmy was more worried about his torn shirt and how he could explain it all. 'Can't go home yet, Ando. Need to think what to say.'

Jimmy's cuts stopped bleeding but were still stinging. He set off for the tyre swings, Andy following. They climbed aboard and sat rocking and bouncing off each other. Andy opened his sandwiches and they were soon spinning yarns, through mouths full of cheese and Marmite, about what should happen to Old Neb the cockerel. Then Andy saw Mrs O go into Mrs Russell's house.

'Come on, Jimbo. You can go indoors now and get those cuts washed or something.' Andy knew all about what Mum called 'secondary infections', ever since that splinter in his finger.

Molly was reading. When she saw Jimmy, she pursed her lips and shook her head. 'Oh, Jimmy, whatever…?' She pulled, none too gently, the remains of his shirt over his head. She dropped it on the floor with an accusing gesture, shaking her head and tut-tutting at her young brother. She turned him around, examining his wounds, then poured hot water from the kettle into a bowl.

Andy looked on. He hurt for Jimbo. His cuts were gross.

Mo looked more worried than cross. 'It needs Dettol, our Jimmy. In the water and then the ointment. Keep still and don't yell if it stings.'

Jimmy looked a bit sulky, but he suffered his big sister's first aid treatment without too many ows and ouches. Wasn't going to look a sissy with Andy watching.

'Got any Betadine, Mo? Mightn't sting so much – my mum swears by it.'

Mo looked at him, thought for a minute, then said, 'What? Oh, iodine, Jimmy? Your choice.'

'No way. That purple stuff stings even worse.'

Mo was genuinely sympathetic. She despised the white leghorn too. They all did. She didn't even quiz Jimmy about why he was in the pen at that time of day. Andy reckoned he'd known other sisters who'd kick up a fuss and dob a bloke in. Not this one.

Mo rubbed a strong-smelling yellowy ointment all over Jimmy's wounds. Andy recognised the smell from when Mrs O tended his splinter. Some of Jimmy's wounds were still bleeding and those she spread thickly with the ointment.

'That'll do, Jimmy. Now go and put a clean shirt on – an old one, mind. It can act as a bandage and let the air get to the cuts a bit. It'll help them heal.' She shook her head and picked up the bowl and towel she'd been using. 'I'll talk to Mam, don't worry, but that bird's called a leghorn for a reason, little brother, and those leg horns are designed for fighting and ripping things to bits. Right. Off you go now and leave me in peace with my book while I've still a chance. Hey, and take a couple of the rock buns. They're just out of the oven.'

Andy chose two of the biggest while Jimmy ran to get a shirt.

Back on the swings, Andy was concerned for his friend. 'Are you okay. Jimbo?'

'Stings like 'ell, Ando. Thanks fer askin'.' Jimmy wasn't a sissy but he didn't have to pretend it didn't hurt at all.

Andy was relieved the cuts had been cleaned up. His mum was always going on about infection. If It'd been him, she would've checked whether he needed another tetanus shot. But in the here and now, Jimmy was muttering about the 'claggy' Dettol ointment stuck to his shirt. Andy chalked up another new word for his mum.

Then Jimmy started muttering about the rooster. 'I hate that bird you call a rooster. It's a bloody *cockerel* in English. And no colonial's gonna tell me how to talk my language.' He shouted and strung together a list of swearing names for the hated bird. Some of them were new to Andy.

'Wow. Them's some swears, Jimbo. Your mum'll have yer guts for garters if she heard.'

'Her ears can't reach this far. I hope.'

Andy laughed and swung in circles so wide and fast in the tyre that his rope twisted and the bough squeaked. Then he joined with Jimmy inventing terrible swear words for the big bird. Some other words they daren't for the life of them speak too loudly. Some of Andy's words came from that horrible Rezzo on the other side of the world but it just felt good to let all the tension of the day go, and it did, flying to the rooks above. Then the humour of the situation caught up with them and they started inventing crazy words that no one listening would ever understand.

'This is sure, certain and f'ra fact good fun,' chortled Andy.

'What's that you keep sayin', Ando? Sure, certain and fat?'

Andy giggled. 'Sure certain and f'ra fact. Mrs Reeves said it an' I liked the sound of it. Guess I just picked it up. How's these: drongo, twit, clown, galah…that's you.'

And the two lads sang out even more of all the silly words they knew and could invent. Loud and tuneless they were, until the rooks up high in the trees above started competing with their cawing.

Andy wanted a game of Holey. He had Aggie with him of course, and a couple of others he'd won off Jimmy. But Jimmy didn't want to play. Truth to tell, his back was stinging, and his shirt was sticky with ointment and pulling on the cuts. They stayed on the swings.

Jimmy ate Andy's banana because they'd finished the sandwiches. Andy was still eating redcurrants and pondering what he'd thought in the orchard, looking at clouds. What did it mean, the here and now? What was his mind suggesting before…and now? Could it really be a time warp?

He promised not to let on to Billy about the goat and stuff before Jimmy himself was ready to tell him.

It started to drizzle, so they walked into the stables for shelter. A few kicks of the football around the stable walls made them both feel a bit brighter.

Billy came looking for his brother when they were just about finished. 'Mum asks if you'd give this note to your mum, Andy.'

'Sure thing.' Andy remembered about the radio. 'Billy, can I see how your crystal set's coming on. I've done robotronics and…'

That Billy face again. 'Not today, Andy. Look, I know you know stuff, but it's at a bit of a tricky stage and I've got to write it up. It's an elective project for school, you see – gets marks. I will ask you to come an' see sometime. Dad's helping me but we usually work at night 'cos that's when we get the best reception for the short wave signals, frequencies and stuff. And Ando', he turned to go back indoors, 'I do know all about radio telegraphy and stuff. This is what we call a wireless, Ando.'

16

Andy was suddenly overcome with embarrassment, remembering about last week. *I don't want to revisit that incident – that's mother talk.* He'd been a stupid dork. It was after he'd checked out crystal sets online. Great stuff but he'd told Billy what he'd found out; that radio was a word from Latin meaning to radiate. Yeah, right, sort of showing off. He then told the lads all about the crystal sets he'd found 'online', in detail, and robotronics… big mistake.

Billy had been livid. He didn't want some other kid, wherever he came from, telling him how to work his project. 'You're nobbut an Aussie know-all. Full o' new ideas and crazy bloomin' schemes, you are, and a liar to boot.'

'I'm no liar. Yes, I do come from another country and I am different, and right now I'm glad I am who I am.'

Andy had fronted up to Billy, his eyes angry and his fists clenched, and Billy jumped on him. They fell and rolled on to the ground. Billy looked to be getting the better of it and, as if he realised it, with Andy still flat on his back on the gravel, he pulled himself up and sat on Andy's belly. He looked as if he thought honour had been satisfied and, starting to grin, he leaned over and pinned both Andy's out-flung arms to the ground.

'Okay, clever clogs, had enough?'

But Andy was seeing not Billy's friendly face above him, but Rezzo's evil grin. Fat bully stinking Rezzo. His memories of that fight, and the injustice he'd felt at his treatment by the school, had come sweeping over him like a cloud of red dust. Billy's grin was widening and he moved one arm away to help Andy get up. Andy swung his left and socked Billy on his chin. Knuckle on bone. Not a game. Not funny.

Billy fell back, rubbing his chin. Jimmy pulled Billy up, then yanked Andy to his feet. He looked shocked. 'What's with this knuckle stuff, Andy? Don't you know the difference between fighting and wrestlin'? We don't fight.'

Andy stood there like a dummy, shivering with tension. His brain was still back in the schoolyard weeks ago, and Rezzo's snotty red face was still before his eyes. He started to sob, then cried real tears of frustration. Then he went to kick Billy. Like a kid.

Jimmy grabbed him from behind and gripped him firmly round his chest. Andy struggled but Jimmy was stronger than he thought and wouldn't let go. Andy quit sobbing and wriggling. He slipped onto his knees, wiped his face and nose with the back of his hands, then ran his fingers through his hair. He was just thankful he hadn't head-butted Billy as he had Rezzo. Head down, bottom on his heels, he stared at the bits of gravel all rucked up by their wrestle.

Billy and Jimmy sat down either side of him. Jimmy looked at Billy and Billy looked back. Somehow they felt that to keep quiet and wait till Andy wanted to talk was the best thing. They liked Andy. Even Billy did, deep down. Fourteen-year-old lads didn't blubber; gotta have a *real* reason if they do. Clearly Andy had a problem; nor was he used to friendly wrestling.

A few more deep breaths and Andy was Andy again but feeling a bit of a dork with the lads sitting, waiting for him to get back to normal. Andy pulled a tissue from his pocket, gave his nose a good blow, and regained enough common sense to realise it was decent of Billy not to hit him back; his chin was an angry red.

Andy wriggled his legs out in front of him. Then, there on the gravel, he told them all about Rezzo. 'He was always a little slime. Not so bleedin' little either. I caught him trying to grab a Grade 6 girl and pull down her knickers. It was in the school garden and the girl was crying. I grabbed him. He kicked me. I lost my feet and fell down. He flung a fist and I head-butted him. A teacher on playground duty saw us. I called him a fat slob. That was that. Once too often, they said. Thinking back, not proud of myself.'

He told the lads how Rezzo was what his mother called his nemesis. He'd tackled Rezzo before but only after a lot of what his dad said was prevarication. Rezzo once took Andy's school bag from his locker and peed inside it. All over his lunch box, his books and everything. Andy hadn't dobbed Rezzo in, though. Not even when old Potts was reading the riot act. All the teachers reckoned Rezzo was the victim because his brother and his dad were in jail. They said he'd had a troubled childhood. Andy's mates knew better. Rezzo was always the one who started the fights. The last time had been one time too many. The injustice of it all had steamed inside Andy for longer than he'd realised. He thought he'd got over it. Till last week.

He'd sat there, in the dust, not quite knowing whether to just go home or what. *Didn't mean to talk about all that. Guess it's out in the open now. Feel a bit of a dill and they'll be disgusted.*

Nobody moved, not sure what to do or who should do anything.

Then Billy scrambled to his feet and held out his hand. 'I'm shaking your hand, Ando. That was a good thing you did, standing up for that girl. But me and Jimmy enjoy wrestling, and wrestling's not fighting. Don't do it so much now, anyway, but sometimes we push and look rough, only ter do what we haveter, to get each other on the floor and keep him there. We don't try to bash each other up. We only wrestle for points. Not to see who gets hurt. Just for fun. That right, Jimmy?'

Jimmy nodded. 'Aye, it is, Billy. If we really get mad, Andy, we don't wrestle because that'd get nasty, as our bad tempers'd take over. We could really do damage to each other. So we clear off out of the way and think about things instead. And we never ever kick or use our fists like you were going to.'

Billy reinforced his brother's argument. 'Fists and feet is fighting, Andy. Our dad would belt us if we had a fight, a real fight. He says we're now old enough and sensible enough to know the difference.'

'That's right, Ando. We're pals, us an' you. Mates in your Aussie language. You can wrestle me any time.' Jimmy grinned. 'You'll not get the better of me, you big Aussie, but wrestling's only ever to score a point, okay? Like playing marbles.' He chuckled. 'That's the best way to score points, but Billy's no good at marbles so we wrestle. Awright, Ando? Let's you an' me do battle over a game of Holey. That's fun.'

***

All that had happened a week ago. Andy hadn't told his mum about it, feeling she didn't need to know. But in some ways. though he still felt awkward about clobbering Billy, he felt that telling the lads all about Rezzo and his sacking had taken away some sort of burden from his brain; there seemed less confusion rattling about inside. And it had all ended in a positive way – Billy still tossed the odd remark his way, but they seemed to be more like equals now and less of rivals.

It was all in the past now, and the lads hadn't mentioned it since but right now other thoughts were nagging Andy – this very minute, on this day of the rooster battle. He idled the football between his feet and dribbled it away from Jimbo.

Billy said it was time and Jimmy said, 'What for?'

Billy meant for tea, but for Andy, that was *it*. The moment of understanding, or realisation, whatever… Suddenly all those little circuits in his head started charging in sync, as his dad would say. He felt his face blush uncontrollably and he wanted to yell out loud. Instead, he hid himself by tucking Mrs O's note deep into his pocket.

Suddenly he knew. Billy called his crystal set 'wireless'. And he, Aussie Andy, had answered, 'Wireless in your time, Billy, is not wireless in my time.'

All this time trying to work things out and I realise what's what in the middle of a kick with Jimbo. Not in bed when I usually do my thinking. Just three words to show me what's what, 'in my time'. That's what I said. An' my time is 'real time', like now, the twenty-first century and not the middle of the twentieth. An' in the orchard, I said 'the here an' now'.

He froze. It was gobsmacking stuff. Those words summed up all the funny feelings, the questions he'd been asking himself in bed at night. Could that be what was at the back of all this; all the differences, the questions he wanted to ask and couldn't? *It really is a time warp, time zone – parallel lives an' that. Research is being done, I know, in my time. Not Mum's sort of research but into past and future. An' they do exist. All that stuff with the crisps and Mr Scott, f'rinstance, gotta be evidence of a sort.*

Jimmy was trying to wrest the football from between Andy's feet.

Andy shook his head at Jimmy. 'Sorry Jimbo. I'm just not with it. Been a mixed-up day. Better head home.'

Jimmy thought he was referring to his rooster fight and his injuries. 'You are a good myte, Ando – the best.'

'No probs, Jimbo. Seeya. I've some emails to write to my rellies so I'd better make a start.'

Jimmy spun around. 'C'mon, Ando, I'm okay. Another game of Holey?'

'Nah. Go nurse your wounds, Jimbo. I'll teach you to talk Orstraylian yet,' Andy joked, 'Have to go, Jimbo.'

He sprinted down to the gate while Jimbo dragged his feet in the gravel towards his home. Jim was reluctant to face his mam – he wondered if Mo had calmed her down?

17

Once over the gate, Andy slowed down to a walk. His thoughts were in that familiar tangle. How could he talk to Mum about Mrs O telling him about the crisps in Scott's shop – that just didn't make sense. Mum was into 'facts' with 'evidence'. She'd say his imagination had gone haywire again, one of her usual cop-outs. And if he told her what he now knew was the truth, the Big House family were in another time, which was it? Gran's time, the nineteen fifties? Crazy stuff. He imagined Mum's face.

As he opened the door of the Barn, she called out, 'Had a good day, Andy? Tea's nearly ready.'

Phew, doesn't want an answer. Just the usual hint to get washed ready to eat. Nice one.

He gave her Mrs O's note. She tucked it into her pants pocket without reading it. Something was getting served up that looked and smelled *great*.

Andy didn't get a chance to talk to his mum after tea. Nor could he look things up on the computer. She worked on it steadily until it was time for bed and there was nothing on TV. He settled for a DVD but his mind couldn't settle to the story. When he did go to bed, he couldn't sleep for thinking about parallel time zones.

He remembered his journal as he curled up under the quilt. *Supposed to be for 'travel experiences and observations' but I've been writing all kinds of stuff in it. Anyway, I might not be allowed back to Sunbury. Who cares? So no point worrying if Mrs McGee or old Potts read it? Could be interesting to have them read about my fight with Rezzo and all that stuff. Like my side of the argument. But how much of all these puzzles and time warp mysteries to put in? Okay, so it'd keep me on the mark, but they – and even Mum – don't need to read all that. Yet it should be recorded safely. Who knows what might happen?*

His light stayed on a long time that night. He wondered how Jimmy was, too. But he needn't have worried.

Mrs O, like all mums, was more concerned about checking his cuts and scratches, and fowls' dirty feet causing infection, than asking how he'd done it. She even told Dad that night that Nebuchadnezzar had to go. 'He's too aggressive, that old cockerel. He'll have someone's eye out one day,' she complained. 'Get in this Dettol bath, Jimmy, and afterwards I'll rub more ointment all over the cuts.'

Billy was asked to collect the eggs that night. He found his brother's old raincoat hanging from the apple tree. Later, when the lads were in bed, and no one else could hear, Jimmy told him all about lassoing Russell's goat. Billy was usually the one to boast about what *he* could do.

Watching Billy's surprise gave Jimmy such a good feeling he nearly forgot his cuts and bruises. Then he turned over too quickly in bed. 'Ouch.'

However, as Jimmy later told Andy, he felt a lot better in the morning. His dad asked him to make a couple more nesting boxes and Jimmy was looking forward to Andy helping. Dad said they were becoming a production line, like Henry Ford's in America, and promised more chocolate and some money for the pictures on Saturday. Jimmy thought that whatever the prizes, it was more fun when he could show Andy how to do stuff instead of the Aussie always having the ideas. Though he thought that last idea about sloping roofs on them was good, so did his dad. Definitely worth a bar of chocolate. But when Jimmy was ready to start on the woodwork, Andy still hadn't arrived.

***

Andy was having breakfast and a talk with his mum. She'd lost Mrs O's note. Well, it was unreadable anyway. It turned up all wet and indecipherable in the pocket of her cargoes after they'd been through the wash.

She wasn't very happy. 'I went to ring Mrs O but realised I don't know her number. I know there's no signal up at the Big House, but honestly, Andy, we're in the space age and yet… Oh, I don't know. How do all those people manage? I thought I'd ring on Mrs Reeves's landline phone. But she's gone out. I need to go into the library in town and I'll phone Mrs O from there. Her number must be in the book. So do you want to come in with me?'

Andy didn't know much about libraries. He hadn't belonged to a library since he was a little kid, when his mum used to borrow coloured picture books to read with him. The one here was a huge place with a terrific bank of computers for members to use and he wondered if the one at home was as vast. He agreed. He'd like some more crisps anyway if the library was near that supermarket.

Mum arranged for the Tolkien books to be held for Andy. He'd seen the movies but last night, mixed in all his thoughts about time travel he suddenly thought he'd like to read the original stories. Today as he looked through other books on the shelves, he asked himself, *What was the last book I read that wasn't a school book? And when?*

He stopped and ticked off on his fingers. *I've got the PS, and my DS. I like the MP3 for my music. There's TV and DVDs. But Dad's got one of those ebook things to download stories and says it's not heavy like a book, easy to carry when he travels. Still reading, though. Reading takes more time because you have to think. Mum goes on and on about me always being in a hurry, always after a quick result. How many times has she called me a typical Aussie-whizz-bang-techno-gizmo-kid? Hmm. Now she asks me what I do to fill my time 'cause I don't use my DS any more. There's just no pleasing parents. Guess I could pick a couple of the books from the young adults shelves and ask Mum to borrow them. Or maybe I could join myself? Wouldn't hurt.*

Afterwards, they sat in Hanratty's eating fish and chips. Mum's mind was on a text from her publisher that came while they were in the library. Andy's mind was on his fish and chips.

'Great chips Mum. Better 'n thin fries, aren't they?'

She just nodded.

Best let her think through all her stuff. Got enough of my own. All this parallel time zone stuff; I know it exists, but how? What's the connection, what's the catalyst, as Mum wrote the other night. Good word – she said it means something that precipitates change.

With every chew he had a thought – and it seemed every question created another question. With every swallow of fish or chips, with every dab into the tomato sauce, another twisted query would turn up.

That gate, f'rinstance – the old gate – seems to be the magic doorway, or portal as the Phantom calls it. The other side is early time, or then, and this side is real time and now. I still can't find the other gate I saw from Gran's tree, those weeks ago. Okay, so what is *the catalyst? My mind? My imagination? Who knows the answers? Who can I talk to? So much to get confused about and it's all just too weird to talk about in a sensible way. How can I start? I can't, not yet. So I think I know the* when *I am but I don't know the* how *of it.*

'Andy, do you have to burp? We aren't at home, you know.'

He was quite relieved to get back home, in a normal routine, whatever 'normal' was. His mum started checking her emails and he switched on the TV. It was the first of the Lord of the Rings movies and the channel was planning to show the whole series again. *Good coincidence; take my mind off all the other stuff for a couple hours.*

Next morning, armed with a note from Mum for Mrs O, a

pocket of marbles, Mum's little digital camera to take photos for her, and some bananas to share with the lads, Andy set off up the drive.

He dawdled up towards the house, thinking but not making any sense of anything.

He heard the lads' voices. They were quarrelling. Loudly. Billy wanted Jimmy to lend his bike to Andy so he and Andy could go for a bike ride; he was declaring he and Andy were both older than Jimmy. But no way was Jimmy going to be left behind. They were deciding to settle things with a scrap on the cobbles as Andy reached them.

They stopped yelling long enough to give him a casual wave; he waited and watched as he peeled a banana. Now he understood about their scrapping or wrestling, they could get on with it. Jimmy declared himself the winner. Their mam came out with a full basket of laundry to hang out. She looked tired and said if they were so bored, her two could carry the basket up to the washing line. The lads and Andy shared the load then fled over to the swings.

Mrs O started to peg the washing on the long line. Andy handed over the note.

She smiled in thanks then turned to her sons again. 'Jimmy, that bike of yours you were quarrelling over has a flat tyre. In fact it has *two* flat tyres. I want you to get those punctures fixed. *now!*

Billy thumbed his nose at his brother in triumph. Jimmy glowered but slumped off to do as he was told. He'd felt his mother's hard hand too often on the back of his legs to ignore her.

Billy turned to Andy. 'C'mon, Ando, let's go and see if the old bull's in t' meadow today. Bet it's bigger than anything you got in Australia. Mum said it's been bellowing enough to drive her mad an' it's by the orchard fence she says and she hears it through the scullery window. It's a real monster. A Friesian. Gets a mask wired on its head when it's put in t' meadow. A real freak. C'mon.' He hared off up the Top Drive, with Andy grumbling after him.

'Hey, Billy, slow down, mate. I've already walked up the long Bottom Drive, you know.'

Top Drive was little more than a quiet lane, stony and overgrown on its banks. It had wheel tracks either side of a long bumpy bit in the middle. *Car tracks, I guess.* He eventually caught up with Billy. He was balancing on the bottom strut of an old iron fence bordering the big meadow. Their orchard was not far down the hill, below where they were, and Andy could hear the chooks chuckling and Old Nebby's raucous crowing. Looking straight ahead, halfway up the hill and about as far away from this fence as it had been from the bottom drive, was the Tree. *Looks smaller than it felt; guess that's because of the distance.* The meadow looked empty. *So where is this bull?*

He clambered onto the top rail of the fence and prepared to jump over.

'Ando, ge' back. Quick,' and Billy pulled Andy's cargo pants.

He fell back, on to his bottom by his friend's feet.

<h1 style="text-align:center">18</h1>

'Hey. Whadyer do tha' for?' gabbled angry Andy. He got up and brushed the wet grass off the seat of his pants.

Billy grabbed him again and pulled him behind a bush. He put his finger to his mouth signalling 'shush'. 'It's Capper's bull,' he whispered.

He pointed to Andy's left and then Andy heard it for himself, a snorting and snuffling noise getting closer.

He peered around the bush then pulled back, a look of horror on his face. Eyes wide, he stared at Billy and whispered, his voice rasping, 'It's bloody 'orrible, Billy. An enormous bull. And that 'orrible tin mask on its face...' Words failed him. He'd never seen a bull as big, not even in the ag show at home.

The bull pulled up, near to where they were standing. Andy hunkered down, hardly daring to breathe. How come he hadn't seen it or heard it earlier? *Surely this is the big meadow that runs all the way down to the hedge behind Mrs Reeves's barn? Their rental?* Here, there was only a thin metal railing fence between them and the monster. Thin and rusty, weak, frail...wouldn't stop a dog.

The animal's head looked nearly as wide as a door and half as high. The mask reminded him of his dad's garden shovel, but bigger. The greyish metal had hammer marks all over it where it had been beaten into shape. It was held on the bull's head by a leather harness that went round two long, curved horns.

'Like Samurai swords,' a hoarse whisper again from Andy.

Billy just grimaced. 'Tall as you, Ando, d'ya think?'

The huge bull lifted up its head. Its wet pink nose was

pointing straight at Billy and its eyes glinted under the mask. Andy realised if he could see the bull's eyes, the bull could see him. The bush was too sparse to give coverage, some camouflage.

Then it bellowed; a deep double bass rattle dragged up from the bottom of its massive stomach. Goosebumps prickled Andy's arms and the back of his neck and the waves of sound slammed with each reverberation against his eardrums.

The bull scraped one of its hooves over the grass – and again and again. Billy moved nearer to the fence, stood still. Andy was open-mouthed in horror. Billy was daring it to charge.

Andy was not impressed. In a hoarse whisper, he warned Billy, 'If that beast charges, Billy, yer on yer own.'

Billy smirked at Andy. 'Scaredy-cat. You're chicken, Aussie,' but he backed off a step.

The bull was now standing still, just staring back at Billy under that mask. It decided, just another silly human to ignore. Grazing was what bulls did very well. It snorted in derision and put its head down again to graze.

Andy laughed in relief. 'C'mon, Billy. It's not interested. It said bugger off.'

Billy thought Andy was mocking him and went red in the face. 'This stupid animal has no right to ignore me. I'm the superior being. I'll strike its heart with fear.'

Andy watched as Billy started to walk along the fence line, then turned, glared at the bull. Eyes wide open, singing 'dah de dah' he danced from one foot to the other waving his arms in the air.

Andy wanted out. 'Billy,' he whispered hoarsely. 'You're not in the movies. No sense getting it all pissed off. Leave it.'

Billy just glowered at him. 'Shurrup, Aussie. If Mum shoulda heard you swear just now, you'd get more 'n her finger wagging at you.'

'Huh – pots and kettles, Billy.'

Still the bull went on munching, ignoring both of them. Lush and juicy grass had its interest, not silly humans. Its leathery tail twitched a few times as it fought a fly. Billy thought he'd been patient long enough. He intended to show this tall and lanky Aussie show-off a thing or two. It still ignored him.

Billy was incensed. He looked around for a small stone, found some bits of flint that swept up off the driveway and threw a handful straight at the bull's mask.

Andy pulled further under the bush and froze to the grass in horror. The bull, startled by the ringing of the stone on the metal, lurched backwards, waving its head from side to side. The massive metal mask slipped sideways but didn't fall off. It was still looped around the two horns. Those sword-like horns. Andy tensed as the monster planted its two front hooves on the ground, lowered its head with a slobbery snort and pointed its horns directly at Billy.

'Oh crikey,' Andy whispered to Billy. 'Come on, walk back a step, slowly.' He knew if the animal charged it would take the fence. And Billy. And he, Andrew from Adelaide, was next in line. Andy moved up onto his haunches, ready to run.

Billy stood as still as a statue – close, too close, to the fence. The bull shook its head from side to side and turned as if to move away. The mask slipped even further to one side of its head.

Billy exploded. How dare this stupid animal make him look such a clot in front of this Australian know-all with his 'online this' and 'online that'. He tossed another handful of gravel onto the bull's mask. It shook and rattled and echoed with a noise that reminded Andy of hailstones on an iron roof. The huge animal spun round. It lifted its massive head to look at the boys with wet, bloodshot eyes and emitted another sound-wave-interrupting bellow.

Andy felt a shiver run up his spine. 'Yoicks. Billy, you dork.'

Bent over, Andy ran to another big bush further back. Billy watched him run but stayed his own ground. Then the bull butted the thin top railing of the fence.

'Oh 'eck. It's comin' through.' Billy forgot about being brave. He turned and ran towards the same bush Andy had already dived under.

They both rolled over and crawled, bottoms in the air, towards the stony driveway where there were a few strong trees between them and the bull. However, the bull stayed at the fence, snorting and spitting through its nostrils, tugging one of its horns back from under the top rail.

Billy rubbed his arms with some long wet grass to cool down some scratches. Andy was already scrambling uphill on the stony driveway. He looked over towards the meadow fence.

His mate was still rubbing his arms and muttering, 'What's a dork?'

Andy was thankful all the panic seemed to be over. Then he heard, and felt, a thud – and another – in rhythm. He swivelled towards the meadow again. He couldn't see because of the trees a little bit down the hill but that noise was from four large cloven hooves. 'Oh, shivers.'

Berrum, kerclop, berrum… The tread of a monster – huge feet on a wet field. The bull was on the move. Berrum, kerclop, berrum. It had followed the lads' sounds as they went up the drive. Andy saw it was still the other side of the fence. And the fence looked as strong as a piece of string. If it saw him, or Billy… He shivered. The bull was snorting and snuffling with the effort of lumbering uphill. A sudden clang as that mask struck the railings. Which side of the fence? Another clang and a shrill squeak as the metal mask ran along the rail. The loose mask had got the bull mad. It wanted revenge.

'C'mon, Billy, hurry up.' Andy ran further up the lane towards a big stone wall edging the road above. He hoped there were enough bushes between him and the fence to act as a blind. *That wall looks strong enough…*

The bull's heavy tread had slowed. As each of the hooves hit the ground, Andy felt it shake under him. For sure, certain and f'ra fact. The monster's skin made a squeaky leathery noise with each step, just like his football after a game on wet grass.

'Billy, you better say your prayers.'

The wall was too far away. The lads lunged under a huge rhododendron bush. It was like a cave inside. The leafy branches hung down on all sides, hiding them.

Billy put his finger to his lips. Andy hoped the bull couldn't see or even smell them. They could hear it breathing. Loudly. Every single breath. It had followed the line of the fence all the way. It was trolling them, baiting them. The two lads tried not to move. Andy even tried not to breathe but he was too puffed from running and couldn't hold it in. The bull's hot breath wafted through the leaves. It smelled of Dad's lawn clippings after rain.

The two lads waited, silently crouching. Billy got cramp in his leg but didn't dare stretch because his shoe would poke out from under the edges of their hidey-hole.

19

Andy wasn't sure how long they'd been hiding. He wished he'd checked his watch before. Then he realised the birds were chattering again in the branches above. The snorting and snuffling had stopped. Had the bull moved away? They peeked out: two heads, one above the other; two sets of wide, anxious eyes.

The animal had fooled them. It was now as determined to get its own back on the lads as Billy had been earlier to tease it into a response. It was still there, every hundredweight, every tonne of it, two wicked horns, a steamy pair of flared nostrils that the brass ring went through and a *huge*, sweaty, shiny black and white leathery body.

I'm only two metres from death, thought Andy. *That stupid, bloody Billy. Two big bull-sized steps at a charge. Too easy.*

The monstrous animal was standing just inside the meadow, its big head nodding up and down, the iron mask slipping further down one side of its massive snout. Its tail was whipping from side to side and over its back with whooshing and slapping noises. The boys fell back into their hidey-hole. The bull was swishing its wet tongue over and around the big ring on its nose. One eye looked straight at their rhodo bush.

'Oh 'eck,' whispered Billy into Andy's sweaty ear. 'What if it can't see 't fence properly? It could easy barge straight through. An' I think it can see me feet.'

'Sssh. You dork, you started all this.'

They hardly dared to peek as the bull nuzzled the top piece of railing. It was an even thinner and weaker-looking rail than the other ones. It scraped the metal mask and the big head jerked back, its one available eye searching for its tormentors. It stepped back a pace or two and lifted its head. It was looking directly at where the boys were crouching. It stepped forward and – horror of horrors – lifted its heavy head slowly over the top of the fence, sniffing the air. They could see thick snot rolling down from its nostrils mixing with the froth around its mouth.

The boys didn't dare even whisper. It seemed ages and ages that they had been waiting there. Billy needed to pee. He was getting desperate. He risked another peek. The bull's massive head was right over the fence, so near he smelled its breath again and saw even more yellow gunge running down from its nose. It stretched its massive throat above the rail, its wet, pink nose breathing snot and steam enough to turn the big brass ring all misty. Long droplets of froth and spit plopped onto the grass.

Tactics, thought Andy. 'Stay or move?' he nudged Billy, daring a whisper.

If they ran like the wind back down the drive, would the bull barge through the fence? Could it barge through without getting tangled? It had such a wide chest and shoulders and such a strong neck he thought it probably could chase after them still with lengths of metal fence attached.

He noticed Billy was looking quite pale and his bare knees had gone clammy. He was in shock, or so Mum would say.

Andy remembered the squashed banana in his cargo pants. Tactic Number One: get Billy back to normal; he needs a sugar kick. The banana was split and gone brown from being in his pocket, rattling around with Aggie and his steelies, but he managed to get it into two pieces and thrust one at Billy so they each had a piece to chew on. No chewing noises. Definitely no talking. Their ears were pricked to hear the bull but it was quiet. Too quiet.

A distant shout and a loud squawking broke the silence. Shouts of anger came from the orchard.

Billy gave a mashed banana grin and whispered, 'That's our Jimmy collecting the eggs. Old cockerel's protesting.'

The bull was distracted by the noise. It turned and they heard the mask clang on the top rail of the fence. Andy peeked cautiously out. Billy thought he'd never been so happy to hear that horrible cockerel's squawk.

The monster had its back to them and was sniffing the air from the direction of the orchard. The heavy mask was now hanging down one side of its head, held only on one horn and around its muzzle. It looked very uncomfortable. Andy even felt sorry for the poor confused beast. He fancied that if the huge animal could speak, it would ask why its peaceful life had to be so disturbed by a cruel and thoughtless human.

They watched as the bull headed off to investigate the new sounds. The heavy tread seemed to shake the ground under its feet and the loose mask was swinging like mad. It picked up its pace, with loud snorting and puffing that faded as it trotted further away.

Andy gave a big breath outwards, spitting chunks of banana he hadn't managed to swallow. 'It knew we were sitting in the bush, Billy. All the time we were in there it just stayed quiet, waiting.'

Billy grinned. He felt brave again.

The two lads raced down the Top Drive's stony surface till they got to the orchard gate. Billy couldn't wait to tell Jimmy about the bull. Billy started reliving the scare with the bull, as if it had really chased him or as if he'd done something heroic. Andy was a bit scornful. As far as he was concerned, Billy had been more foolish than brave.

Anyway, Jimmy was too busy moaning to his brother about the punctures in his bike tyres to listen to any tales of derring-do from them. 'Not my tyres, our Billy, yours. An' I had to fix 'em.'

Jimmy counted five eggs in his bucket. He ignored the bull,

which by now was trotting along the sturdier orchard fence. Its mask was hanging straight down one side of its head. Its nose was tilted up as it tried to see with its one eye, the other one still covered by the strap holding the mask. Its tongue licked upwards at the gunky brass ring impaling its nostrils. The brothers ignored it – this fence was good and strong – as Billy regaled his brother with tales of his exploit.

'I hate that bloomin' cockerel,' was Jimmy's only retort.

'Rooster,' chivvied Andy and ducked a friendly swipe from Billy.

He was feeling hungry. A few bits of banana had only touched the edges. Billy wanted to tell his brother all about their bull scare. Andy wanted his tea and the safety of his little room to have a think. Maybe he could read one of the library books to take his mind off things. 'I'm off home, lads. See you tomorrow.'

Mrs O called out to Andy as he headed past the backyard. She had an answer for his mum. Great. He took it from her, then hared down the drive.

Pickles jumped up to lick him. Andy hunkered down and rubbed his ears. 'What a welcome, Pickles! Did you know about that monster bull attacking us? Dogs have extrasensory perception, so Mum says. If you don't know what that means, I'll just let you think about it. I'm here now and I'm hungry. End of another day. Time for tea. I'm coming, Mum!'

20

Andy's mum was in a bossy mood next day. He thought she was having a problem with her publisher or editor or somebody because she was on the phone a lot. She was all cranky with Andy and told him to bring his journal up to date; that meant he had to remember what he'd been doing and where he'd gone. Oops. It sure was up to date but what was in it he wanted to talk with her about before she went and found it and read it for herself. She wasn't sneaky that way, though, not like some mothers, but he really wanted to talk some things over with her first.

He ran to his room and put his journal deep under his mattress, then ran back outside. He grumbled about his mum to Pickles. She'd been furious with Andy when he admitted he forgot to take photos as she had asked. She kept mentioning things about old Mr Scott, too.

'Mum, what did Mrs O write to you in the note yesterday? Can't you ask her all about this stuff?'

'I'm going to walk up there this afternoon. It's a lovely day. She's asked me for afternoon tea. I'll enjoy that and I'm really looking forward to meeting her. She's seen a lot of you these last few weeks and I feel it's been a bit rude of me not to walk up and introduce myself.'

'Hey, great. We can walk back home together. You'll like Mrs O, and you'll meet the lads and there's Mo and young David and the littl'un just learning to walk. You like little kids, right?'

She smiled. 'Off you go then. I've put your lunch in your pack. I'll see you later.' She turned to go. 'Oh, Andy, have you got that new marbles bag Mrs Reeves sewed up for you?'

He held it out for her to see.

'Great, see you later on, Bloke.'

When he got up to the Big House, Billy was fixing a new axle on the dinky. 'Hello, Ando. Wanna give us a hand?'

It meant quite a bit of work. Billy had already measured up some timber and Jimmy was drilling two holes for the axle in the side boards.

'What's with the old drill, Jimbo? You're winding that thing like my mum when she uses her old egg whisk to make meringue.'

'Huh? You're a smarty pants you are. This is my dad's old drill.'

'Aren't you allowed to use his electric one?'

'Whaddya mean, electric? My dad's got all sorts of stuff down in his workshop in the town. Has to have, to fix all the engines and stuff. He lets us use what he's got in his shed here at home.'

'Yeah…if we're careful and put it back all clean, like,' argued Billy. He was waiting to hear what marvellous piece of equipment Andy would now dredge out of his imagination. Sure enough…

'My dad has a twelve-volt one, made in Switzerland, I think. You can put the different bits in and it's great for putting screws in timber, *and* undoing them again.'

Billy had had enough talk about all the wonderful things in Australia. 'I dunno about bits, Ando, but if you wanna give us a hand, just do it, eh?'

Andy asked Jim if they still needed more nesting boxes.

'Nah, did a couple t' other day, so got enough. Till Dad says diff. Thanks, myte.'

Andy was given the job of tightening the spokes in two of the wheels. Old wheels, bit bent, weird spokey things. Such small ones he thought would've been better moulded out of rigid plastic like the ones on his scooter at home. *When did I last ride down our street on that scooter?* He looked closely at the wheels.

Okay. He knew Billy was touchy about stuff, but surely people here had electric drills as well.

He tackled the spokes in the way Billy instructed. He was no stranger to pliers and he helped fit the rods in a way that pleased him. He found that in some ways it was good not to have the router, the sander, the drills like his dad used; how it came about he wasn't sure, but he had more time to just think about what he was doing and how to do it better. Also, he liked the fat-sounding clunk of the mallet on the wood frame. It was a good feeling too, using his own strength to twist the spokes. 'Back to basics' his mum would call it.

Time passed. The dinky was looking good. Andy looked at the watch his mum had bought him in that cheap shop in the town. Half-past two and they hadn't eaten lunch yet. Then David came out of the house with some sandwiches and a bottle of homemade lemonade.

'Mam says it's good you are all so busy an' you can have a picnic out here 'cos she's got Andy's mum coming and you're all too dirty to come in.' He prattled it like he'd memorised what to say.

Andy thought it good timing but Billy put his tongue out at his little brother, who retaliated with a grin.

'Ohkey-dokey lads, let's eat,' sang Jimmy. He wiped his greasy hands on his shorts and chose a sandwich. 'Huh, egg and lettuce or egg and lettuce.'

Andy put his Vegemite sandwiches out to share and watched for his mum. No sign yet; he hoped she wouldn't be late. Jimbo suggested she would have walked up through the meadow and used the orchard gate.

'Meadow's quiet. T' bull's back in t' farm. Old Capper asked me if I knew why its mask was nearly off. I telt him I'd seen nowt. That wasn't a lie either.' He chewed a crust with his mouth wide open. 'He didn't ask our Billy.' He laughed so much that he almost choked on his share of the big banana from Andy's backpack.

With its new axle and the wheels fixed, the little dinky whizzed down to the big old gate at a whacking pace. Then they each had a few rides down the gravel.

'Spins good,' sang Billy. 'Good tracks in the gravel, Ando.' High praise from Billy.

Sure was a gravelly, dusty game. The one who pulled it back up the slope quickest got the last bag of crisps. It was Jimmy, but he shared.

'That's enough. I'm knackered. Let's 'ave a threesome game of Boss.'

Andy felt greasy, dusty and very happy. It'd been good making something again. Like this little dinky. As they ran and skipped over to the stables, he wondered about making one when he got back to Australia. Even as he thought, he knew his mum would prob'ly buy him a go-cart. *She's not good with mess in the garden, an' stuff like that.* Then he realised that no cart would be as much fun as using one you made, and making it was the best fun of all. *It's not only Mum's fault. Honest true, do I ever think of making stuff if I can go an' buy it? No. No excuse really. I do have electric tools handy to make a job easier.*

'Shame, Ando'. He spoke aloud as they ran into the stables and Jimmy looked sideways at him.

'Just thinking, mate,' and he settled on his knees to send the first marble.

He even scored a couple more. A steely off Jim and a glassy off Billy. He knew that was because of his lucky green Aggie. *She's a good mascot, that one.*

Then he remembered the time and checked his watch. 'Hey, better go and see if our mothers have finished their talking. I'll walk home with Mum.'

Mum wasn't there. She had not arrived. The lads' mam

and Mo were cutting a piece of cake for themselves as the lads breezed in. Andy felt a bit embarrassed. He could guess what had happened; he knew what his mum was like if she'd got onto her computer – she forgot all about time.

He wasn't sure what to say, so just thanked Mrs O for lunch, said, 'Bye, lads, p'raps tomorrow?' and ran out, down the gravel and over the gate.

***

His Mum was not at her computer. She was sitting with Mrs Reeves having a cuppa.

'Mum, where were you today?'

'Andy, where were you today?' Mum explained how she'd walked up the drive and thought it very pretty. She came to the big gate and walked up the driveway through the lovely landscaped gardens just as it was coming up to three o'clock.

'How did you climb over the big gate?'

'Andy, I didn't – it was wide open.'

'Mum, three o'clock was when me and the lads were fixing the dinky and testing it out down that bit of drive…'

She looked at him, noting the puzzled look on his face, the state of his clothes, grease on his pants, pocket bulging with marbles… 'Andy, I walked around the back of the house. I could not find a green door. There were three doors at ground level and black wrought-iron staircases twisting up to what looked like little flats above. The middle door on the ground had a big brass number 2 on it but an old lady lives there and she's not a Mrs O or Mrs anything beginning with O.'

She switched on her camera. 'I took this with me, seeing as you kept forgetting and, look, this is what I took. See? All the house and gardens.'

Andy gaped, open-mouthed, at the little screen. One by one

they were pictures of the Big House but not how he knew it. The lads' back door was different. He shuddered – Mum had been there at the same time he had. This was creepy. This was a new problem to solve – parallel time zones. How could he break the subject to his mother. Now they *had* to talk about it. He reversed the view the gallery of pics again.

'Mum, I…' He looked up his mother. 'I dunno what to say.'

She waved her hand, to stop him. 'The old lady in number two told me some young families live over in the converted stables but she thought they'd gone to Spain for the summer holidays. They must be the ones Mrs Reeves knows about. No other boys live up there as far as she knows.'

Mrs Reeves nodded as his mum continued. 'Andy, I don't know if I'm worried or plain furious. I want the truth. Just where have you been all these weeks, most days and nearly all day long?'

21

Mrs Reeves spoke up. 'Andy, love, I've been on the phone to that Mrs Hooper, she who lives in number two up there and as she knows me – well, a bit anyway – she's really intrigued. She telt me that renovations to the house were back in t' seventies and eighties, and she's the second tenant in her part. She understands that the Big House used to have just the three houses in it but that it stood empty for a long time before the renovations.' She shook her head at Andy. 'My husband as a young fella was friendly wi' t' young Knollys who farmed off Paddy Lane and he used to talk about some lads who lived in t' Big House and who'd come for billycan of milk most nights. He used to knock about a bit wi' t' eldest lad and he were called Billy. But that was way, way, back, Andy. He was talking about fifty years ago.'

'This is really weird, Mum. Every day I've been with the lads, and the Big House is where we've been. True.' He thought of something else. 'That note Mrs O sent you, didn't it have her house number on it and stuff?'

'No, Andy, she would know that you would know and that I would know – sort of thing.' She looked as irritated as she sounded, as if she didn't believe him, and waved him away. 'Oh, just go and get a good wash before tea, Andy. Maybe we can talk some more later.'

Andy ran up his little paddle staircase and sat down heavily on his bed. This was really creepy. Weird stuff – again. Though it was all starting to add up. *But ter what? And how? Better change out of these greasy strides 'n' keep Mum sweet…* He drew the little drawstring marble bag from his pocket and angrily clunked a

125

couple of the steelies together on the quilt. One was Jimmy's till today; dear old Aggie won…

He sat up straight. Aggie. Gran's special marble. *Of course. Mum would say it's just coincidence but it's more than that. Got to be. The old marble's brought me good luck most times I've used it. Yeh. Gotta be down to Aggie…*

He stood up. '*No!*'

That first day when he'd climbed Gran's Tree, and looked over the Big House at all the TV aerials, saw the big gate open wide – he didn't take the aggie that day. The next day he had and every day since. Today he had Aggie with him but Mum didn't. Gran had called Aggie special. Just how special? It was crazy, but he knew how to put Aggie to the test.

He tipped the rest of the marbles onto the quilt, picked up the little aggie and zipped it into the little bag again and left it carefully on his bed. Now to find out, once and for all.

He scrambled down stairs to the living room. 'Mum, just going out for a quick walk, be back before tea's ready.'

He was out of the house before she could argue. He ran up the drive faster than he'd ever done before. This time, Pickles followed him, tongue dangling and keeping pace with Andy. Together they reached the fork in the driveway and there was the big white gate. Smartly painted. Wide open. He didn't even think about Pickles getting into a fight with other dogs. He had to solve this mystery, once and for all. He ran up the slope, over the gravel where he and the lads had made all those tracks only – what? An hour ago? The only tracks now to be seen were of car tyres near the big four-wheel drive parked up the top; all the rest was raked. Neatly.

He stopped and looked around. He was sweating because of running, his cheeks felt hot, but inside he was chilled all over. He hunkered down and stroked Pickles's silky ears, over and over. 'This isn't the same place, Pickles. Yes, it is the same house but this is where Mum came. Not where I was. Yet we were both here, at the same time of the day, but the days were years apart.' He sat down and hugged Pickles. 'Only this afternoon,' he checked his watch, 'me and the lads fixed the dinky here. Just here. Right where I'm sitting and you're lying down.'

He scrambled to his feet and Pickles looked at him, his ears lopsided. Even a doggy face can show a curious expression when his human friend is upset.

Andy toed his sneaker on the gravel. There was no grease spill underneath, no little pool from when he squirted the oil on the dinky's wheels. *I dropped quite a bit and worried about the mess, and Jimbo said nothing to fret about. That was just about right here.* He scraped his foot sideways in the gravel. *There's nothing here; no chips of timber and bits of wire to show for it. I know we made a bit of a mess. I saw it when I ran home to the gate. Not long ago…not an hour ago. Well, maybe… There's nothing.*

He turned round and round, looking at how neatly the lawns were mown and their edges trimmed. The gravel pathways in front of the Big House were raked, neat and tidy. Big ceramic pots filled with vivid flowers were balanced on the stone steps between the upper and lower lawns. Andy felt a chilly tickly sensation crawl slowly up his spine to the back of his neck. Unstoppable tears welled up in his eyes and he rubbed them with the bottom of his T-shirt.

He walked slowly around to the backyard. He saw what he now expected to see, what his mother had seen: the big wall, the big gates. They looked just the same but the wall of the house, its doors and the number of small windows with neatly painted frames, he had never seen before. Sure, certain an' f'r a fact.

The hair on the back of his neck prickled and he shivered. He was thinking ghosts. Suddenly, he took to his heels, Pickles loping ahead of him, and ran back through the open gate and down the drive, tears running down his cheeks.

He ran indoors.

Mum was waiting. 'Andy, how dare you go off like that. I showed you the photos…'

'Mum, shush, *please*. I just been up there an' it's like your photos. No grease and mess on the gravel either, like the lads and me made. Mum, that was only a coupla hours ago. And the difference is Aggie, Mum, Gran's old green marble.'

Mum saw he was upset, but couldn't restrain herself. 'Andy, for goodness sake.'

'Mum, remember? Gran said it was *really* special – the aggie marble. In my email about the Tree when I sent her the photo, I said how I'd counted all the aerials and discs on the roof of the Big House and all she said when she answered was "That was because you didn't have my green marble with you." I didn't understand what she meant, Mum. After all, she is an old lady – okay, okay, Mum don't get mad – but now I do. She asked me to take Aggie back where she came from, right? So I did, I do, but it's not just to *where*, it's to *when*. and when I don't take Aggie it's *now* not *then*. Mum, d'ya see?'

His mum shook her head from side to side. 'Andy, stop a minute. I'm quite flummoxed. There has to be a logical reason, an explanation, for all this. I don't believe in magic stuff, you know that. Now you're trying to tell me it's time travel – and without the science.'

She flopped onto the nearest chair. 'Oh, Andy, if you were up there at the same time I was, because of the green marble, where was I? In a parallel time zone? Is that what you're telling me? You're expecting me to believe the old agate marble is a catalyst… And for what, Andy, tell me – *what?* C'mon, Andy, talk sense. This is mad, crazy Doctor Who stuff.'

Andy sniffed. Wasn't that just what he'd known his mother would say?

After tea and even later, she was still trying to make sense of it all. Talk about going on and on, and on…

'You're also expecting me to believe, Andy – and this is crazy – that you were there in the same place at the same time as me. Yet you weren't. Or I wasn't. Oh dear, this is confusing.'

Andy gave his nose a good blow on a tissue. She had to listen. 'Mum, try to believe me, please. They talked of the Queen's Coronation, right? I didn't get it then. I do now. The girls waited outside one of the London palaces in a crowd when Princess Anne was born. And when I talked about the moon walks, Neil Armstrong, NASA and stuff, the lads laughed at me and then even hinted I was telling lies. They said I'd been reading too much Dan Dare, that I was telling tales. Billy got really cross when I talked of Dad's electric drill, like I was making it all up. Today, Mum, I was there umpteen years before you, but at the same time of the day. If we'd gone up to the Big House together, Aggie would have worked for you as well as me. Let's go up tomorrow with Aggie and be together and see where – and when – we end up.'

She rushed across and held his face in her hands. 'Andy, calm down, please. Tomorrow we're going to visit some old friends of Gran's and half-cousins of mine who lived near Manchester. I can't change our plans this late. We've to drive down the motorway, leave about half past ten…'

'Aah, Mum…'

'Don't start, Andrew. There will be other boys there, some about your age. Some are distant cousins, some quite unrelated.'

Well, at least she's stopped harping on about not trusting me. Andy didn't know whether to be excited or scared about what he'd found out – and he was sure he *had* found out – about Aggie.

Later as they packed their clothes for the Manchester trip, it seemed his mother was ready to believe him, or some of what he had said. She talked of catalysts and what they were and, though she was reluctant to admit the existence of a magic marble, she did agree they would both pay a visit to the Big House, as soon as possible and together, with Aggie.

'If it'll settle your mind once and for all, Andy.'

He knew that she wouldn't let herself believe in magic and time travel – she thought it all nonsense. *She always reckons a rational explanation can be found if we apply our minds to it.*

When he finally got into his bed that night, he lay awake trying to make sense of it all in his head. *One thing for sure certain and f'r a fact is those lads are* real. *All of 'em are real. I* do *know I can go into the past and just how it's done. What I* don't *know is, if Billy and Jimmy are ghosts, how can they look so real? What* is *'real' anyway? 3D? Sure, what they've got in the Big House and what we do there is maybe old-fashioned stuff – or greenie stuff as Mum calls it. But it's all real when I'm there, more than the 'reality' of the egames and when I invent war games.*

He lay awake for a long time thinking and trying to make sense of it all. He just knew that if the lads were from, were in, the past, then he was able to cross into that past – with Aggie. And if that place was the past, it explained why his mobile wouldn't work there. Because mobile phones had not yet been invented. And all that talk about his crisps being from between the wars… Andy finally fell asleep.

22

He woke early, even as the autumn sun awoke. He'd made up his mind: another test was needed. Mum was planning for them to be away for three days. He couldn't wait that long to find out the truth. After pulling on his clothes, he sneaked out, leaving a note on the table for Mum. Aggie was carefully zipped into his pocket.

The Tree, Gran's tree. Cautiously he scanned the meadow: only a few silly sheep to scatter, no masked bull to be seen. He ran over to the tree and started the climb. Shouldn't it be lower down, easier to reach between boughs, if it's *then*? The tree should be fifty years smaller if I'm right.

Uncertain, he didn't count, just looked for the 'deformed bole' as Gran called it on the email. Ugly words for a lovely-looking thing. *Be good to stop an' get my breath back. Yeah, found it.* He rubbed his hand over its shiny surface. It felt just the same as it had on his first day. That day he hadn't brought the aggie. His fingers tested the bark for those letters that were carved in. His Gran's initials were not there.

'I knew it. Well, Mr Tree, whaddya reckon?'

He sat and watched the weak reddening of sunrise over the hills to the east. Deep down, he had known the initials would not be there under his fingers. They couldn't be, because she hadn't carved them yet. With the aggie in his pocket, he was in the time span before whatever day it was in nineteen fifty-something when Gran had carved them before she sailed to Australia in a big ship, a liner. The lads' talk of the Queen's Coronation being recent meant this was – really was – the mid-nineteen fifties,

Gran's time when Gran was a teenage girl. He put his hand over his mouth. His face felt hot as excitement swept over him like the beam of a big torch.

He clambered down and ran over the meadow, scattering the silly black-faced sheep again. Grandparent sheep, these, if not great-great-great-grandparent sheep.

His mother was waiting for him, stony-faced.

'I got your note, Andy. Please get your breakfast inside you and you can tell me all about it in the car. We had better not be late. I hope I'm going to like what you'll tell me.'

Andy tucked his aggie with the other marbles in his bedroom drawer. She belonged in Singleton Park. He knew that now.

Mrs Reeves was curious too. She came running across to the car to tell them, 'I'm going up to the farm Saturday for some eggs. I'll pop across and tell the lads' mam you've gone to Manchester, shall I? If she's there, that is.' So that was settled.

When they were well on their way, Andy told Mum about the initials not being there in the Tree. 'Aggie was with me, and I was back in the early time with her; in the lads' time, Mum. I reckon the earlier time to be sometime in the middle nineteen fifties, depending just what recent meant when the girls were talking of the Coronation. The shiny bole was there in the trunk but that had probably grown there since the tree was a sapling. There were no carved initials around it. I sort of didn't expect them to be there because they couldn't be if I was right, Mum. And because when I went up the Tree this morning I was in earlier time, with Aggie, and before Gran carved her initials there. That first day, I didn't have Aggie and saw the carving because I was in *real* time, *now* time and Gran had carved her initials ages ago, so they were there to be found. Mum, it's just got to be, it *must* be, Aggie who takes me into the past. Think about it, Mum.'

His mum went quite pale. She drove very carefully and deliberately, puzzlement written all over her face. After quite a few minutes, she asked the same question Andy had asked himself up the Tree. 'Where does my mother fit into all this other life of yours, Andy? No, don't answer. I need to concentrate on my driving.'

He could see she was thinking hard but she didn't say any more. Nor did he. *Better let her work it out for herself.*

***

Andy had a great time in Manchester. Same chatty sort of stuff as with some of the other people they'd visited, but this time there was a good mix of ages. Cool.

Andy found it tedious when people kept remarking he looked like someone else or 'took after' Esther's Robert or some such. Thankfully, a big kid called Alex, a second cousin once removed and a bit older – old enough to drive a car, lucky duffer – suggested leaving the oldies to their memories, Andy was one of the first to agree. Another lad was called Jason. Jason and Alex knew each other and were quite thrilled to meet Andy – another second cousin. Andy felt he was family and it was a good feeling. Alex drove five of them to one of Jason's favourite haunts, what he called an amusement arcade in the city. It was a blast.

Andy had a great time on all the machines, specially the Formula One. He and Jason competed and though Jason beat him, Andy didn't care.

Alex was reeling in some game that featured a bright yellow Lamborghini – his favourite car. He won his race and yelled out, 'Hey, lookit the Lambo, guys. I'll have one of those one day. Yeah.'

They all laughed. A couple of the others were plotting their tracks on the massive wide screens and at their spectacular crashes, a group gathered round cheering them on. Music was drumming loudly through the place, screens and neon flashing, beeps and pings as players scored or lost their game. It was great. He'd nearly forgotten how much fun these electronic gizmos (Mum's word) were. By the time they returned to the oldies, he'd spent nearly all his funds but he thought it was really a something place.

How Andy wished he could tell Jimmy and Billy about it. He wished they could go with him to a place like this. They'd love it.

<h1 style="text-align:center">23</h1>

Andy hoped for another trip to the arcade but they ran out of time. Alex was okay, though, and asked if, when he finished school next July, could he come to Aussie for his gap year or on an exchange, and Mum invited him to stay. Cool.

On the Sunday, they were expected at another of Mum's relatives' place with another side of the family relatives he didn't know. But these distant relatives remembered Granny and Grandad and had been to Singleton Park to visit 'before your Granny and Grandad went to Australia', so he talked about their rental and they marvelled over how the old lodge must have changed.

Andy left Mum to do most of the talking and when they suggested he went out into the garden he took his DS out with him – thankfully he'd remembered to charge its battery – and the time passed quickly enough. The lady brought him out a plateful of cakes and a Coke. *Okay!*

Then on Monday they visited Gran's very old Uncle Sydney and Aunty Jean, who were retired and home all day. He quickly found out they were the cup-and-saucer kind but he had a Coke and could let his thoughts drift off now and again to the previous day's car chases.

'I'm ninety-two,' were Uncle Sydney's proud first words on being introduced to Andy. He was really keen to know how Andy had been keeping busy at Singleton Park. 'Bet it's different from what you're used to, young 'un.'

He asked Andy how many flats there were in the Big House now and seemed astonished when Andy said he only knew of three. Andy didn't mention about the marble, time travel and all that. He thought it was best just to listen. He could see that Mum was determined to catch every word.

'Did you know Mr Scott of the grocer's shop, Aunty Jean?'

'I think so, lad. But I did most of my shopping at Co-op – that was in my end of town, y'see.'

'Did you, Uncle Sydney?'

'Nay, lad, never went shopping, me. And I bet you spend most of your time outdoors, young fella me lad,' Uncle Sydney surmised, rubbing Andy's hair.

Why do people do that? Andy answered politely enough and then told him about Farmer Capper's bull.

The uncle laughed out loud at Andy's story then asked, 'The Cappers are never still there? I'd a thought they'd have sold up since the old fella died. Well, I never…'

His wife, Aunty Jean, heard the story and admitted she was gobsmacked. Andy had heard that word quite a few times in England but usually from the lads. He quoted it while they were chatting on the drive home.

'Andy, please don't use that word. You know I don't like it and it does sound a bit, well, vulgar.'

He couldn't resist teasing her. 'Mum, Mrs Reeves says it and you know you told me to collect new words, didn't you? This is a lovely, fat sort of word and it fits.'

'I prefer flummoxed or flabbergasted, Andy. They mean the same thing and they're good words, they're in the dictionary…'

'So's fart, Mum. And one of those uncles was an expert, wasn't he? Good word, fart.' He laughed for a good few minutes as Mum struggled to retaliate and drive the car.

'Andy, please. Be sensible, you're not a little kid any more. We've about another half hour if you want to have a game on your DS. I want to think. I've a lot to try and get written up when we get home – well, tomorrow anyway.'

So she needed to think. So did he. He had a few answers to find, too. Serious ones.

Later, after they unloaded their bags, Mum suggested Andy had his shower while she checked her emails. She took her time but eventually brought her wine over to the sofa with a chilled Coke for him. He was recharging the DS.

'A techno-gizmo. You haven't played with that for a while, Andy. Look, can we talk?'

'Course. I had this the second visit in Manchester, Mum. And I haven't played on the DS because I haven't had time. Not here anyway. That game place with Alex and Jason was the biz, though, pretty decent. Okay, what's the prob?'

'Well, this last weekend we've visited those old friends and relatives of your gran. Some of them knew Singleton Park and all of them described it as now being very different to how you have told me. Their descriptions match what I found when I went up to have afternoon tea with Mrs O and she wasn't there. Only a few days ago, do you remember?'

'Mum – I ran up without Aggie afterwards, remember? I saw what you saw and that's how I know…'

'Andy, please don't interrupt me. When we got home, I found this note from Mrs Reeves. Seems when she called over to Singleton Park on Saturday to tell the lads' mother we'd gone away, she, erm, couldn't find their house. Mrs Hooper – Hopper? – she'd spoken on the phone to her, remember – wasn't at home so she asked at one of the flats and an old lady answered and said yes, there were a few boys but they lived upstairs in the stables and she didn't know their family name.'

'Mum, I can't explain how things have happened except that Aggie seems to be the big clue and I still don't get it. Remember how I went back there the other day and how it looked so different and it'd only been an hour since I was there with the lads? And you were there the same day, same time, and what you saw is what Mrs Reeves's talking about, no? I've been there lots of days over the last few weeks, and I know that Billy and Jimmy have a sister and two younger brothers I've seen but they don't do much with the older two, so not me either. There's a baby who's not walking yet, Molly said he sleeps a lot, and a dog called Panty who looks like Pickles and they're all substantial and not ghosts.'

Mum sipped her drink.

He could see she was really listening and he sensed she either knew something or was still worried, so he went on. 'They live in the middle of the house, a green door and a couple of stone steps up to it. I've been upstairs in the lads' bedrooms and there are some more stairs up to an empty flat in the attic. That's where Billy builds the crystal set with his dad helping. It's got a door to go up to the roof, Mum. I'm sure, certain and f'r a fact they have *all* the middle bit. Their mum told me that first day...'

'Andy, there are twelve flats or apartments in the Big House. Some are up high and have fancy black wrought-iron stairs winding up the outside walls to get to little balconies. I saw no green front door downstairs. That all tallies with my photos, Andy, and with what you saw that day when you left your aggie at home and ran up to check things out. Like you just said. That day I had seen no sign of you and the lads having been there – not at all, Andy. I remember very well because I'd gone up there expecting to see you, to have afternoon tea with Mrs O and then walk back with you.'

Andy was becoming desperate to prove to his mum that he really was able to visit but in an earlier time, half a century ago. 'Mum, I listened to the old people too, and what some of them remembered of Singleton Park from when they were young. That's how it was – is – when I go up there and hang about with the lads. What's that saying – "Evidence isn't always truth"? Come with me tomorrow. You needn't climb over the gate, we can walk through from the farm. That's the way Mrs Reeves would have gone with the pram. It's a huge mansion of a house, maybe she went to the wrong bit.'

Mum looked at Andy. 'Look, son, you're clutching at straws. You've seen it as it is now and I don't know how but you're lucky enough to have seen it as it was, with Mo, Billy, Jimmy and Davo and Mrs O. I know that a lot of what you describe Uncle Sydney remembers too clearly for it all to be make-believe, but…'

'Mum. Granny's Tree, her initials, the stables, the swings, the mushroom barn and, well, I've told you everything. Look, remember those mushrooms?'

'Andy, it's a real puzzle. I know I'm a writer but I have scientific and logical training. I simply cannot believe in a magic marble. As you know, I just don't believe in magic, full stop. There has to be a rational explanation for all this. The packets of crisps and old Mr Scott no longer having a shop, Farmer Capper with the awful dog, and everyone last weekend told me that Farmer Capper died ages ago and I remember that funny poultice you had over your splinter. Weird. These boys who don't have any games, any TV… Andy, I'm starting to get some crazy ideas myself and it's all just too incredible.'

Mum went into the little kitchen, wearing her deep-thinking face. Then she came out and gave Andy a big hug. 'Are you so terribly lonely, Andy, when I work all day?'

Andy was shocked. He stared at his mother, stunned for words. 'Mum, you're thinking I'm like *inventing* friends, family and stuff? You really, deep down, don't believe me. What else can I do to convince you?'

He pulled away from her, and stood up straight with his fists clenched and a defiant chin thrust forward. As tall as his mother, he stretched to seem taller and lean over her. She looked almost frightened and he didn't care. He was angry. *This is unbelievable. After the tests I made and the proofs I offered, she not only thinks I'm a liar, she isn't even trying to believe. She says I'm imagining it all.* He breathed deeply to calm himself down.

'Look, Mum. Because you can't explain things, you refuse to even try. You're rooted in your principles. Isn't that what Dad used to complain of?'

It was his mother's turn to look furious. He knew he'd gone too far but also too far to back down. *She has to take notice of what I'm saying. She must believe me because, strange though it may be, it's true.*

He was determined to get through to her and made a last effort. 'Mum, come up to see the Big House with me tomorrow. I'll have Aggie in my pocket, like I usually do, and you'll meet the lads and all the family for yourself.'

She was looking at him, squeezing her eyes and pouting her lips.

'Unbelievable! You are, Mother, and that's what you think of everything I say to you. No, don't you raise your hand at me. I'm not into smacks any more. It's supposed to be natural to strike out when challenged – okay, I feel like that myself right now.'

His mother flopped onto a chair, her mouth wide…

'What? Going to tell me I'm being cheeky, Mum? Well I'm fourteen, and you can drop the word only in front of it – I can see it hovering on your lips, Mum. I know why I have to be here with you and I think you know deep down that it wasn't my fault. It's so hard for you to believe anything you can't explain that it's easier for you to think I'm a liar. Okay, Mother, isn't that what you've always really thought, deep down? Even about the school stuff?'

Andy couldn't know it but his mother was just stunned at this tirade coming from her son. Not just a silly kid, after all. But she still could not believe him. It was all too incredible.

He saw she was so angry she couldn't find the words. *Well, so am I, but I have found the words.* 'That's what all this is about,

Mum, isn't it? You won't believe me because there's no evidence except what I tell you. You need evidence. You're scared of the unknown. Well, shit happens, Mother.'

She found her tongue. 'Andy, no need for that language.'

Andy agreed. It was a futile argument. He ran into his own room and turned at the door to yell, 'Just for the record, shit is in your precious dictionary, Mum, and so is gobsmacked and that's how you look right now.' He slammed the door so hard he heard the picture on the other wall fall onto the floor.

24

As it happened, Andy and his Mum didn't go up to the Big House next day. In fact, Mum had lain awake deciding on new tactics. She greeted him at breakfast with the words 'We need to see if we can enrol you for the new term, Andy.'

'Hm. Change of plan, eh, Mum? Lay awake working out how to separate me from the Big House, did you?'

She frowned. 'Andy, let's strike a truce. What you tell me and where you've spent so much of your time is beyond my understanding. I'm trying hard and I don't believe you willingly live out a lie – not for so many weeks. That's one thing. Being practical is another. The new school term's getting closer and I'd like to be sure of a place for you well before it starts. They have half term in October, which is when school at home starts term four. We could perhaps be home in time for that, Andy. I prefer you don't lose out on your education, son.'

Aha – an olive branch. I'm her son again. Huh. But okay. Andy knew she was actually recognising he wasn't a little kid any more. She'd had enough talk of times past and wanted to connect with a recognisable present. Okay, he'd go along with her for now…

A doctor, not mister, Preston was the school principal. 'We can accommodate our young visitor, no problem.'

Andy thought he was pomposity personified (one of Mum's favourite sayings). Andy's school reports were examined and finally Dr Pomposity said Andy could be fitted into Fifth Form. He was given a list of books to read, the library was suggested, and Mum had a list of uniform recommendations.

He had little more than two weeks of holiday left before

term started. *Wow, thought it was longer.* 'Mum, is this a private school? You know, do you have to pay? I'd be quite happy with another school. It's only for a few weeks.'

His mother was relieved Andy had a place. 'I think Fifth Form is roughly equivalent to our Year Ten, Andy, but the books seem more detailed than what you had at home. It's perhaps a different numbering system. And, no, it's not private as such. Though I do have some charges to pay, and basic uniform to buy, your books come free… Mrs Reeves says it has a good reputation. It'll do for the short time that the law requires you to go to school and it could be a valuable experience before you get back to Sunbury. Deal?'

The old bargaining routine. 'Okay, deal. But what if I can't go back to finish at Sunbury?'

But his mother had had enough of hypotheticals; lips tightly shut, they drove back home in comparative silence.

Andy didn't sleep well that night. He dreamt of big new school buildings and strange blocks of flats that Mrs Reeves called the Big House. He fought the big white rooster with a spear made from a black iron staircase. He shared a swing with Billy and Jimmy but the lads' faces kept melting and going all runny like chocolate in a pan, then coming together again and grinning horribly at him. He'd had this horrible dream before. Pickles and Panty kept melting one into the other and he could see their faces clearly but not the lads'. He woke up at one stage and he was crying. Crying real tears that wet his pillow.

***

Next morning while eating his breakfast, he wondered what to do. Should he pester Mum into coming up to the Big House? No, she wasn't in the mood. He'd pack his backpack and take the camera to take photos of the lads. *That'll show her. And I can tell them all about the amusement arcade – no, perhaps not. But I can take Aggie and the steelies and alleys I've won off Jimmy. It'd be good to thrash Jimbo at a game of Boss today. He's no ghost, he's real as.*

Mum really was not in the best of moods. She'd charged up his mobile and insisted he had to have it on at all times. He promised to wear his watch so he'd always know the time. She'd charged the digital camera too. He promised to take photos of the lads and anything else of interest. Whatever. By the time he left home, it was nearly eleven o'clock. Late.

Walking up the drive seemed hard work today. Somehow he couldn't feel excited at seeing his new friends. He so wanted to tell them about the arcade in Lymm, but he knew that wasn't on. Well, he'd talk to all these copper-whatsit trees, instead…

'The lads can't possibly understand about electronic games machines. Did they even have the Formula One motor race in the fifties? If I talk about things like that, Billy will only get touchy again. Maybe I can talk about time warps and stuff and see what they know because I know their Dan Dare comic mentions rockets and future. Mum reckons I shouldn't push it, not till she can come up to the Big House and she can meet Mrs O. Huh, when she's ready.'

He turned and did a mock bow to the trees overhead and on the driveway banks. 'Okay trees, I didn't expect you to answer. It's only Gran who believes you know things. Not me.'

He threw his pack over the gate before he remembered the camera was in it. Oh heck. Still, Mum had dropped it at Singapore and it worked okay. He was thinking how he could mention Jason and the other rellies; that should be okay.

He knocked on the back door of Number 2. Strange the lads were not around. Mo came to the door. He knew she preferred to be called Molly.

'G'day, Molly. Are Billy and Jimmy around?'

'Hello, Andy. Thought you'd gone back to Australia.' She

laughed. 'The lads are in Milnthorpe today, Andy. Something to do with school. They're staying with Uncle Maurice tonight and then coming back tomorrow. But do come in. I've just made some biscuits and we're having some of Mum's homemade ginger beer if you like it.'

Who's we? Ahah. Inside, playing the upright piano, was cousin Joan. Andy was pleased to see her again. Her lovely green eyes went all crinkly when she smiled at him. Crikey – he was going to blush. He bent down and made out to fasten the long lace in his sneakers till his face – and his other interested bits – diminished. Fourteen and I'm blushing – freaky.

Sitting next to her as the three of them chatted over the ginger beer, he discovered Joan was really interested in going to Australia one day. He talked happily about his own country and soon any embarrassment was forgotten. She was just another friendly teenager. She said she was fascinated by the marsupial wildlife and really wanted to see kangaroos, wombats and emus in their natural environment. She said it must be strange living in a country where nothing was built before Captain Cook landed.

'Lots of people think that.' Andy felt he had to put the record straight. 'Perhaps not houses and monster buildings of bricks and stones and streets and things, but the first Australians lived all over the country, and they knew how to live in it without lots of buildings. They had their own shelters that suited their lifestyle and the climate. I went on a camp once to Uluru, in the middle of the continent, and we slept in the bush under the stars – and if you ever want to see stars, well, wow, that's the place. And we were taught what plants and animals the local tribes would eat and cook. It was really great. And if you ever visit, you must come and see me.'

Mo broke in. 'This house was built more than a hundred years ago and it has its own ghost.'

Andy stared at her, wide-eyed. 'Have you seen it?'

They shook their heads, but Joan said, as Mo grinned at her, 'We've all heard him, though. Every night about eleven o'clock, the footsteps start. Heavy footsteps, one by one up the main staircase in our hall. I was sleeping here one night and I tried to keep awake because Mo had warned me and I was interested. I could count the stairs and hear the pause as he turned round each landing. The funny thing is that when he reaches the top by the door to the passage outside our bedrooms, he goes straight on through the wall and you can hear him continuing up the neighbour's stairs.'

'Yes, Andy,' Mo went on. 'You see, this used to be one big house, and now three families live here. When the dividing wall was put in, the little staircase was added off the top landing to make an entrance to Mam and Dad's bedroom at the front of the house.' She paused for effect. 'The ghost doesn't go on those stairs. He walks through that dividing wall.'

'Crikey, Mo, aren't you scared?'

'Not any more. To use one of your words, Andy, it was weird at first but we got used to it. Mam says it must be a man as the noise is heavy-footed.' She grinned. 'It's good fun for scaring any friends staying from school, though.'

That started the girls talking about their school. Andy listened, with half of his mind on the ghost. He'd love to hear its footsteps himself…

'Andy, you're miles away. What level did you say you're in at school?'

Oops, not concentrating, Andrew. 'I'm in Year 9 and I've three more years to do before I leave. After that, dunno.'

The girls seemed to have their futures all mapped out. Their school year started with the start of this next term. Weird to start a year at the end of one. Joan was going into Upper Fourth level at her school. Andy remembered Jimbo saying he was going into a Lower Fourth. Seemed odd, but then… He just listened. Mo would be going into Upper Fifth at the same school as Joan, whatever that difference meant. They were both aiming for high marks over the coming year; Molly because she wanted to qualify for entry to Manchester Teacher Training College which, she said, required a high entry score.

'But my dad's not too keen on my going to live away, even though it's in college accommodation. And I have to be over eighteen, he says. When I've finished training, though, I'll be of age, as they say, like twenty-one, then I can make up my own mind where I go.'

'Twenty-one? In Australia, eighteen is when we can vote, be treated as adults, an' that.'

The two girls looked at him in surprise.

Joan spoke first. 'Australia seems to be so ahead of us in many ways, Andy. You know, you gave women the vote many years before they could vote here.'

That didn't really interest Andy, though. He was thinking about different attitudes to school. 'You girls are so different from the lads. You like school and think of it as a challenge and you both want to be teachers.' Molly wanted to teach biology and science and Joan wanted to be a primary school teacher. *Wow.*

It was good sitting with the girls and talking about things. Andy thought how his mother would call them high achievers. They could talk about lots of things like music and movies – which they called films or the pictures – as Andy had already learned, and had similar thoughts about gaining an education. There was no jigsaw puzzle today; Andy learned it had been finished and packed away.

He pulled his MP 3 from his pocket. 'Like to hear some Aussie music? I've some fabulous country stuff on here. He clicked through, reading the screen, then took the earplugs from his camo pockets. 'Blast. It's flat. Needs a recharge. I'll bring it back tomorrow.' He noticed Joan and Molly's expressions. *Oh, crikey, you duffer, Andrew. He rolled up the earplugs and stashed it all back in his pocket.*

'Andy, how do you listen to music from that tiny little thing? My goodness. Like I said earlier, Australia does seem to be ahead of us in many ways. I do have a record player, and a few decent records. The 33s are much better than the old 78s…'

Andy was nonplussed. Sure, he knew record players, and cassettes and CDs but old celluloids…nah.

Joan thought he was out of his depth. 'Come on, Andy,' she gestured. 'I'll teach you how to play Chopsticks on the piano.'

Andy didn't want to make a duffer of himself but they perched closely together on the piano stool and even though he was very conscious of her warm thigh pressing against his through her cotton skirt, he had to concentrate on the keys. Despite himself, he started to enjoy it and before too long they were clunking away on the keys even more quickly and he was remembering to press the correct ones. He did admire her lovely long fingers and the deeper tone of her laugh. Then it became an infectious giggle as Andy – not concentrating – stabbed the wrong note, BOYNG. Molly laughed out loud and soon they were all having a fit of the giggles.

More fizzy ginger pop then they clustered round the table for a game of cards called Beggar Thy Neighbour. Andy knew it as Strip Jack Naked but didn't feel like saying so in front of the girls. They chatted throughout, and Mo was the quickest at picking up the cards.

Andy asked her about the cinemas. Now he understood about time differences, what he called earlier and real times, he wasn't surprised when she confirmed that the Palladium and the Roxy did exist. No argument. They both liked going to the pictures, and the Palladium was where the lads went for matinees. *That's something to tell Mum. Not great. She'll take some convincing.*

Both girls liked reading a lot and Andy asked if they'd read

Lord of the Rings. He was stuck for words when they didn't know the books. These were girls who enjoyed reading. When he mentioned J.R.R. Tolkien, Molly said her dad had a copy of *The Hobbit* but she didn't know of any other books he'd written.

'What about Harry Potter, Hogwarts and all that?' Oh heck,, Andy, bite off your tongue.

'Hogs' warts? Andy, they're farming books, are they? We aren't farmers.'

Proves me right. No way a kid in real time would *not* know about Harry Potter. Then he remembered: Mum told him the Lord of the Rings books weren't published till the mid-fifties or thereabouts. Molly didn't know them and now Andy knew why. *This is proof of everything I've told Mum. She's just gotta believe me now. Oops. What's Joan saying?*

'Don't you want to come up to see the badger, Molly? Good chance of a sighting.'

He realised Joan was talking about going up to the copse in the meadow tonight. There had been sightings of a badger in there. Mo wasn't fussed about going. She'd seen them before and she had a good book she wanted to finish.

Joan turned to Andy. 'Are you interested, Andy? The copse is halfway to your house anyway. Early mornings are the best time but evening's possible for a sighting.'

He nodded. *What's special about a badger? But I like Joan, oh yeah. If you're going, you of the lovely green eyes, I'll be there.* He stifled a smile as Mo gave him a look like she sometimes gave Billy. *Oops – smack your fingers, Ando.*

'Mr Capper's given his permission, Andy. He'd like to know if there is a living burrow. He actually likes the animals, though many don't, and he said he'd make sure that bull of his is tucked up safe in its stall.'

That's a relief. It'll be good but I'd better look up a few things on badgers.

Actions speaking louder than words, Andy excused himself to go home. 'I'll have a bit of tea and meet you there later, Joan. Okay? And I'll see you next time, Molly.'

25

The first thing Mum wanted was the camera. *Oh, bugg-ah.* He'd forgotten to take photos and Mother was not amused. He told her about the lads being away and about the girls and also about the badger sett.

'Guess I can't stop you, Andy. I know that copse in the middle of the meadow. With this Joan, is that right?' As he nodded, she looked at him over the top of her computer specs. 'If it is the fifties again this evening, Andy, you'd better behave yourself, okay?'

'Moth-*er.*'

Andy got onto the computer and googled 'badgers'. *Better know something about them when we meet up. Ahh, says they grow to nearly a metre long, live about five years and they're omnivorous. 'Rare and protected.' Rare, eh? Hmm. So they're sort of like a wombat but black and white, not a dusty grey.*

He gobbled his tea and ran up the meadow to meet Joan at the copse. At this time of the year, it was still not dark at half-past seven and English 'dusk', as they called it, was a gentle, slow fading of daylight, unlike Australia where it could go from daylight to dark in half an hour. So he reckoned there was a fair chance they'd actually see one of these creatures. Then he stopped, as he realised he hadn't crossed over the gate. *That means the gate is definitely not the catalyst. If Joan turns up, I'll know it's the aggie, only Aggie, takes us back. Time travel without the science. Yep.*

She *was* there; waiting at the copse. She gave him a big, warm smile and those eyes of hers sparkled like jewels.

Wow, she looks good. Pity she's wearing that fat, woolly jacket, can't see her shape… Cool it, Andrew, it is chilly autumn.

She was so excited about seeing a badger; he was glad he'd looked them up. He told her what Google had brought up and she just laughed.

'Whatever's Google? Do you mean "gobbledegook"?'

Oh heck, slipped up there…but it's more evidence for Mum. Computers were just not known in nineteen fifty-whatever. Joan's done research in natural history books, the museum and the library. I've been to the library and there are computers there, in my *time. Enough about this time travel thing for now, Ando. Concentrate on badgers, and this girl.*

She was a few paces ahead of him as they pushed their way into the old copse. The tall trees, beeches, elms and ash, he could recognise. Other bushes and trees fought for space to seed and grow. There were lots of tangled branches to wriggle around. Underfoot was layer on layer of crackly leaf litter. Tree roots were spread like cobwebs beneath it and too easy to trip over. He stumbled once, making the aggie and the other marble in his pocket rattle and clatter.

Joan pulled his jacket sleeve in caution. 'Ssh. Why ever did you bring your marbles, Andy? They're too noisy. And put your feet down gently or the badgers can hear our tread from below.'

Maybe could have brought only the aggie – didn't think. At least the little marble has brought me into the early time without climbing that gate. So that is definitely not the portal. Cool.

He couldn't help wondering whether he would see a badger in his 'real' time but he didn't think too hard – he saw a squirrel. A shaft of light from the setting sun picked up the bark on an elm and there it was, a red squirrel scuttling up to wherever it had its hole. He couldn't help himself and whistled in delight. His mum had said they were extinct now – that is, in real time – only grey ones left.

Joan was annoyed at him. 'Andy, you have to be quiet.' She whispered right into his ear. 'We have to find the sett and then we sit down and wait, no talking, no moving around.'

Andy hadn't thought she would take it as seriously as this. She was some committed nature lover.

They came to a small clearing. Paths trailed through the dead leaves. Something had been digging in the soil but he didn't think it significant until Joan grabbed his arm in excitement. She signalled him to be quiet and sit down – a soft-looking pile of old leaves looked okay… Then he saw what had excited her, a round dark hole into the bank of soil, a burrow. He finished his apple and threw the core over towards a tree. It rolled back and Joan frowned at him – again. *What is it about females and frowns?*

'Shush, Andy. There's its sett,' whispered Joan. 'Now we wait. If we see one come right out, I'll shine my torch on it but not until it's really out or it'll vanish back underground and stay there.'

Hmm, speaking not allowed and I want to get to know more about this girl. However, with his usual good nature, he helped find a suitable spot to sit down.

The sun by now was casting only a few very low, long shadows along the cleared soil. Soon those shadows lost definition and disappeared altogether. Gradually his eyes adjusted to the semi-darkness. The bushes and tree trunks were streaked with moving shafts of starlight; or moonlight. Andy couldn't work out from his seat among the leaves which it could be. Then Andy heard the distant call of an owl, 'Woohooo, woohooo.' Yoicks. He wished Joan could switch her torch on. Even though it was now more dim than dark, it was a bit creepy. And cold. And the leaves or bits of sticks and stuff tickled and scratched. He bent to rub his leg. Something moved near his foot. Oh crikey. It was a little mouse sniffing at his sneaker laces.

'It's a vole,' whispered Joan, so very quietly in his ear. 'Don't move your foot.'

Even such a gentle sound as her whisper startled the little vole. It just vanished. Andy wasn't sorry. It might be called a vole but it looked like a mouse to him and he didn't fancy it sniffing up his leg and getting into his pants.

Joan elbowed him gently in the ribs. He reached out and gave her hand a squeeze. Still gripping it, he looked at the mouth of the burrow. A black nose with a wide centre stripe of a startling white, and two little glinting eyes above, was snuffling gently around the entry. They sat rigid, hardly daring to breathe, hands clasped. It was Brock the badger. It moved forward till almost all its body was out of the sett. He – it was a he– was only about a metre from Andy's foot; a foot that immediately wanted to twitch.

He was big and sturdy and moved slowly. *Ponderous*, thought Andy, pleased at the word. He determined to keep his legs, feet and toes rigid. Brock's body outline was camouflaged in silver-grey hair and he blended superbly with the silver streaks on the trees and the tops of the bushes. *Genuine camouflage, his; not just a printed pattern on my camos.*

The two spectators didn't dare move a muscle. *This is really something.*

Andy wondered which was best, holding Joan's warm hand in his or seeing the badger. Then, as Brock started to move from his burrow opening, Joan withdrew her hand. Andy looked sideways at her. She was staring, fascinated, at the lumbering animal as Brock started grubbing around among the leaves. He found the apple core and emitted a whinnying sound and, thrilled, Joan grasped Andy's hand again and leaned nearer, elbows well tucked in, to point with a hesitant finger at the sight. From the snorting the badger made as it tackled and slopped around at the apple core, Andy reckoned the animal was as delighted with his find as he was, sitting so close to Joan. *It's a communion of spirits – who said that?*

He sensed he couldn't prejudice the moment by moving to give her a kiss or even a hug. He tried hard to give the badger his undivided attention and that way he might gain some Brownie points. The badger really did look magnificent, the moonlight shimmering like silver on its coat.

He wondered if the animal would hunker back. Joan pulled her hands away and dabbed her eyes with a handkerchief. *She's literally moved to tears.*

Oblivious of his audience, Brock waddled along, slowly, belly close to the ground then turned its back, presenting them with a view of its fat little tail.

Andy was peering at its tail, trying hard to determine whether it was one that would swing from side to side, when Joan elbowed him in the ribs again. He nearly whistled in excitement as another stripy snout protruded from the sett. Then this was pushed out of the way by two smaller ones with excited eyes. The two little ones scuttled over towards the boar. They sniffed at his snout and copied his movements. With an eye on their father, they copied his rooting around under the soil. Meanwhile, the mother badger edged towards Joan's feet. Online she was called the sow. *Just like pigs.* He wiggled his fingers across the ground between them and gripped Joan's hand with excitement. She smiled widely back at him, her eyes sparkling in the night's light. *Wow.* The animals didn't seem to have smelled them or sensed them in any way.

He was really thrilled to see the badger. Joan had opened his eyes about the wonder of things which, in his 'real' time, were so rare as to be considered endangered. *And she's some interesting girl.* A whole family of these animals had allowed Joan and himself to watch them going about their normal nocturnal business; quite unafraid, the little ones snuffling and snorting around the parents' feet with such solemn yet comical intent. *Not many people get the chance to see them in this natural state.*

Joan said in about fifty years' time there'll only be a few left in the whole of England. Many farmers uproot their burrows and some people even hunt them. That time-scale of fifty years means Mrs Reeves has probably never seen a badger and never will. So I'm luckier than I ever expected because I'm able to see things in an earlier time. Thanks to Aggie.

He flinched as the owl hooted again, much closer now. Mr and Mrs Brock turned towards their shelter, the little ones scuttling to go first.

Joan whispered close to his ear, 'Perhaps they took that as a warning, a signal, that a fox or some other predator's near, do you think?'

Andy had been trying so hard to breathe quietly and now he felt Joan's warm breath on his cheek and simply had to let a breath out. He managed a smile back at her, though. Her breath smelled of the peppermints she'd offered him while they were waiting. He felt his face warming again – blasted hormones.

Peering towards the sett, he bent forwards, over his feet, onto his knees and picked up a bunch of coarse grey hair. Looking intently at it in a shaft of moonlight, he held it up to show Joan.

'Oh, Andy, what have you got? Oh, I'm so tickled pink at seeing the badger. And a whole family.'

'Joan, that was terrific.' *So are you.* He nearly spoke out loud. 'Er, weren't they just magnificent. Stunning. I never dreamt…'

Joan rubbed her fingers over the badger whiskers. 'Aren't these coarse and wiry? You know, we've been so lucky, Andy. I knew of the sett, sure, but I wasn't a hundred per cent sure it wasn't deserted.' She laughed. 'Why are we still whispering? Let's go. Follow the torchlight on the ground till we're back in the meadow.'

'Hey, Joan. It's not late. Come and meet my mum. Then we could get our notes onto the laptop and I can do a printout for you.'

Joan looked a bit puzzled then laughed. 'You are a joker, Andy. I doubt if I could fit on your mother's lap. Thanks, though. I'm staying at Molly's tonight so I'd better get back. She'll be mad to know what she missed.' She leaned over and gave him a quick kiss on his cheek, stood back and smiled, then gave a little wiggle of her fingers and set off up the hill.

Andy headed down, his mind whirling, and muttering to himself in the dark. *Kiss on the cheek? Why does that feel sexier than grabbing a real pasher from girls at home in Oz? And my hand only wandered to her hand, nowhere else because Mum had warned me. Sometimes she's right. But things are sure different back in this time. Makes me look forward to next time. Wow, have to fix up a date…*

He checked his pockets. The marbles were safe. Best not tangle the badgers' whiskers with them. The hairs were really wiry; in proper light he might tie them carefully together.

Mum was ready with her questions.

<h1 style="text-align:center">26</h1>

'Hey, no Joan? Why didn't you bring her back to say hi? Or couldn't you?'

'Ahah. Mum, you're now thinking time zones and stuff. I did invite her but she had to get back to Molly's. But I'm wondering if she could have, really could have come back, you know, into our time, with me?'

Mum was still a bit flummoxed. 'I guess Aggie was necessary. Okay, but I wish you'd taken the camera with you.'

'Mum, how could we have used a flash? We even had to put the torch off.'

She shrugged and suggested he get his notes onto the computer. 'You can send emails too, if you want. I'm not using it any more tonight.'

Later, as he brought up the home page, he wondered how Joan would have taken to the computer. *She's one cluey girl — well, pretty and cluey. If anyone here would know about computers, it'd be her. And she doesn't. She thinks Google means gobbledegook and as for her thinking that about a laptop… More proof I'm right about all this. Don't want to risk not seeing her again.*

He stopped his fingers on the keyboard, thinking he had to keep such thoughts to himself. He knew that emails weren't as open to public view as Facebook but his mum might get to read some. *Interesting, though, Mum guessed I had to have the aggie with me. Yes, she really is starting to think time zones and that Aggie really is the key to it all. What's that word of hers — 'catalyst'?*

He didn't want to think how old Joan would be in sixty years' time.

The next day was Thursday. Molly had said the boys would not be home till late, so he took Pickles for a walk up the Sedbergh Road. He didn't take his marbles, but Mum stuffed his pack with a snack and even some biscuits for Pickles. And a big bottle of water to share with the dog and a plastic dish to lick it from.

He really enjoyed wandering along the lanes and seeing the different birds – even some pheasants nesting in the bracken. He never used to look around at the countryside when they went for a drive anywhere at home, in Aussie. He preferred to play his DS in the back seat. Somehow, watching nature – animals, trees, everything in the natural world – seemed good. He used to think all country areas were huge empty places, but they're not. You only have to sit quietly and wait and watch and listen and they're full of tiny animals, insects, plants – and big ones. Or going for a walk and watching a dog being free.

He'd changed his ideas a lot since coming here. He realised that. *The lads and their family, how they all stick together, makes me a bit jealous. But the lads seem to fit with me like as if they were my brothers; bit weird but I like it. Then all Gran's old rellies love me like close family, though I hadn't known they existed and yet they knew all about my family's history, in this country and back home. P'raps when we get home our family over there could get together sometimes; more than we have done till now. Mum's uncles and aunts have lots of grandchildren; not all are little kids. We just don't visit. That second cousin, Jake – we hung out once at Gran's when his mother was in hospital – he was okay. Plays B Grade, not bad. Doesn't live far away from me either. Yeah, p'raps when…*

'*Pickles!* Come here, Pickles, come. Silly mutt, don't run off like that, I'll get shot if you get lost. Hey, you got a rabbit. Good dog.'

Pickles dropped the rabbit at Andy's feet then turned and ran off as Andy was distracted.

'Oh crikey. What am I supposed to do with this, dog? Poor little bunny. Looks so small. Take it back, I guess. Mrs Reeves'll know what to do with it.'

He had a big plastic bag in his pack. He smiled to himself, remembering how his mother had folded it up and said, 'In case you find any more mushrooms, Andy.' Tongue in cheek, natch. She knew about the mushie barn and Capper.

'Oh, Pickles. Another? Look, doggie mate, time we went home, I think. You've enough roast bunny here to last you a week.'

As if Pickles knew, he flopped down on the grass by Andy's feet, tongue lolling, panting.

'Okay, mate, here's some nice cool water for you. Lap it up mate, that's the ticket.' He stroked the dog's ears while Pickles licked the plastic bowl clean. Andy went to pack it away with the rabbits when the thought struck him. 'Y'know, dog, that Panty doesn't have a dog bowl like this. In fact, none of them have a plastic anything. How would they?'

Pickles cocked his head on one side as if he was understanding what the nice-tall-human-who-takes-him-walks was saying, then dutifully stood up and pushed his head through the loop of the big leash hanging from Andy's hand.

'Clever dog. You're ready for home, too. Okay. Let's get these dead animals out of my pack asap, shall we?

They set off on the return route, Pickles content just to walk at Andy's pace, Andy musing about what plasticky substances would be around in this early time. *Well, they have perspex, because that was in all the planes in the war they're always talking about. They have a bakelite telephone and I know they have bakelite rings holding light bulbs on – because I changed a bulb for Mrs O. Guess you have ter give time for new ideas to take hold to use the stuff.*

It was well into the middle of the afternoon before they arrived home. Mrs Reeves and Mum were sitting in the back garden enjoying the sun.

Little Jacynta gave a yell, 'Andy.'

Mrs Reeves laughed indulgently. 'She knows tha name, Andy. Hey, don't tell me the dog actually caught a rabbit. Goodness me, two of them. Pickles, you've never bin as lucky before. I'll make him up a lovely few dinners as a reward.'

She took the rabbits indoors, returning soon after with a chunk of her crusty homemade bread lathered with strawberry jam for Andy. Andy had to repeat a lot of his story so she could hear it too, so of course he told her good juicy stuff about Pickles's rabbit chases, through big chews of delicious strawberry goo.

Mrs Reeves asked how far he'd walked. 'Did you see the gypsies at all, Andy? Fred says they're on t' Lane – usual time of year for 'em. Big smelly caravans they 'ave, all-in-ones they are, engine with a house behind.'

Andy shook his head but his mother got in first.

'Gypsies, Mrs Reeves? Are they a nuisance?'

'Not really. Travellers they call themselves now. Fred's old mother used to like 'em coming and some of 'em were good blacksmiths for shoeing hosses. These ones just come, stay a couple of nights and move on.' She turned back to Andy. 'You went in direction of the Knott, Andy. Did you see t' telephone tower? Up near the tarn, it is. Fred says it's a big, ugly thing. Spoils scenery, he reckons. I've read all about microwaves being dangerous so I'm glad it's not near 'ere.'

Andy agreed it was an ugly tower. 'My dad always says all the telcos should get together and share a tower. We get too many near where I live. You see them sticking up from hills and walking tracks, an' I think they're just ugly things.' Then he thought about it. 'I do like my mobile, though, so guess you have to have 'em.' He laughed. 'That one's got a massive mesh wire fence round it, be good for chooks.' He licked his jammy fingers. 'That's where Pickles caught the first rabbit.'

Pickles heard his name and started performing by rolling

around on the lawn. The women were laughing at his antics. Andy was still grinning at Mrs Reeves's comments about microwaves – she was always using her microwave oven.

As the day started to cool, Andy's mum was feeling the cold so she gave little Jacynta a cuddle and they made their way back to the Barn. Indoors, she said she wasn't using the computer any more today, she'd had enough of it for a while. From what she went on to say, it seemed she was getting close to finishing all her editing.

Andy thought he would check for emails, one from Tom would be good. Also, he was waiting for some replies from Gran and didn't necessarily want his mother to read them.

He'd asked Gran some questions about her life at Singleton Park, questions Mum had been reluctant to ask. She was shy of getting information she really didn't want to have to process, he knew that. He thought a few clues as to what and why and where would help, so why not ask? He hoped Gran would answer soon but there was nothing from her when he checked. Nothing from Tom either. He had an idea Tom was more into Facebook than emails now. *Bummer. What's the good of havin' any of this communication wizardry as Mum calls it if it's not used? Communication wizardry. That huge phone tower I saw today. Yet my mobile's dead as a dodo when I'm at the Big House. Suppose, of course, that's when I'm in past time and the power hasn't been organised, collated, channelled or whatever. It simply wasn't known how to connect that way, then.*

Despite his constant questioning and pondering, Andy didn't take long to fall asleep that night. Nor did he wake with any of those melting-face nightmare horrors.

He slept in late next morning and when he scrambled down his little stairway for his breakfast, Mum already had a snack in his backpack – and the camera ready and charged, waiting on the table.

'I knew you'd be eager to get up to see the lads, luv.'

Jimmy was sitting on the dinky the other side of the gate. 'Hello, Ando. Haven't seen yer for a week. Mo said you were back. Guess what? The Lees are here.'

Andy wasn't really happy to hear that. Visitors? He'd brought Aggie and the other seven marbles – steelies and alleys – that he'd won off Jimmy. He'd got so much to tell the lads about his days in Lymm, and the badger – been nearly a week. He would have preferred to win some more of Jimmy's steelies in a game of Boss, to keep his hand in. He knew he was getting better at the game; he'd read up on some tactics shown on an American website and had even explored some philosophical theories on the psychology of losing. Many of his wins he owed to the aggie, he knew that, because she was a prize shooter despite her uneven surface – or perhaps because of it. However, he couldn't get a word in while his pal was prattling on about the Lees.

'Hey, Jimbo. The Lees are gypsies, yeh? Mrs Reeves said she thought the gypsies were here.' *So not just ordinary visitors. Could be interesting. Different, anyway.* He thought he could always talk about the gizmo-games tomorrow.

Billy sauntered over from the house. 'Hi, Andy. We thought you'd gone back to Aussie. Good timing, mate. Mr and Mrs Lee and all the little Lees, Romanies, real gypsies, have come. They're camped on the lane.'

As they ambled up towards the swings, Billy told Andy more about them. 'Every year they come. They make what Mr Lee calls a slow return from the Appleby Horse Fair. They bought a new horse for their van last year but Dad says the Lees just like to get together with other Romanies from all over England. It's their tradition. Anyway, they're heading down south somewhere in time for their young 'uns to go to a special school for travellers, an' that doesn't close all winter 'cept for Christmas Day.'

Jimmy butted in. 'They camp on t' lane up Top Drive.'

Andy knew the lane was really an old Roman Road.

'Wait till you see their van, Ando, it's wonderful, really okay. It's got a round roof, with curly edges, it's all painted blue and yellow and it has pots and pans all round it dangling and clanging as it goes along. And even t' wheels are painted round t' edges with flower patterns, Ando.'

'Mrs Reeves said they had all-in-ones. Yer know, like those big American mobile home things.'

Billy had that look on his face again so Andy didn't go on about different vans. The Lees' van sounded nothing like his Pop's in Australia that Pop was so proud of. Custom-built and air-conditioned, he towed it behind their big four-wheel drive.

'Do the Lees have a four-wheel drive, Jimbo?'

'Huh? Four wheels? O' course they do, you clot. An' it's towed by their horse.'

Leave it, Ando. Share the crisps. It's safer.

Andy offered a bag of crisps to each of the lads and the three of them walked up the Top Drive, munching and chatting non-stop as they went. They passed where he and Billy had teased the bull the other week, and by the time they turned onto the Top Lane, Andy felt he knew the Lees almost as well as the lads.

Billy said how Mrs O passed on to Mrs Lee some of Molly's old clothes for her little girls. Billy and Jimmy's old clothes were usually too torn and mended to give away. Andy grinned when Billy said that. His mum grumbled regularly that he got dirtier here than ever he did at home.

'So what's new? My mum always grumbles at me when I get home, after cricket specially, with red ball colour and grass stains on m' strides. And I do get dirty here, rust marks, playing marbles in your stable on the concrete. Got oil on my shirt t' other day, she wasn't too pleased about that. But she's good at fixing stuff even if she loses her cool sometimes. When I tore my camos once she mended them quick smart, and the sleeve seam on my Darwin Croc T-shirt when I wrestled with you, Billy, that time.' *Oops, that's enough of that. Heck, I'm not a kid, look after my gear when I can, and at least she can wash my dirty gear in a washing machine, not like the lads' mam.*

Jimmy elbowed Andy. 'By gum, Andy. You 'ave funny names for yer trousers. I know camos now for camouflage but strides is new.' He thought for a minute. 'Strides fits really. Good name that. Tell you what, though, yer wouldn't dare give yer funny shirts away to anyone, Ando, would yer? Well, not that one with the electricity thing on the front. That's daft, that is.'

'Whadya talking about, Jimbo?'

'That AC/DC one – big black letters an 'all.'

'It's for Acca-Dacca. A band.'

'Huh? Our Uncle Maurice plays the trumpet in the Silver Band,' started Billy, so Andy just wrinkled his nose at him. It could wait. So many things in Singleton Park were very different from home in Australia. Sure, certain and f'r a fact.

As they walked along towards where the Lees were camped, Andy was only listening to the lads' chatter with half an ear. He felt his brain was overloaded with information these days and questions no one could answer because he couldn't work out what to ask. *Okay, so I tell 'em about the badgers and going to Lymm to visit cousins there, but I can't explain the huge buzz in that amusement arcade, its electronic and robotic machines – all the whizz-bang gizmos as Mum calls 'em. Wish I could.*

Jimbo and Billy were too excited about the Lees to notice Andy wasn't joining in their argument about the Lees' last visit. As if he would know anyway.

Then Jimmy elbowed him – again – and pointed up ahead. 'It's them. There's Sam and Tommo.' He broke into a run.

***

The Romany camp was on a flattened stretch of grass just off the laneway. It was a splendid van, with four huge wooden wheels with big spokes and iron rims. One end of it was blocked in up to its rounded rooftop, except for a little window. Andy thought the door had to be at the other end. It was like something out of an old fairy tale book he had when he was a kid. It was certainly nothing like Nana and Pop's twenty-footer back in Aussie.

Oh crikey – I left the camera at home and this would have been a perfect shot. Mum'll crack a fruity, this time.

Sam came running over and gave Jimmy and Billy a big hug in welcome. 'Who's your new pal, lads?'

Andy stuck his hand out straight. 'Hi. I'm Andy,' as the lads competed with each other to tell Sam he came from Australia.

Sam gave his hand a hearty shake then he had to shake hands with the smaller kids who came running over – all his six brothers and sisters except the baby.

'She's asleep in t' van. Come and meet Ma, Andy. Pa's gone to the Top Farm – horse trouble.'

'Pa knows horses inside out,' Sam explained to Andy.

Andy already knew from an excited Jimbo about Pa setting traps to catch wild rabbits for the cooking pot and cleaning the skins for Ma to stitch them into warm hats and mittens to keep them warm in winter.

Ma Lee stood up slowly from a three-legged stool, a wide, welcoming smile on her suntanned face. She was a tall woman, taller than his mum, but Andy reckoned he was taller – just. She was wearing a red and white spotted scarf tied around her head with curly bits of dark hair escaping over her ears.

'By gum. You lads have grown.' She shook hands with them both then turned to Andy. Her smile faded, slowly. She stared at him, her face growing solemn. She put out both her hands, lifted them up onto his shoulders and then gazed intently into his eyes.

Andy felt awkward, embarrassed, and tried to smile. Her eyes were almost on a level with his; she held her head up proudly and held his gaze. He looked deeper and deeper into hers; they were a beautiful seawater-green and could see right to the back of them… He felt he was sinking, no spinning, yes sinking – down and down into a whirlpool – a green and white and purple vortex ring – and revolving and tilting far away from this place and this time, into somewhere different, somewhere else.

Her hands rested heavier and warmer on his shoulders. A heat spread from her fingers across his back and up the back of his neck. Andy closed his eyes and that seemed to be a signal to spin, dizzily, around and around. I'm not moving. I can't be. I c'n feel my feet on the grass. This is only an illusion, magic…

His protests and questions were stuck in his head. He couldn't find his voice; he couldn't feel his mouth. *It's hypnotism. Not really happening, Ando.* Though he could feel his feet firm on the grass, he felt he was spinning, around, and around, gaining momentum and boring downwards into a massive tunnel, a dark place with a wind that tousled his hair and drove him down, and down…

The spinning slowed; the wind changed direction and started humming and echoing in his head. It gentled and became a whisper fanning into his ears as his head seemed to stay still again, steady on his neck. The warm heaviness lifted from his shoulders.

Andy took a deep breath, lifted his head and opened his eyes. Hers were twinkling back at him, just as before. His feet were still on the grass by the cook pot, just as before. They had not moved. The other lads were still chatting behind him, as if nothing had happened. To them, nothing had.

Billy elbowed him in the ribs. 'C'mon, Andy. Yer gone ter sleep. Say hello to Ma Lee.'

Andy blinked, put his hands over his ears and brought them to under his nose. Ma Lee leaned forward again and took hold of his two hands, together in hers. From something he saw deep in her eyes, he knew that she knew what he was thinking. He coughed and she spoke.

'You are the boy from far away.'

'… from Australia,' interrupted Jimmy.

'From far away,' Ma repeated. 'You're a time traveller, Andy. Am I right?'

Jimmy again interjected. 'Tha's right Ma. When it's day here, it's night where Andy comes from. That right, Ando?'

Andy didn't know what to say. He felt glued to the ground. *This is what it means when writers in books talk about being brought back to earth by an event. Sure, the clocks are different between my real-time home and here and it's clocks that measure time, but how?*

Then he saw on Ma's face the same sort of grown-up wise look he'd seen in his mum's face the other night when she was asking questions about the lads. Like she really knew more about him than he did himself; had the answers to all the questions in the universe.

Then Ma smiled, a big lovely smile that lit up her whole face. 'Andy, you're welcome to our hearth.'

28

She gestured them all to sit, and they scrambled to a place, each one of them cross-legged on a striped blanket spread over the grass. In the big metal cook pot over the fire was bubbling a thick pea-green soup. Ma ladled portions into bowls and handed them round. It smelled delicious, like pea and ham. Andy's stomach gurgled loudly as he sipped a delicious mouthful. Some bits of green stuff looked like stinging nettles.

Ma knew what he was thinking. 'Them's *chitries* in our tongue, Andrew. *Chitries* add flavour.' She turned to Sam. 'Rake the big cob from the fire, Sam.'

This turned out to be a round loaf of bread cooked in a pottery basin. Sam tipped it onto the grass, where Ma Lee broke it into chunks and gave everyone a small portion to dip in the soup.

The food restored Andy to the here and now. 'This is *great*, Mrs Lee.'

The lads joined in with a chorus of smashing.

Then, even better, because the clouds were coming over and a brisk wind was scattering the old horse's hay, she handed them all a baked potato.

'Rest it on t' grass till it cools a little and then dob some butter on to run down the cut,' advised Sam.

They were the very tastiest baked potatoes Andy had ever bitten into. *This is a bit of Jimmy's awright.*

He looked at some clay-covered parcels baking slowly in the ashes.

Billy had the same idea. 'What's inside the clay, Ma?'

'Them's for our tea later, lad. It's pig. Eat pig, do you?'

'Pork?' asked Billy.

'Come back later, lad, and you'll find out.'

Andy was checking out these new lads. Hard to tell how old they were. He reckoned Billy and Sam were about the same age, though Sam could be a bit older. He'd got a few muscles in his arms and had a bit of a moustache on his lip, more than Billy's little shadow.

Billy started telling Andy how Sam had last time shown him how to carve the best catapults using his knife; how to find the most supple tree shoots for making a bow and the best ones for the arrows. 'I'm hopin' he'll show me where the best water grasses are for making the best twine to prime my bow. I tried other string an' it's no good. Think we can, Sam?'

'Aye, should. Mine's good, though, an' I want a pheasant or two. We'll take 'em wi' us. Could do wi' some tail feathers to fletch ends of my new arrows. Gives 'em flight, Billy. An' Ma's fond of the taste of pheasant.'

Ma looked at him and smiled.

Andy listened with interest. Mrs Reeves had warned him not to let Pickles chase the pheasants in the bracken, but here was Sam saying he wanted to catch some.

Sam picked up his bow and arrows, sure he'd get a rabbit or two if not the game birds. 'Rabbits get silly in t' bracken. Easy to find. If rabbits have to be eaten, our way his way of catching 'em is better than traps. Traps are cruel things. Creatures die too slowly. Me and Pa hate traps. We've both rescued quite a few drummers, that's rabbits, from traps before today, and let 'em go if they weren't too badly hurt.' He turned to Billy 'Let's be off, Bill.'

Tommo was the second son. Andy reckoned he looked about thirteen – about the same as Jimbo. They were similar heights. He looked to be a more thoughtful sort, though, not so outward-looking. Tommo opted to stay with Jimmy and Andy. He wasn't keen on killing anything, not even for food. His own job was to look after Groi, the horse that pulled the cart. But – paradoxically – he did enjoy fishing, and he wondered if this new lad would like to go if he and Jimmy went this arvo.

Then Jimmy piped up. 'Tommo, can you show Andy how yer do the bird calls?'

Ma looked up. 'We call birds *chirilos*, Jimmy. Like lots of our words, they roll around your tongue. You and Billy and Andy we call *gorjer* – that means not gypsy. That's what you call us – gypsies – no?'

Jimmy nodded and hoped she didn't think it rude.

She smiled. 'Actually, we're Romany. Say it Roh-mah-nee. We're a proud people. Not didikoi. They're travellers too, but not Romany. Now you know.'

Andy didn't but he nodded. *Mrs Lee's just like my mother, into words and ways of speaking. What is it with mothers? They're like teachers. Languages, dialects, accents – so many names for different ways of talking.*

Ma nodded at Tommo. 'Do the *chirilos*, *chav*. I like to listen, too.'

Andy was growing really interested in this language talk. *Chav* must be like Mrs Reeves calling me 'love'. He thought that people here in England did that a lot, to each other as well as to kids. He didn't mind. Mrs Reeves pronounced it as loov. He could see Tommo was happy enough with *chav*.

Then Tommo started to whistle. Andy listened in amazement. It was so clever, so like the real birds, the sound so musical and gentle, yet it seemed to reach over the hill and back again. And the wild birds were hearing Tommo's call. *It's incredible that he can attract wild birds.* One answered, but stayed hidden.

'Thrush' said another little brother, then 'Blackbird.'

A thrush with its speckled breast flew onto Tommo's outstretched hand but then took off as Jimmy moved nearby.

'Got yer *mooikosht*, Tommo?' called Ma.

Tommo shook his head. 'Gotta mek another, Ma. Lost it.'

It was a cherry stone, Jim explained, but Andy thought how titchy-little a cherry stone was. They gotta be kidding.

Ma signalled the end of the bird recital. 'Tommo, *chav*, you must take the horse to some fresh grass.'

'Oh, Ma…' He shrugged as if to protest, then changed his mind. 'Come with us, lads, to find a good spot, eh?' We'll do some fishin'. Just 'ang on while I get me rod, and Sam'll not mind us takin' 'is.'

'Yeah,' whooped Andy, so they set off together.

It was slow work as old Groi liked to stop and pull up whatever clump of grass he fancied. *If this Groi's a new horse, he was no young 'un. He's big, legs are thick and got massive feet. Like Cooper's draught horses. An' this Tommo's got muscles somewhere, because this old horse takes some pulling away from a feed.*

The lads chatted about lots of things but Tommo wanted to know about Australia.

'Andy talks funny,' laughed Jimmy. ''E says myte instead o' mate and he's always saying okay.'

Andy let them get on with it but when Jimmy started singing 'okay, okay, okay' to the tune of 'D' ye ken John Peel' he joined in, as loudly as the two of them together.

''Ow do you know that tune, Ando?'

Andy reckoned explaining could wait and started singing the words. Their voices echoed around the lane and they sang the verses again and again, just for being happy, together and under a lovely warm sun. They manoeuvred the horse through a narrow wooden gate leading to the lower slopes, then started running upwards, through the bracken, with Groi clop, clopping alongside. Andy jumped and Groi whinnied as suddenly two frightened pheasants flew out of the bracken in front of them.

'This larl hill is called Benson Knott,' said Jimmy. 'Dunno who Benson was.'

Andy reckoned today was a real language day. He'd learned

that larl was another funny Singleton Park word and it meant little, like titch.

Jimmy continued his instructions, proving he knew his way around his home patch. 'Let's go up to top and you'll see Big House and Tommo's van from up high. Then we'll go down t' other side to larl tarn.'

'Tarn?' asked Andy. He'd heard that word from Mrs Reeves; the phone tower was near to it, she had told him. He couldn't see the tall, ugly phone tower that he and Pickles had passed by only the previous day. There was no sign of it. *'Course it's not here, I'm in their time, not mine.*

Jimmy was explaining about the tarn. 'It's like a dam, like a big pond, very deep, though. 'Ere, look over 'ere, Andy.'

They stopped and Andy let go of Groi's long rein. Tommo wandered over to some bushes where little birds were fluttering about now the wind had dropped. The horse was happy, snuffling in the bracken for hidden tender shoots of whatever was growing down there.

They were at the highest point. Jimmy pointed over to the distant skyline, where they could see a thin silver glint of the sea. 'That's Morecambe Bay, that is. Holiday place. Well, really it's where River Kent runs into sea. Dad says it's the estuary. We went there one summer holiday and it rained and rained. Dad said never again.'

They could see up the lane, northwards, to the Lees' caravan, and the smoke from Ma's cooking fire. Then back and down the hill over the grey stone wall and the green meadow. Beyond the Tree, was the Big House with its orchards and gardens.

Andy thought the grass was so green it looked painted. *It's so different from at home in Aussie, where hills go purply pink in the distance and the land is reddish or sandy-coloured and the mallee and gum trees have narrow leaves in a kind of grey-green that curl over in hot weather.*

For about half a minute he felt homesick, missing it all. Then he thought what Mum had said:, 'Enjoy everything here, son. Look around you and note how things look and when you get home you'll remember and know that ours is a wonderful world.'

He laughed. 'It's a fabulous lookout. Like when I climbed that big horse chestnut down there,' and he pointed. 'I was up so high and I could see right over to that same sea. I wasn't scared, though. Well, not till I started climbing down again. You beaut.'

Jimmy said he'd climbed the tree once. 'I didn't get far. I didn't really like having to climb down again after. Easier going up. Our Billy's up that tree as often as he can. Our Molly too.'

Then Andy remembered: when he was up the Tree, he'd counted all the TV aerials on the roof of the Big House. He could see the Big House roof from here. *Even at this distance I should see the aerials if I were in real time. They aren't there. The chimneys are, those fancy brick ones, but the metal ones with caps – they're missing.*

He turned to look again for the big phone tower and the wind farms Mrs Reeves spoke about yesterday. From this point, he could see for miles around; no phone tower, no windmills. *Looks nicer here without them. From here, I couldn't miss 'em but I know, positively sure, certain an' f'r a fact, they aren't built yet.*

He put his hand into his pocket and rubbed the aggie between his finger and thumb. She was quite warm to the touch. *It is Aggie. The little marble is the secret. Mum's gonna have to believe me.*

29

Tommo was shouting. 'Andy. Jimmy. Catch t' old horse, will ya?'

Groi was trotting eagerly down towards the tarn, trailing his long rain. Andy caught up with him to pull on the rein just before they reached the flat around the water. Groi halted and snorted with a half-hearted protest. He didn't protest for long.

The lads flopped down on the thick lush grass by the tarn where the water was shallow and lapping at the edges.

Tommo hunkered down and lifted up a fist of the icy cold water and drank. 'Come on, Andy. It's fresher than any out of a tap.'

It did taste good.

Jimmy nudged Andy. 'Aye, we'd best drink before the horse snuffs an' snorts in it.'

Tommo pulled an old tobacco tin from his pocket. It was full of maggots and worms to use as bait.

'My dad calls them gents,' declared Andy. 'Good for little fish.'

They skewered two or three of these onto each line. Andy cast first.

Tommo was surprised. 'Hey, you're okay. Done this before?'

'Sure I have. Me an' Dad went fishing off the jetty in Darwin. We always hoped we'd catch a barra – that's a barramundi. Lovely eating fish, for sure, certain an' f'r a fact.

As he watched over his line, Andy told the lads how big the barra can grow.

Tommo whistled again, loudly and shouted 'Okaaaay,' which made Andy burst into laugher.

'You'll both soon sound like Aussies,' he laughed. 'Hey, let's see if you can whistle this.' He licked his lips and started 'Waltzing Matilda'.

'I know that from school.' Jimmy started singing the first line and he'd a pretty good voice, so Andy stopped his whistle to start again to be in tune with him.

Tommo listened for a bit then joined in with his lovely chirpy whistles. Groi snuffled and snorted as he drank from the icy water of the dam.

Jimmy stopped singing as he thought of something. 'Hey, Ando. That's your song, listen… "Andy sang, Andy sat. Andy waited till his billy boiled".'

Andy ran at him and tackled him to the grass, 'An' it's all about a billy, you duffer.'

Jimmy sang on, 'Andy's voice can be heard… Owf, uff, owf, uff,' as they wrestled, laughing as if they couldn't stop.

Tommo shook his head as he watched his two *gorjer* mates roll around on the grass. 'C'mon, you two. You're scaring all t' fish.'

Jimmy sat up, suddenly remembering. 'Hey, Andy, you singing about billy reminds me, I hope our Billy remembers he's gorra help old Capper with the milking this arvo.'

Tommo asked why he was doin' that and Jimmy explained about raiding the mushrooms. 'This is his punishment from Dad. It's mainly because of 'im teasing Capper's ol' bull t' other day as well. Its mask got broke.'

Andy looked conscience-stricken and Jimmy passed him a sly wink.

'But ol' Capper's paying Billy five shillings for helping mornings and arvos this week. Not bad.'

Tommo laughed. 'Then 'e won't forget milking, not when 'e's getting paid.'

Andy really enjoyed feeling lazy in the sun, sitting on the

grass by the water, whistling and waiting for the fish to bite. *This is good. Feels so right somehow, like I belong here. Like the lads, they're so different from me and they know stuff I don't and they're good fun. So enjoy, Ando. This is cool.*

Jimmy was moaning they'd have to go to school 'in a coupla weeks'. Tommo looked at him.

'Wish I could go to school like you do. We get to Kent, down south, an' we go then. We move on after winter and I 'ave to miss it.' Jimmy curled his lip at Andy. Jimmy would much rather have only half a year at school.

'Hey, look you two. No fish, see?' He pulled his line out of the water. 'Told ya. That's 'cos we been whistling and singing. Let's go back an' see what's for tea.'

Within a few minutes, Tommo was tugging a reluctant Groi up the slope and down the other side. It seemed a long time since lunch. Andy was thinking about all the differences in this very bit of scenery between yesterday and today. *Today I'm about fifty years before yesterday; yesterday when me and Pickles were near here I was about fifty years in the future.* He staggered and felt staggered. *Tomorrow, in my future, I'll still be me but Tommo and Jimmy, if they're still alive in my time, will be really old men. Oh, I don't want that to happen.*

When they got back to the van, Tommo rewarded Groi with some sweet, dry hay. Andy kept out of arm's reach of Ma Lee. He didn't want any more spinning down dark holes.

Ma said the other two had returned with some rabbits and Sam had gone down to the farm with Billy to bring some milk back. 'You two can have tea with us if you like.'

But Andy had realised what the things were he'd seen earlier wrapped in clay. 'When you said pig, you meant hog, didn't you, Mrs Ma? I mean, hedgehog?' Ma smiled and nodded. She showed them the inside of one she'd cracked open.

Tommo smacked his lips together, 'Yum.'

Andy was reminded of echidnas. He quickly explained, 'I think I'm expected at home, thank you, Mrs Ma.'

Jimmy started moaning about the end of the holidays again. 'I wish I lived like you, Tommo.'

'Nay, lad,' said Ma Lee. 'Tha's got a better life than our lads. Tha can stay put in one spot. Nice house, big country to play in, gardens to grow food in, hens and eggs. That big White leghorn now, that'll be a good dinner for you all come Christmas.'

Over the wall and down the hill to the orchard wasn't very far away at all, and they had all been listening to Nebuchadnezzar doing his usual raucous cock-a-doodle-doo call.

'We hate him,' spat Jimmy. 'He wants to fight and bite and nip whenever we have to go into the pen. Getting the eggs every day is *murder*. He attacked me and I got really cut and marked. 'Orrible thing.'

Andy nodded, remembering.

'Well, why keep 'im?' asked Tommo.

'That's right, lad. If yon *kanni*'s trouble, you get rid of him,' nodded Ma. 'I'll take him off yer hands, any time.'

Jimmy looked at Andy and winked. Andy looked back. *Now this is interesting. I bet Jimmy likes the idea; it's a horrible bird. And that's another name besides cockerel and rooster – it's kanni in Romany.*

'Mmm,' he muttered. 'We'll see you tomorrow, p'raps, Tommo. Come on, Jimbo, it's started raining, just enough for me to get wet going all the way home.'

Jimmy didn't like getting wet. 'Hop over t' wall, Ando. I'll come down to the orchard while you go over to the tree, then yer c'n cut across to Mrs Reeves's place. Let's away home.'

Ma scraped up the little clay pots containing hot pig to keep warm in the ashes till Sam and Pa Lee came back. One by one, the others disappeared into the van for shelter. Tommo too, after putting a canvas sailcloth over Groi to keep him dry.

'See ya, old chap,' he said, and patted the old horse's neck.

Groi snickered his pleasure at being left in peace to finish his hay.

***

Andy and Jimmy ran down over the grass. They stopped by the orchard fence under the shelter of an apple tree. Jimmy pulled a couple of apples and held one out to Andy.

Then Andy saw Jimmy's bare feet. 'Where are your sandals, Jimbo?'

'I swapped them with Tommo. He's going to make me a bird whistle like his, that one he calls a *mooikosht*, or summat like that, Ando. You aren't the only one with funny words.' He looked at his bare toes curling around the wet grass. 'My ol' sandals are too small for me anyhow, an' I've got new ones ready for school. Look, Ando, it's not really late. Shall us 'ave a quick game in t' stables?

Andy nodded and grinned as he thought of all the 'funny words' the lads used that he'd never heard before. 'Cool. Race you to the stables then.'

Jimbo was laughing. 'Just had a thought, Ando. Our Billy was telt – sorry, told – by the headmaster that he has to speak proper when he's at school. Nobody's pulled me up – yet. Tommo has words we don't know, hasn't 'e? Mam thinks it's about time someone else and not just her and Dad made us think about how common we sound at times.'

'Common? My mum loves local dialects. She says they're individual and part of someone's identity.'

'By 'eck, Ando. Reckon you got marbles in your mouth when you talk like that. Come on, get 'em out of your pocket. I'm in a winning mood.'

The rain beat down on the stained-glass roof panes as they

179

decided what to play. Scraggy Aggie was a bit damp and Andy realised he must have put his wet hands in his pockets after drinking at the tarn. But when he thumbed her off, she didn't seem to roll as well as usual. Then, horror of horrors. Jimmy's alley hit her and she was his. Oh no! She was his mascot. More 'n that, without Aggie he would not be able to see the lads again.

'One more, Jimbo?'

Jimmy was a good-natured lad, and knew the green aggie was Andy's special. Andy took such care of her, and she was always with him, even when he left the steelies and alleys at home.

'Okay, old myte,' he grinned, mimicking Andy's Aussie accent. 'Here, I've got an old crooky made of pot that my dad gave me. That'll be our target. You get that eight out of ten an' I'll swap you for Aggie.'

That was fair, but it took longer than either lad thought. Nor had the apples prevented their tummies rumbling. It seemed a long time since that nettle soup, cob and baked potato. Then Andy whacked the target crooky and took possession of his precious Aggie once more.

'Phew. I'd better get home now. Dunno what the time is but it must be late. Mum got me a cheap watch but I forgot to wear it. There's no signal here for my mobile, see.'

Jimmy had often wondered about that strange thing Andy called his mobile that didn't tell the time or anything but he hadn't time to ask.

Andy gave him a wave then raced down to the gate and scrambled over into the drive. He had a stitch in his side so he stopped to get his breath back and checked his mobile again.

Mum was halfway up the drive. She'd come looking for him.

<h1 style="text-align:center">30</h1>

'When I say four o'clock, I *mean* four o'clock, Andy. That's why I bought that watch.'

'Sorry, Mum, but listen, please, this business about no signals. We get good reception at the Barn, don't we? So there has to be a tower, and there is, I saw it yesterday. The Big House doesn't get reception but okay, some places in the Adelaide Hills don't get reception, do they? And they're high on hills above the city. I looked for a tower while I was up the Knott today but there simply isn't one. Not today, because today I was in the nineteen fifties, Mum.'

Mum stopped and looked at him, shaking her finger. 'Andy…'

'Mum, Mrs Reeves said it was near the tarn, didn't she? And I saw it when I took Pickles for a walk. Well, it wasn't there today because the tarn is where we've just been. But that's no proof of anything is it, because today, if I was in nineteen fifty-whatever, mobiles hadn't been invented, had they?'

'You were up Benson Knott, Andy, near the tarn?'

So he told her about the Big House roof with no aerials on the roof like he';d seen from the Tree. Then of course he had to tell her all about the Romany family.

'Gypsies? Oh, Andy.' Mum wasn't sure about gypsies, nor was Mrs Reeves too complimentary about the travellers.

However, as they walked home and she listened to Andy telling her about the Lees and repeating the lovely names they used for birds and animals and describing what he'd learned of their culture, she sensed these were the true Romany people, not at all as Mrs Reeves described them. She had a comforting thought: 'Mum'll know. I'll email her tonight.'

So while Andy washed his hands and face before his TV quiz programme started, she checked her clock: five-thirty in the afternoon in England would be, she calculated, horribly early in the morning in Adelaide. Mum would be asleep.

She grinned. 'Wonder if she sleeps with her phone by the bed? I'll send her a text and wake her up. Goodness knows she does it to me.'

Within a few minutes came the reply. 'Good educ'n for boy. Not asleep. They true Romany & OK.' It was followed by a smiley face symbol. That, translated, was a relief for Mum.

She texted Gran back. 'Thanks, Mum. I'll let the lad have his fun then.' She thought she had some other questions for her mother. But they'd better wait until she knew how to ask the right ones. What was that word of Andy's? Dork. Well, that's how she felt – summed up her feelings quite neatly.

***

After tea, Mum had a phone call inviting Andy to spend the following day in the Church Children's Home with a crowd of other kids of his own age. Mrs Reeves had apparently put his name forward some time ago when she thought he might be lonely. She was on some supporting committee or something. It was an open day and Mrs Reeves knew some of the lads and lasses who lived there.

His mother thought it could be a good move – might bring Andy back into the twenty-first century. Despite her renewed faith in Andy, and his tales seemingly true about where he went all day, his mother couldn't help having a few doubts. This whole business of travelling backwards in time was just too hard to believe – a hundred per cent, that is. His gran in Australia was no help either, accepting everything Andy told her in emails about his experiences as being absolutely natural, not at all unexpected. She couldn't get her head around it at all. Worse still, there was no one she could talk to – certainly not Mrs Reeves, who was eminently practical. However, this suggestion of Andy spending a day with the local kids – real-time kids – might be the perfect antidote to all this time warp stuff. 'Even having to think about it gives me indigestion,' she protested to herself.

She shared a cuppa with Mrs Reeves, who reassured her that the home was a very well-run place. She went on to say that many of the lads and lasses in the home were Andy's age and shared a lot of his interests. They might like to see his DS if he would allow that – probably quite a few were used there already. Andy's Mum thought it a great idea.

Andy was not so certain. 'I know you got a problem, Mum, with me going up to the Big House so often, but that's just unfair. You've got on with your book faster than you thought because I've been away with the lads a lot. Why should I go off to this home just because Mrs Reeves put my name down? I want to go 'n' see the lads tomorrow instead. Prob'ly catch up with the Lees again.'

But Mum had made up her mind.

Mrs Reeves drove Andy to the home and, after introducing him around, left him in the care of a bunch of guys (as Andy thought of them) to spend the day. He'd given his mother a hard time earlier that morning; objected to being organised and had been quite truculent – even to Mrs Reeves. She was the one who'd done the organising, after all.

Yet after he got talking to a couple of the other guys, he started to enjoy himself. Some of the kids went to the school he'd be going to and they all showed him, and some other visitors, all round the home. He was told that when they turned eighteen, the kids in the home moved on, usually to what was called a halfway hostel while they found jobs or found accommodation with their apprenticeships.

He had a great game of soccer as a member of the red team, watched DVDs, played pool and seemed to be frequently called in for something to eat. Also, he met up with one kid, Steve, and they found out they shared a birthday. Steve was a hot batsman and they had a session in the nets. Andy borrowed a bat from the cricket store, well used but okay for a bit of a knock about. They took turns bowling to each other and Steve said Andy was a natural and he'd be seeing him in the Ashes series one day. Cool comment. As they talked, they thought they'd be in the same class at the same school after the holidays ended. This really pleased Andy; there'd be someone at that school he would know.

31

What Andy did not know was that his mum had decided it was time to act on her intentions and meet the Big House family. With Andy at the home, the chance was there that very day. Gran had answered a recent email with strange hints about people at Singleton Park that were just *so* confusing and she needed to get her head around this place and Andy's fascination with it. She would also test his fanciful theory about the magic of that marble.

She borrowed it, Andy's prized aggie, from his sock drawer. She returned the marble bag to the drawer after taking the aggie, then carefully zipped it into the leg pocket on her cargo pants. 'I'll find out the truth of this, once and for all,' she muttered as she tapped the warm little bump under the denim.

Andy insisted the aggie had the magic. She had taken photos of the house last time she was up there. If it was different this time, she would take photos of it again. She needed to know what was going on in Andy's mind. She also needed some proof – though wasn't really certain what she wanted to prove. Andy's stories were too rich in detail not to be real and she knew, deep down, Andy did not tell lies. So today was her chance to meet this woman at last. Apart from everything else, Mrs O seemed to be an ecological and environmental marvel. Her techniques in reducing the family's carbon footprint were something Andy's Mum was eager to learn, and learn she would with Andy safely out of the way. Mrs Reeves was still in town shopping, so Pickles got locked in the yard and she set off up the drive, a basket of freshly baked muffins as a cup-of-tea-time offering.

She really enjoyed the walk. She had been busy indoors too much, she realised. The sounds, the smells, the autumn colours now replacing the summer green of the canopies, and the rich bronze of the turning copper beeches, were just what she needed to calm her. Only one strange thing: the surface of the drive under her feet was surely not as bumpy, as broken-up as this, when she walked up it before. Even only yesterday when she'd walked up a way to meet Andy, she thought it was bitumen. The stones today felt quite sharp, or else her sandal soles were wearing thin. Then she remembered, of course she had firm rubber soles under her feet yesterday, her proper walking shoes.

She sang out loud, if tunelessly. 'Problem solved and oh, hello, little speckle-chested bird. Isn't it a lovely, sunny day? This is such a bee-uuu-tiful part of the world. Dum de dum…' Suddenly she felt that everything was going her way. Her book was in its final editing, whizzed off electronically to her agent in Manchester. More to the point, Andy's exploits – or at least the stories he told – were about to be corroborated. Or not. Either way, solved, because meeting the mysterious Mrs O should provide all the answers.

Despite Andy's assurances about earlier time versus real time, she wasn't a hundred per cent convinced. All this talk about the green marble was just too improbable but now, today, it would be put to the test. For instance, after that afternoon tea arrangement she missed that day a couple of weeks ago, Andy rounded on her saying she'd been in one time warp while he was in another and they'd been in the same place. Her initial reaction was that it was all rubbish, yet how to explain that Andy had later that day run up to the Big House without the marble and found the house just as she had seen it earlier – minus lads, minus everyone he'd talked about. Also, when Andy had the marble, Gran's initials were not carved on the tree. Because she hadn't done them yet. That very first day when he'd climbed it, minus marble, they were. It was all too unlikely, a very scary situation. This was not the time to allow those feelings to get to her.

'Hey, there's a squirrel – a red one. I thought they were extinct. Ah, it heard me and scuttled away.' She looked up the tree but it had vanished.

Continuing her walk, she started worrying again, chatting aloud in her concern. 'I'm like Pickles when he gets a bone – won't leave it alone. The connection of this place with my mother is easy to explain, quite logical. She did live here once, but the family similarities Andy drones on about are plainly quite impossible. As for this Molly having a smile just like Andy's Gran and, ergo, my own mother: just not probable. If it was, does that mean that Andy has been given a miraculous insight into a childhood different from his own, one designed to carry many messages, influences for the good? And just whose childhood? If Molly is – was – my mother, the lads must be her brothers. My uncles. Crazy. Dreamtime stuff. Isn't that what I said to Andy? Now I'm as bad. Stop speculating and get there and find out.'

She passed through a section of driveway where the big beeches on either side grew over and met in the middle. She didn't remember such canopies from the day before but she hadn't really looked, she decided. 'They'll start thinning out soon; all those copper leaves will drop. It's autumn, after all.' The green marble bobbed against her thigh with every step as if to remind her of its presence. She walked on to where the canopies cleared a bit and there was the big white gate.

She exhaled, gave a little whistle. 'You know, green marble, this gate is just as Andy insists it looks when he sees the lads. Locked tight and scruffy. Yet it has to be the same gate I saw last time – there isn't another around here. Last time this was painted white, and it was wide open, a sensible access to an attractive property. This one is just *so* not the same.'

She remembered how Andy vowed they'd been in parallel

time zones, when he'd been fixing wheels on a cart or something. She shivered, and felt goosebumps pop up in her arms and tickle the little hairs above her wrist.

She unzipped her pocket and rolled the battered green marble around in her palm. It felt quite warm to her skin. How could this little old chunk of quartz really have magical properties? Like travelling into the past? Well, she would soon know. The aggie was carefully replaced and zipped in.

Glad she was wearing her three-quarter denim cargo pants, Andy's mum clambered over the gate and walked up the roughly gravelled approach to the side of the house. Yes, she should have worn her rubber-soled walkers again. She turned around a high stone wall and found herself in the cobbled backyard. The door to Number 2 had green paintwork as Andy had insisted. The large brass number 2 she remembered knocking when she came before was not in evidence. There were no wrought-iron stairs leading above to second-floor flats. No rows of second-floor windows. No little balconies and potted plants. She took a deep breath. Just for a moment, she wanted to turn round and go home. 'No, I've come this far…'

She approached Number 2 and knocked with determination on the green timber.

A teenage girl, hazel eyes and hair to match, opened the door and smiled enquiringly. 'Hello.'

'Hello. I'm Andy's mother. I really thought I should come and apologise for not turning up the other day.'

The girl stood to one side, her smile even wider. 'Please come in. I'll get Mam.' She directed Andy's mum to a small chair, disappeared into a central hall and then ran upstairs.

Some muffled conversation, then rapid steps running down the stairs and in walked Mrs O. She was a tall woman, busily untying a wrap-around apron. It went onto a chair back as she came forward and put out her hand to take the visitor's in a friendly grip. 'It's grand to meet you at last. Andrew's a lovely lad. You must be very proud of him.' She looked around, 'He's not with you today?'

Andy's mum explained about the children's home.

'That's just like Mrs Reeves. She's done a lot for that place in the past. Now she's retired o' course.'

'Retired? But – oh of course,' stammered Andy's Mum, trying to work out in her head how old Mrs Reeves would have been – before. She accepted a cup of tea, made with loose tea leaves spooned into a big brown teapot.

Mo-Molly put cups and saucers onto the table. Not mugs. And not tea bags but proper tea. When she was offered a homemade biscuit from a selection in a tin, she remembered the muffins. While Mo busied herself pouring the tea, Mrs O sampled one.

'Lovely. Please tell me the recipe.'

Andy's mum admitted they were a packet mix, then laughed. 'I know it's idle of me, but that way they only take a few minutes.' Oops. She stopped in time, suddenly realising she couldn't confess to cooking them in a microwave oven. Microwaves were not known for cooking in the fifties; if this *was* the fifties.

It was then she knew this had to be Andy's time warp. Maybe there is no rational explanation to be had. Perhaps I'm *in* it, the time warp. And he hasn't been telling lies. She let out a calming breath.

Fortunately at the moment Mrs O was distracted by a spill from the teapot.

As Mrs O asked Mo to get a cloth for the spill, Andy's Mum breathed a bit easier. She thought how surprised Andy would be if he knew she was feeling as much at home in Mrs O's kitchen as if she'd been there many times before. At the thought, his mother smiled to herself and her own mother's words came spontaneously to her lips. 'There's nothing like a lovely cuppa.'

Mrs O smiled in ready agreement and proffered a small jug of milk.

'Oh yes, please. Thank you. Just a drop.' She looked at Molly and smiled. That smile flashed again in return. Dear God. Not logical. Not possible…

Mrs O was looking at her enquiringly. 'Are you all right, Mrs…?

'Oh please, call me Karen, everyone does. Just had a sudden thought, you know how it is – did I leave the oven on…and so on. But I'm sure I didn't.' She laughed to cover her confusion.

Big smile. 'And I'm Mary.'

So that was all settled. Andy's Mum explained about her writing, how they'd found the rental online.

'Sorry, what line, the railway line? I know they have holiday adverts over all the stations.'

It was like the cartoon light bulb above her head – Andy's Mum now knew for certain that however illogical it seemed, she was now back in a time well before she was even born. What's more, in a place she'd heard spoken of throughout her life. Like hypnosis or mass hysteria or…she sipped her tea and gave a hesitant smile. This scenario – or whatever it was – was all so strange yet, paradoxically, so hauntingly familiar.

The conversation moved back to writing, then reading habits, then books. Mrs O spoke of her own love of books as a teenager and asked if Karen had heard of the Arthur Ransome books, set locally in the Lake District.

'Oh yes. I have an old edition of *Swallows and Amazons*. It was my mother's and as I was always a reader, she passed it to me.'

Molly smiled and left the two parents swapping favourite titles. Within a few minutes she was back and holding out a book to Andy's Mum.

'Why. This is just so familiar to me. How I wished I could have a boat…' she chuckled as she flicked through the pages.

She stopped. It couldn't be. There on the title page – in a lovely inky script, 'With love from Mam'.

32

The signature was exactly as she knew it, had seen it so many times, as it was back home in her study in Adelaide; was even now while she was in England, back home in her study in Adelaide. The book had been published in 1930 or thereabouts. This could *not* be her copy, not the same book, not logical, yet somehow she knew it was: this one didn't have her name and address in it but hers at home on the shelf in Adelaide has – or had. Also, hers at home had a vivid accidental texta stroke on the front; she remembered trying to wash it off. Yet this cleaner one, newer one, was the same book, the very same book, she had read as a child of twelve or so. On the other side of the world.

Molly was still talking. 'I loaned it to Billy and he used to turn the corners over, so I took it off him.' She extended her hand to take it back and Andy's mother was reluctant to let it go.

Mrs O had a sister in Melbourne and was asking about places 'over there' so Andy's mum gathered her senses together hoping she sounded intelligent. They spoke of boys' mischief and of the white leghorn cockerel that, as it turned out, Mrs O hated with a passion.

Mrs O exclaimed at Andy's mum's camera and posed for a shot and eagerly approved it when it was played back. 'It's in colour. You do have lovely things in Australia.'

They spoke of how Britain and the British were still playing catch up after the Second World War.

'Winners can be losers,' said Mrs O and that reminded them both of the lads' current keenness in playing marbles.

Mrs O spoke of her fun with a little Box Brownie. Andy's

Mum promised to print out a copy of her photo and send it up with Andy. Mrs O envied so much of what she called Andy's American influences, and Andy's mum asked for environmentally friendly household tips.

Mo was sent to find the lads to come and meet Andy's mum. It wasn't long before Billy and Jimmy came hustling through the door, a bit hot and grubby, just as Andy frequently described them. They stood politely and shook hands and answered her questions intelligently. She had to stop herself from staring; and wondering. She was sure she had seen them before – somewhere. In the town maybe?

They asked where Andy was and she explained. Mo led in David and the little lad Chris who looked about four or five years old and they were each given a muffin and asked to sit quietly. Mrs O said she had another boy, Mike, about nine months old, who was sleeping upstairs. She spoke of her husband's motor garage business and how Billy was as mad on engines as his father. Jimmy she described as the family 'fixer' and laughed. Andy's mum knew of his making stuff from Andy.

The lads asked many questions about Australia and kangaroos and koala bears and were surprised Andy's mum had never seen them in the wild. They told her how Andy said there were pandas in his home town zoo in Australia and she said they were only recent arrivals and yes, they had refrigerated rocks to keep them cool. Billy commented that sounded quite incredible. However, the chilled rocks intrigued Jimmy and he asked loads of questions as to how the rocks stayed cool.

After saying her goodbyes and promising to visit again, Andy's mum decided to walk over to see the stables. Jimmy pointed the way then headed off towards some tractor tyre swings among the trees.

Molly came running after her and handed her a crisp paper bag. 'My biscuits for Andy. I know he likes them.'

'Oh, thank you.' Then she saw it on the young woman's outstretched arm. A long curved scar. Not new. Can't be two of those. Dear God. 'What did you do to your arm, Molly?' It was stark against Molly's suntanned skin.

'Oh, it's nothing now. Jimmy scratched me once in a fight. I was a silly kid back then. He was a little beast.' That wide smile, oh, goodness me.

She returned the smile. 'See you again, Molly.'

'I hope so, Andy's mum.' She gave a little wave and walked back to the house

Andy's mother was totally discombobulated. She turned to the stables. Today it was a huge open-sided building with a flat concrete floor and dirty big mouldy panes of glass for a roof. Run-down but friendly. There was no evidence of planning a conversion to apartments; no potted plants. Pigeons flapped out from the beams. 'So this is where Aggie won marble games for my mum and is now winning them for my son.'

She unzipped the little pocket and wrapped her fingers around the aggie. It felt quite warm – like a new-laid egg. She zipped it in again and headed for the gate, the driveway and home, her mind challenging the probable with the impossible. *Swallows and Amazons* – that first edition. That scar above Molly's wrist; it had to be unique. She couldn't talk to Andy about what she was thinking. No way. Not all of it. Too hard for him to take in. No proof anyway. Proof, evidence at least, was needed.

At least she knew now that her son was telling the truth – all of it and about all of it. She blew her nose vigorously. Now it was time to return to the real world and the twenty-first century; time to drive down to the children's home and collect Andy. She must tell him where she had spent her afternoon – he'd be so excited.

***

He was. He was rapt. 'Mum, now I *know* you believe me. That's great. I wonder what they'll say? I'll just run up and see them – oh, there's so much to talk about.'

'Andy, love, chill out. It's getting a bit late now. It's their teatime and it gets dark earlier now, remember. Why not make an early start tomorrow?'

'Oh, okay, I guess.'

She went over to their little fridge. 'You know, Andy, I'm quite happy now to hear all about the Os now because I can place them, match faces to names and things like that. A lovely mother, pleasant kids, and very well-mannered ones too.'

'Mum, that's so cool.'

She took a bottle of Coke, and poured a wine for herself. 'Y'know, Andy, I realise now, but don't ask me to explain, Aggie is certainly the catalyst in bringing two time zones together. And Mrs O – who asked me to call her Mary – explained a few dates and things that'd been worrying me, talked of the Coronation earlier that same summer, so this year for Mrs O and her family was definitely 1953.'

'We're talking of Queen Elizabeth, Mum, and she's just had a birthday. It was on TV at home, remember?' He did a rapid calculation 'That's about sixty years ago.'

Mum recounted to Andy what Billy had told her of his crystal set. 'I was to tell you he's getting a reasonable reception and next time you're there he'll show you.' He told me all about you blowing your top one day when he spoke of wireless and you got him mixed up with Rezzo…

'Oh, Mum, what else did he tell you?'

'Not much. But I was touched to hear of your scrap with Billy when you socked him. You obviously needed to talk about your hurt with Sunbury and Rezzo, love. But I am sorry you didn't open up to me.'

'Mum, it was what you'd call spontaneous, y' know?

Impetuous, or something like that. It was just like turning a switch. I guess I needed to talk it out, though I did with that counsellor bloke, didn't I? But I'd buried it – well, almost – at the back of my mind because of all these other questions about time warps and the rest. I've never sort of wrestled in fun, you know? The Singleton Park lads feel almost like family, and even though it burst out of me to them, they were good about it, and it really helped me think straight about things.'

She gave him a quick hug. 'I'm glad, really glad you've exorcised your demon, Andy. But you know, this business with Billy, can I explain to you what I think?'

'Okay, Mum.'

'I did get the impression you talk so much of what we have and can do that isn't known in their time. You really must avoid making comparisons, Andy. They're really very well situated as far as families go – from that time, you know. Try talking more of their interests and what you know is in their now, not yours. As for Billy, he's the big brother of the family and maybe not quite as old as you but…here's a comparison: he seems to have a much more stringent routine of chores and responsibilities than is expected of you. Don't you think? For instance, how about his school finishing at four o'clock each day and lessons on Saturdays? And from what his mother says, he's expected to do most of the more specialised outdoor jobs to help his father, like that massive generator for the electricity and other really heavy stuff. Now you don't know anything about that, do you. And when you talk of rockets, Mars probes and NASA stuff – well, how can you expect him to know about such stuff, Andy? He might feel you're displacing him in the family, because you do seem to have fitted in so well in most respects, and he may worry that you make him look small in Jimmy's eyes.'

'Okay, Mum. I get the message.' *What a bloomin' lecture. Give Mum a word and you get a page back.*

'Andy, if we are right about all this – yes, I say we – and their now is different from ours, like sixty years ago, how can Billy and the others be expected to know about rocket science, electric drills, microwave ovens and all that? It's all about compromise, love.'

Andy was delighted. She actually said 'we' and from 'that time' and 'their now'. 'Cool. You really do accept there is an earlier-time and a real-time situation here, Mum – that's fabulous.'

Mum's face was twisting into all kinds of expressions. Her mouth had dropped at the corners. *She's not hundred-per-cent-happy.*

'I seem to be linking past with present, Andy, and getting some very strange results. Not answers exactly – ideas that could be answers but are just not logical.

'Mum, it's *so* great, really great, to know you believe all I've been telling you. You even treated me like a deranged little kid with imaginary friends, remember? Then you thought I was just lying, and I really was going into the past where Aggie came from. It's magic, Mum, nothing scientific and frightening, just another word – m a g i c – magic. So drop the doom and gloom, hey? Sure, certain an' f'r a fact, having the little magic marble has to be a good thing.'

'Andy, I'm not sad. Just a bit mixed-up about it all. It's just that – well, you know me, I've always believed in rational explanations, and for all this, I can't find one. And now I'm sort of thrilled like you are, but it's so hard to accept. But oh, Andy, one thing I do know for sure, we have to take the very greatest care of Aggie. If we lose her…'

She didn't need to finish the sentence; Andy's face showed he understood only too well.

'I'll take great care of her, Mum. No worries.'

Lying on his bed that evening thinking, then later actually under the quilt, Andy was so relieved his mother was believing him at last he enjoyed reliving some of his experiences at the children's home.

The kids at the home, all ages I met, have computers, have seen and read the Harry Potters, seen most of the Star Wars movies and are just like me. They live in the real time, in the twenty-first century and we have lots of stuff in common. We share the same world. That kid Steve spoke of the war and he meant Iraq and Afghanistan, not World War Two. Also, they've got parents and mothers who go to work. Some even have parents who don't get on well, like me, or no parents at all. But they're all twenty-first century, like me. Steve's mother is a journalist and does a column in the Gazette.

He flopped over onto his back and tugged the pillow under his neck to get comfy for sleep.

It all felt so normal today being there, yet I had Billy and Jimmy in the back of my mind a lot of the time, just comparing things. It's not just about belonging to the real time. The Singleton Park family is in the past but to them it's their here and now and I'm seeing them as they really are, or were. Mum says that by rights they should be ghosts, but they are not. Confusing it IS. That old bloke Scott is now, in real time, the same age as the lads' dad will be if he's still alive in my real time. As for Billy and Jimbo, well, they…oh blast, they could still be alive but they'd be old…

Eventually he fell asleep.

***

Andy's mother couldn't get to sleep either – she was doing her own tossing and turning. A believer in evidence-based rational explanations, she always sought logical answers. Reasoned ones. She picked up the photo of her mother, Andy's gran, from the bedside table and held it above her head.

'Wish you could talk with me, Mum. That scar of Molly's – irrefutable. You know all about it, don't you? That smile on

Molly's face, too. But how can I have been served a cup of tea by my own mother – that's you – as a teenage girl? When I know that you're aged seventy something and over there in Oz?'

She tossed and turned, twisting her sheet and becoming irritable. Then she slid the photo of her mother under the pillow and talked to her through the stuffing. 'Mustn't let Andy hear me, he's mixed-up enough without worrying about me. You know, Mum, this whole scenario is playing out as something extraordinary, the highly improbable stuff of dreams. And yet, paradoxically, so real. And moving up a notch, how could I have shared a cuppa with my grandmother – she who died before I was actually born? As for Molly, Mo, whoever she is, was, well, I know I'll see you again, for sure, certain and for a fact.'

Returning the photograph in its frame to the table, she dabbed an affectionate finger on her mother's snapshot nose, as if seeking there an assurance that the impossible was not only possible but even beyond probable, to be true, she fell asleep at last.

33

Next morning when Andy got to the gate, Jimmy was sitting on the gravel the other side.

On seeing his mate, he jumped to his feet, practically busting with excitement. 'Ando, been waiting. Met your mum yesterday. She's all right, isn't she? She said you'd come up today. Okay.' He grabbed his mate's arm before Andy could comment. 'Guess what, Ando. We've done it.'

Andy wasn't sure what that meant but Jimmy was obviously very excited and unwilling to allow his mate to get a word in edgewise. They walked across the lawns through the back gate of the orchard, Jimmy running as usual, Andy, sauntering along with his long strides, keeping up with him. Billy was waiting, sitting on an old box and holding on tightly to the neck of a wriggling, bulging, squawking sack.

Andy looked over to the chook pen. He knew immediately. 'Wow. Holy cow, Billy, what you gonna do with 'im?'

Billy stood up, held as far away from his body as possible the sack from which a frenzied kicking and crowing scratched and screeched. 'Grab t' neck with me, Jimbo. He's flamin' heavy.'

Puffing with the effort, the lads lumped and bumped the heavy, heaving sack up to the Romany caravan, telling Andy all about the capture on the way. With every bump on the driveway came a furious 'squawk, aroodledoo, squawk'.

'Blimey Charlie, lads,' worried Andy. 'Sure, certain and f'r a fact, this is what my mother would call a desperate measure.'

Ma Lee emerged from her van to see what was disturbing her peace. The lads thrust the squirming and cackling burden towards her. She nearly dropped it. She knew exactly what 'thing' was protesting inside. She looked at the lads very seriously and nodded to Pa.

Like a signal to come and rule his roost. Andy grinned at his own joke then tried to look very serious as Pa Lee stood up from his wooden stool, thumbs tucked in the scarlet braces that held up his trousers.

'Aha. Lads, did tha' faither give thee permission to bring up his prize white leghorn?'

Billy didn't hesitate; the lads had it all worked out. 'He's getting to be more trouble than he's worth, Pa. Only the other day, me mam said we should get rid of him.'

Andy thought that was nearly true. He didn't think their dad would be so ready to agree, though.

Esther, the eldest Lee daughter, came out of the van with the baby just as Ma thrust her hand into the sack. 'Careful, Ma. Yon's vicious.'

There was a lot of wriggling and a lot of squawking. Ma nodded then walked round and behind their van. Pa Lee signalled to the lads to stay where they were and then he picked up a huge kettle of water from the fire and followed her.

It only seemed like minutes and they came back, Pa holding the still hot but empty kettle and Ma holding an upside-down cockerel, his wings widespread and dripping sadly, some skin and bony lumps showing. He was *not* wriggling and *not* squawking. Andy looked at Jimbo and Billy.

Billy was looking, with a thoughtful expression, at what used to be Nebuchadnezzar. He was remembering all the times Nebby had attacked him; how Jimmy still had some nasty scratches on his back; how Mam was afraid of the old cockerel, too. Then Andy looked at Jimmy. Jimmy's usual grin was wiped from his face. He was biting his lip. He was remembering too.

It was all okay till Ma sat down on her stool and started to pluck the cockerel. Wet feathers fell onto the grass and the little kids chased around, giggling and picking them up.

Billy's stomach gave a lurch. 'Oh, 'eck.' He needed a change of scenery. 'Hey, shall us go looking for otters in the beck?'

Jimmy also wanted to get away from the evidence of their dirty deed. 'Yowieeee. Let's go to Spindle Woods. Can Sammy and Tommo come as well, Ma Lee? With t' cockerel, you'll not need to catch rabbits for tea, will yer?'

Pa nodded. 'Off you go and 'ave a last bit o' fun, lads. Tomorrer we're settin' off again. Got to get down south, Ando. Our lot'll get some schooling. Last time together for a year, eh?'

Billy was off, leading the way and leaving their white-feathered enemy's remains behind. He wished he hadn't worn his wellies, couldn't run so fast. He was remembering as he ran, Mam called Nebby her nemesis. He'd have to look it up.

Going to Spindle Woods, Andy ran with Tommo. He hadn't realised Tommo would be leaving so soon. 'I'll be in Aussie before you come back, Tommo. This'll be my last day with you.'

Tommo gave him a friendly wink and a slap on the back. 'We'll remember each other, eh, Andy? For ever.' Andy blinked. He hated goodbyes.

Then Sam yelled out, 'C'mon, Aussie Ando, we're off to the beck. It's a mile, tha knows. Gotta catch up.'

Andy knew by now that a beck was a creek and they'd mentioned otters. So he was as keen as the others. He and Tommo broke into a run.

***

Andy thought Spindle Woods terrific. The sun had broken out, the clouds were clearing, showing the sky as that pale English blue (as Mum called it). Tall trees were scattered over the grassy acres, and the water in the creek was icy and very fast flowing.

'Wicked. What a beaut creek.'

'It's a beck, you clot,' jibed Billy. 'In t' south I think they call it a brook. And nowt wicked about it.' He waved to the distant hills over to the north. 'It comes down from t' fells, high up. It's a breakaway bit of t' big river that goes through t' town. Down there,' pointing along the water's course, 'below where we'll be, it runs underground and stays that way for a heck of a distance till it hits t' river again under one of the big bridges. From a culvert.' He leaned over to whisper, eyes open in excitement. 'A body washed out into river once. Caused no heck of a fuss.'

Andy was intrigued. 'Who was it? Was it murder?'

Billy laughed and ran down the slope. 'A bloody big sheep it were. Silly animals, sheep.' Laughing, and quite unworried about the fate of a lonely sheep, he ran to join the others, Andy striding behind.

Andy wondered about otters. No otters here that he could see. Not even further down where the grassland levelled out a bit and the beck widened to a deeper pool. There were reeds and long grass round the edges and they could hear frogs, jibber-jabbering from every direction. He liked frogs; he once had a green tree frog from the pet shop but one winter it died of cold.

The lads planned great fun damming the beck. Sam and Billy found a spot further down near the pool and Jimbo and Andy chose another one where there were lots of small rocks. Tommo wandered off to whistle to the birds and see which ones were around the water. He'd only been to Spindle Woods once before.

'Frogs'll like the pools even if otters don't,' declared Andy. 'Have you ever seen otters in the tarn over at Benson Knott, Jimbo?'

Billy answered from his dam, as he heaved up a big chunk of rock to deepen the hole, 'Otters don't go in t' tarn.'

Tommo came back. 'That's not otter water,' he asserted and laughed out loud. 'No fish there, Andy.'

Andy laughed, thinking of the tarn. Billy, having planned already how he would block the water, was huffing and puffing and heaving rocks and splashing. He made a big noise about it. Tommo wandered off again, whistling.

Andy sat back on his heels. 'This is terrific, this water. So cold and so clear. I can see the bottom. Creeks near my home are fast when they've got water in, but dry up every summer. My school makes lists of when frogs are seen, and where they are, 'cos they're getting rare.'

Jimmy looked shocked. 'No frogs? Blimey. We've got 'em all over. I dropped one in Dad's wellies t' other day an' yer shoulda seen him hop.' He cackled. 'I mean me dad, not the frog. Hey, you ever collect spawn, Ando? Grow taddies?' He didn't wait for an answer. He shook his head towards Sam and Billy and lowered his voice. 'Let's you and me block t' water from t' others.' He moved over to the opposite bank.

Andy grinned. He hadn't done this in a creek for yonks. No need to watch out for snakes here either. Sneakily, moving as carefully as they could and not make loud splashes, they shifted as many rocks of the right size as they could in order to make an effective dam, hoping to stop the water getting down to Billy's chosen place. He and Sam were busy lifting much bigger rocks than Andy's and Jimmy's, big ones from under the water. Sammy was piling the rocks with care to get them to fit together.

Jimmy winked at Andy and they worked harder and found enough stones eventually to score quite a wall across bank to bank. 'Nearly a yard and a half,' Jimmy whispered hoarsely, 'This'll show 'em.'

'About a hundred and thirty-seven centimetres,' calculated our modern Aussie.

Downstream, Billy was heaving a big stone onto his wall and yelled, 'Hey, water's slowed.'

Sam leaned back and pointed upriver. 'It's your Jimbo an'

Andy. Their dam's a good big 'un, Billy.' He sat back on the bank and laughed.

Billy didn't see what was funny. 'Oy, you rotten spoilsports. I'm making a pool for frogs and you two are stopping the water.' But he grinned as he said it, picked up a bit of branch, ran up the bank towards them, whacking the water and spraying himself in a sunlit shower.

'Drops and plops, lads, drops and plops.' Jimmy ran to his brother and jumped in, feet first.

Laughing together, the two lads wrestled to see who'd be the first to lose their feet and sit down in the water. Andy thought of Aggie and the other marbles in his zip pockets and even though they were safe twice over in Mrs Reeves's little bag, he decided to stay clear. Didn't fancy getting his wellies full of water.

Fat chance. By the time each of the brothers was sitting in a muddy puddle, hands behind and knees akimbo, they were all four of them laughing till their sides ached. Andy and Sam stayed dry – well, almost – on the bank.

'You two are all muddy from eyeballs to breakfast time,' cried Andy. 'Let's share this lemonade. I've another bag of chippy-crisps in my pack…'

Tommo joined them on the warm grass. He'd found an old bird's nest, delicately made and quite small, and they all gathered round, admiring the dainty thing.

'Was a chaffinch's, I think,' asserted Tommo, and put it carefully to one side.

Jimmy and Billy spread their shirts over a bush to dry in the sun.

'Look at it steamin',' called Jimbo.

The five lads sat on the grass, swapping stories as they shared three packets of crisps and Marmite sandwiches with swigs of lemonade. Tommo emptied his pockets of some early blackberries.

'Nice brambles over there,' he pointed, 'but not really ready yet; give us gripes in the gut, too many would.'

Andy told them about the children's home. 'I was there yest'day. Mrs Reeves said it was a special charity day or something.'

'Aye,' said Billy, 'she does a lot for them lads an' lasses, does t' old lady.'

Andy wondered what Billy would think of the real-time Mrs Reeves he knew who wasn't as old his own mum. 'Hey, they can play a good game of football, those kids. Said they have their own team. I didn't do too well, been outta practice.

'Preston North End' said Billy, spitting out an unripe blackberry. 'That's my dad's team in the league.'

Andy told them all about the A League in Australia.

'I thought Australians only played cricket,' protested Jimmy, 'because it's summer all year round. I like cricket and they play at school. Our Billy's good at bowling, aren't yer, Billy? When it's in season o' course. An' Andy, why you call 'em kids – we're not baby goats, tha knows.'

'Huh? Well, it's just the word we use at home, in Aussie. You aren't children any more, not really, are you? It's just a word. An' I do like cricket. I'm in one of my school teams. I've missed it while I've been over here. At home I play the indoor game in winter and, well, our summers are good an' long too. I had a few hits in the nets at the home yesterday, though, and met a guy who'll be at my school.

'Guy?' Sam laughed. You and yer words, Andy. We burn guys here on Guy Fawkes Night.'

'Hah, hah, hah. I play soccer in winter…'

'Football,' chorused the English lads.

'Soccer,' corrected Andy.

'Football,' came a chorus.

They all got the giggles and lay back on the grass kicking their muddy legs in the air.

Billy's wellie flew in the beck. 'Oh, 'eck. Gotta unplug dams anyways. Farmers get cranky, else. Come on, lads, then let's go home.'

Andy checked his watch. 'Crikey, it's after four o'clock.'

'Be late when us gets back,' muttered Jimbo.

'*Kanni* stew for us supper,' carolled Tommo.

The other lads were silent. Tommo shrugged and strode on ahead, having just thought that of course Jimmy and Billy were nervous about sacrificing Nebuchadnezzar. They had to face their dad and mum.

<h1 style="text-align:center">34</h1>

It was lucky the lads couldn't see what was already going on at the Big House.

Mr O had come home a bit earlier than usual. He blew his top when Mum told him the cockerel was missing. 'That blasted fox,' he shouted.

'No, Bill. The gate was locked and there are no holes in the fence. Got me thinking…' Mum hesitated.

'Those gypsies then – the Lees,' yelled Dad, and strode off up to the orchard to find out.

His anger cooled a little bit with the effort of striding quickly up the stony Top Drive all the way to Paddy Lane. Nevertheless, he marched along the lane with a frown cutting deep lines above his long nose. He reached the yellow caravan just as Pa Lee was sipping a cup of something.

Ma had the baby on her knee, feeding her sweet-smelling chicken gravy. The scent of wild herbs and prime chicken meat emanating from the big pan over the fire was delicious and even Dad felt his stomach grumble. He wanted his own tea. Then the hundreds of white feathers fluttering all over the grass under and around the caravan reminded him why he'd come. Those feathers, wind-dried and fluffy again, were the ones Sam wouldn't want for his arrows and Ma wouldn't need to make cushions. They were proof. Mr O knew exactly where old Nebuchadnezzar had gone.

Pa stood up as Dad approached. 'Greetings, friend. My wife and I wish to thank you for your very welcome gift. Your lovely children brought this proud old *kanni* up to us today and we have made the best possible use of it. We thank you and your wife for your generosity.'

Well, well. Spoken in a truly old-fashioned way. Dad just stopped himself from making a deep bow. What could he say in response? No way would he rant and rave. He found himself fighting a grin, as he met in Pa's eye a similar twinkle to one he knew was in his own. Those cheeky young beggars. The old cockerel had been more trouble than it was worth. It was well past its best, anyway. His anger was quashed as quickly as it had flared up. He put his head back and laughed.

Pa Lee joined in. 'Join me for a pipe, friend? Ma, fetch us a cup, *chav*.' The two men had known each other for many years, after all.

Dad tapped down the baccy in his pipe. 'Have to deal with the lads somehow, though, Lee. Stealin's stealin', when all's said and done.'

They nodded over the pipes and discussed what would be an appropriate action.

Pa Lee offered to mend Mum's saucepans and sharpen her kitchen knives – his stock in trade, he told Dad. 'Just send one o' t' lads up with 'em this night because we're setting off after sunup.'

'Nay, it's all right, Mr Lee. I think pot and pans are, too. I'll tan their bloomin' backsides, though. Mebbes. Let them say their piece first.' He grinned. 'Truth to tell, I'm not unhappy you've got the bird and put it to good use. My wife would never have cooked it even if I'd killed the beggar. She's soft that way.'

As the spicy acorn coffee came their way, they shared stories about their sons' antics and many other little items of local gossip, as men do when enjoying each other's company.

Dad eventually shook hands with Pa Lee, said to enjoy the chicken, nodded goodbye to Ma Lee and stood up and stretched, ready to walk home. Then he recognised Jimmy's sandals on the caravan step. He raised his eyebrows, tapped his pipe against a stone, and rose to go home.

Ma produced a big bunch of lovely artificial chrysanthemums, which she placed in his arms. 'These are for tha missus. My thanks, tha knows.'

Dad left the Lees, carrying the brightly sculpted flowers. He walked slowly home, deep in thought. He'd known the Lees for years. They were decent people. He was pretty sure they believed the lads' argument for giving them the old cockerel – its reputation over the years, its viciousness, was well known to the Lees, and many others.

However, the lads had to know they went too far giving it away like that. They must need to recognise right from wrong. The cockerel may have been a nuisance but he was valuable breeding stock, in spite of his foul temper. He laughed aloud at the quip, 'Fowl temper, more like.' But the principle remained. There was also the matter of Jimmy's sandals. A new thought struck him: was it that new Aussie friend of theirs who put them up to all this?

***

That Aussie friend had long gone to his home. So had the lads. Jimmy had crept into the bathroom early, hoping to be in bed when Dad got back. Billy had done a quick chore at the farm and told Jimmy to hurry up; he hoped to avoid Dad as well. However, even in their pyjamas they copped the flak (Billy's phrase from the Spitfires) and learnt what their punishment was to be.

Dad asked them each to explain themselves and, to be fair, he did listen. 'Well, you two, there has to be a reckoning. That bird was very valuable.'

Jimmy's cuts were still very fresh in his memory. 'But Dad, he was vicious. Even Mum called him her nemesis.'

Dad ignored him. 'I have considered that, and that he was getting old. But more important, you've let me down – and yourselves. What about trust and responsibility? You can't take matters into your own hands. Tomorrow's Friday and almost the end of school holidays. I know that new friend of yours from Australia plans to come up again. I now know he wasn't in on the plan so I'm not blaming him at all. But you two either stay indoors tomorrow and the weekend or forfeit all your pocket money on Saturday. What'll it be?'

***

Next day, Andy came up to the Big House as early as his mum said was reasonable. He was so curious about what the lads' parents had said about Nebby the *kanni*. He knocked the brass sailing ship knocker for quite a few minutes before the door opened.

It was Mo. 'Hello, Andy. You know about the cockerel of course?'

Andy was so used to teasing the boys about rooster that he had to bite his tongue. 'Yes, I was there, Mo, er Molly. Er, are they coming out today?'

She smiled. 'Don't look so pathetic, Andy. Yes, they are allowed but only if they finish their chores, and Dad gave them a very long list. But before they start on the list they have to finish their breakfast.' She smiled. 'Orders from above. Come on in. Want some pobs?'

Andy didn't know 'pobs' and had to ask.

She looked at him pityingly, like only big sisters can. 'My mother's homemade bread and butter, chopped into pieces with sugar and hot milk. It's delish on a cold morning.'

Very soon, Andy was at the kitchen table with the lads and the younger ones. He declined the pobs but a number of slices of brown toast looked very inviting, standing on edge in a toast rack in the middle of the table.

'Ando,' exclaimed Billy. 'Have some toast. Mo, pass him the butter and Mum's marmalade please. Or there's redcurrant jelly, if you'd rather have that, Ando,' and he grinned. He knew all about the redcurrants and the goat and the white leghorn doing battle.

Andy grinned back. Sounded good. He sat down amid the noisy family. He'd only noticed little Chris a few times, and never as clean as this. The baby was there too, in a high chair eating a piece of toast. They all looked newly washed, with their hair combed. Molly was the boss of this outfit. He helped himself to a piece of toast off the rack.

'Where's your Mam?'

Mo replied, 'Upstairs, getting ready. She's off to the town, one of her committees today.'

Andy raised his eyebrows. As far as he knew, women on committees, in the public eye as his own Mum often said, weren't usually short of money. So that was more evidence this family weren't in dire straits like some people in the papers were complaining. The Os had a good car, a modern one for the nineteen fifties, a Standard Vanguard.

'Ando, you're dreaming again.' That was Jimmy. 'You'll miss all the toast.'

Mrs O came downstairs. Andy looked at her to say 'Good morning' and tried not to show his surprise. Gone was that wrap-around overall. She was wearing a dress-up suit like his own mum liked to wear for appointments, and her hair was all brushed up into something very tidy. She looked very different from the Mrs O he'd seen nearly every day. Then he realised he was staring.

'Can I have another piece of toast please, Jimbo?'

Molly started to clear the breakfast table, delegating the two elder lads and young David to go into the orchard as she did so.

'Molly, have you got a minute, love? Are my stocking seams straight?'

Andy couldn't help it but to look. His mum didn't have lines up the back of her legs when she dressed up. *Fashions are different here, for sure.*

Molly and her mam were chatting in the corner, then her mam pulled on her gloves, picked up a leather briefcase and waved to them all.

'Be good, now. No shenanigans. Molly's in charge. Must go, Mr Russell's waiting.' She turned. 'I'll catch the bus back, Mo. Mr Russell's staying in town till later.'

Molly turned to the table. 'Right, lads. Mam wants some apples off the little Bramley tree. She says they're mostly ready and she can do apple sauce to put away. A lot of the apples have got a beetle and she wants you to put the bitten ones in a pile and the others that aren't bitten or eaten, carefully in the big buckets in the greenhouse. She says there's a lot of windfalls.'

This didn't sound very interesting to Andy.

Jimmy saw his face and whispered. 'Sorry, myte, but Dad said it's a penance for yesterday – old Nebby, tha knows? Mum's got a list of jobs as long as your arm. But if we'd kicked up about it, we wouldn't have been allowed to come out with yer at all and it's school next week.'

Andy nodded. 'Yep. Okay, mate. Count me in, and maybe we'll finish sooner.'

Jimmy grinned and gave him a friendly knuckle knock.

It was more fun than he expected. Billy had brought an old wheelbarrow to put the apples in. First they had to be thrown onto an old sheet spread on the soft grass. Molly would tell them off if too many got bruised. Because Andy was the best at climbing – they all knew he'd gone up the big horse chestnut tree – he had the first go at picking the apples up top. There were some damaged ones, some still on the tree but soggy and squishy. These were thrown onto the grass and the old billy goat ate them almost as soon as they landed. Then apples lower down the tree were added to the ones on the sheet. Billy and Andy poured them into the wheelbarrow. It was nearly full and sank into the damp earth and grass.

'We can't shift this,' Andy protested, shoving and tilting the old wheelbarrow and getting sweaty with the effort.

Billy took the other handle and they pushed and Jimmy pulled the wheel out of the grass. Just as it lurched forward, Andy spotted the goat.

35

The old billy goat was hopping up in the air from all four feet at once. He gave his body a twist in mid-air then landed on all fours. A silly grin on his bony face and he was jumping again.

'Look, he's laughing,' shouted Billy.

Jimmy pulled a face. 'Dunno about that but 'e's farting.'

'I reckon he's shickered, stonkered, drunk,' whooped Andy. He pulled Mum's little camera from his pocket. His mobile one was no good here, he knew that now. But the digital camera didn't need a signal. It'd be a great photo for Mum

He yelled to his mates as he turned the camera on. 'He's been eating all the fallen fruit, right, even before we got here. I read a story not long ago about a pig that ate fermented fruit and it was drunk.'

The lads giggled as they watched the old goat wobbling around on his spindly legs.

Jimmy mimicked him from behind. 'I've cider inside me insides,' he sang.

Andy was laughing so much, he cried.

Andy got a quick shot of Jimbo mucking about with the goat. Excellent. It worked. He was glad he'd shoved it in his pocket after all. He stood back and took another few of the lads and the goat.

Then Billy yelled out, 'C'mon, you lot. That goat's really pooey. Let's get the barrer home. Hey, Andy, that your mum's fancy camera? She showed it us when she came up. She took some of us all.'

Andy turned the camera onto Billy.

'Hey, it's me. Howdya do it, Ando?'

The lads crowded round.

Davo cried, 'What about me?'

Andy took one of the chubby youngster with the wide grin, then showed him.

'Ow. It's me. In colour. Like I am really.'

The lads all laughed, then Billy asked seriously, 'That's a great camera, Ando. I thought it was that watch thing you used to wear that never worked. This is just so small and flat to take photos. Is it Australian?'

Andy laughed. 'Prob'ly made in Japan or China or Taiwan. The man in the phone shop said they make good ones, but you're talking of my mobile phone, I think. That's more for calls than taking shots.'

'What yer on about, Ando? That's no telephone. It's got no wires.'

Andy was stuck for words. He put Mum's camera back carefully into his front zipped pocket as he wondered how to respond.

'That's why it's called a mobile – supposed to work without 'em. Bit of a gimmick really an' not much good…erm… Hey, what about these apples, Billy? Let's finish with 'em and get on to what's next. Leave Stinky Billy Goat here.'

Sticky moment was over.

Billy took charge. 'Barrer wasn't a good idea, lads. Too full to move. Let's put some in t' buckets and I'll come back later for what's left.'

Andy filled his bucket. Made of galvo, it was heavy even when empty. Took a while to fill as he had to check each apple for flaws. Gave him time to think.

Didn't like telling fibs about my mobile phone but what can I do? Can't explain. And this bloomin' bucket – wish plastic had been invented by this time. That started him on another tack as he lifted apple after apple into the bucket. All that carbon footprint and global warming Mum talks about, only the people in my real time could have caused it. People in these nineteen fifties don't have all the implements, the household appliances, the electronic gadgets we have at home.

He remembered talking about being an electrician with Jimbo, because that's something Jimmy wanted to do when he grew up. *He's never heard of electronics or robotronics. Or even electric tools – well, not like ours. They're happy with the things they have, but wouldn't it be easier for Mrs O to have a washing machine and a tumble dryer – and a TV and…*

Billy called out to them all to get a move on. 'We'll be stuck with flamin' chores all day if we don't.'

Andy dragged his bucket along behind the lads, feeling the whole weight of modern inventions and the damage they cause to the environment heavy on his shoulders.

Okay, they can't have mobiles and TVs are very expensive and with only tiny screens, but they've got movies. They listen to radios called wirelesses that are in cupboards like sideboards, they have a phone for using in their own time, but Mrs O said not every house has one. They have a wind-up gramophone that plays big old vinyl records that Mrs O sings along to, and they're not short of money because their mam dresses up lovely for meetings, and they go to private schools for Secondary. But they don't have freezers and fridges either, and not DVDs or even old videos. It's sad, really sad, to think that it's my own time, people in my real time, that are to blame for all the CO_2 that Mum goes on about – our freezers and fridges and what she calls techno-gizmo gear.

He realised there'd been more than sixty years for things to be invented between now and then. *Whichever. But they're all happy, they do things, make things and they don't miss the things I have, 'cos they don't know what they are.*

They'd reached the greenhouse.

'Ando, you gone to sleep, myte?' Jimmy took his bucket. 'We're done with apples, it's eggs now. Our Billy's gone off to clear up rest of t' apples.'

'Okay. You say eggs?' He looked around; couldn't see any. 'From the chook pen?'

'Nah. These ones are in t' old scullery. Mum wants us to wipe 'em and put 'em in t' isinglass.'

'Where?'

'Isinglass. It stores 'em, keeps 'em fresh. Don't you store eggs in Australia?'

He couldn't mention the fridge. 'Erm, we don't keep chooks any more, Jimmy.'

'All right, Ando. Well, it's a fishy jelly stuff and the eggs are sealed an' air can't get in them and they stay fresh longer.'

'Sounds gross.'

'No, not too much of it.' Jimmy didn't understand 'gross'. 'Not too big a job. Quickly done anyways. Then we can 'ave something to eat. We have to go to the old scullery. They're on the slate shelf to keep cool, Mum said. Molly said when we're finished she'll mek us some sandwiches.'

'And rock buns,' sang Davo. 'With lots of sultanas in.'

Jimmy piped up as he led the way through a passage to the old scullery. 'Our sultanas come from Australia, Andy.'

Andy told the lads about Grandad's grapevine and how the summer heat last year dried his grapes into currants.

He got a sideways look from Jimmy. 'You do tell us some funny tales, Andy. I think you just enjoy pulling our legs, eh? You've allus got a sharp answer.' He opened the door into a dark, room with a cold stone floor. 'This is the old scullery. Mum says years ago the servants would do their cooking in here.'

'Yeah, now she's got us,' chimed Davo.

'Oy, Titch, don't be cheeky. You better not do this anyway. You'll break the eggs, you will.'

'Don't call me Titch. I'm not so much smaller than you,' sulked Davo.

Billy was already there, turning a heavy brass tap over a long concrete sink. 'I'll wipe 'em, you lads can put 'em in the bucket, one by one, gently. It's that big bucket with the lid, over there.'

Andy looked. Another huge galvo bucket. He took the clean eggs off Billy and passed them to Jimmy to put in the bucket, one at a time. It was hard work, living in the nineteen fifties.

'Hey, come on, Andy, catch up with Billy, won't yer? My belly's grumbling like 'eck and it must be time for those sandwiches.' Jimmy still looked a bit sour-faced as if he really did think Andy told porkies.

'Sorry, Jimbo. Hey, I'm hungry too. Still got some chips, I mean crisps, in my pack. Let's eat 'em when we finish this, get rid of that smell of fish from that goo you put the eggs in. Phew.'

That made Jimmy's face crinkle into his wide, friendly smile again.

'We can't, you twerp, Ando. You left that back in t' kitchen earlier. C'mon, let's go. Job's done.'

Back around the table, hands washed and hair combed at Molly's insistence, they tucked into big fat sandwiches of cold beef. A bowl of lettuce and other salad bits from the garden was in the middle of the table.

'I didn't think you'd like sardines and eggs after what you've just been up to,' Molly laughed. 'Put some healthy lettuce and tomatoes on your sandwich, lads. You too, Andy, but I'll give you the choice.' She laughed out loud as Jimmy, who hated cucumbers, complained that even lettuce smelled like cucumber.

'Brighten up, Jimmy, there's chocolate cake for afters, so eat up. My special recipe.'

Andy smiled. He liked her laugh. It was more of a chuckle, like his Gran's. He grinned and put the crisps on the table. 'Let's share.'

Billy told his sister about Andy's little camera and she asked to see the photos.

'I'll get them printed and give you a copy. Sure, certain an' f'r a fact.' He was pretty sure Mum had bought some of the photo paper for the printer, the way she'd been pestering him to take photos. He grinned. 'Look, Molly, these are the ones my mum took of your mam and all of you when she came up that day.'

Molly was delighted to see again the coloured pics as Andy backtracked on the camera's gallery to show her. 'Hey, just a sec.' She brought her photo album from the living room. 'I've a Box Brownie now but Mum says I can have one of the new Kodaks for my next birthday. This little camera's been good but it's a bit old.'

You're telling me. Andy remembered Gran's little black and white photos. All square with wavy white borders. Just like these. He froze. Exactly like these. There were photos of the lads, Molly and their dog, in the snow – Molly was ready to throw a snowball. It was the same shot – he'd seen it before – but missing a certain little scratchy mark. He had held it before. No, not before – after. Half a world and half a century away. For a minute or two, he felt almost sick. This business about time swapping was getting just too much to cope with. How he wished he could talk about it with the lads. But they could never, never, understand.

Molly tapped his arm. 'Look, Andy. Look, lads…'

Andy knew these pictures so well. *Oh crikey, oh heck…*

Molly was describing her photos. 'These are from last winter, Andy. Look, lads, there's Panty and that's you lads on your sledges.' There was Molly at the back in a coat with a fur hood, her arms poised ready to throw that snowball.

Andy looked at Molly. 'Is this your album?'

'Yes, mostly, but Mum took most of the photos.'

Andy felt goosebumps pop up all over his arms and up the

back of his neck. He leaned over, covering up his confusion by pointing at one little photo after another as Molly continued describing them, his thoughts whirling madly in his head.

This isn't just the nineteen fifties, this is Gran's collection too; this is all about her. Weird. Spooky. Last time I saw this snap, and that one, and this one – Gran had taken them out of a box to show me. No album, though. Gran had been looking for a snap of the Tree.

He turned away, pretending to cough as he blinked a few times and shook his head. *These photos are a dead spit of Gran's old ones. That means that Gran's photos are of these lads, and Mo, and Singleton Park. Well, she lived here, didn't she? But how can Mo have a copy of Gran's photo that I know is, right now, back home in Adelaide? This is doing my head in.*

'You all right, Andy?'

'Sorry, Molly. They're great pics but I better go.' He made a show of looking at his watch.

'Sorry, guys. I'm late an' I'd better go. See ya.' He ran from the house.

'Sounds more like an American every day,' stated Jimmy.

36

It was Saturday but Andy and his mum weren't visiting relatives and friends today. Mum started to cook scrambled eggs but Andy didn't want any.

She was surprised until he told her about the eggs yesterday. And the fishy glass stuff they put them in. She went strangely quiet. 'I think I've heard of that stuff, Andy.' Then she slowly turned the camera over.

'Mum, some photos. I took them on your camera 'cos I need a signal to take photos on my mobile and, well, this way seemed safer. Can we print them a copy to take up on Monday?'

His mum was in a funny mood. *She's not with it. Like she's got something else on her mind. Can't be her book, though. That's finished. Down in London or Manchester or…*

'I thought you'd be pleased about the photos, Mum. That I'd finally remembered.'

She gave a slow smile. He'd expected her to be all excited. *Is she on those headache tablets again?*

'I am, Andy – excited, that is. The ones I took on my first visit to the Big House came out lovely and clear on the computer. I took shots of the family the other day. I need to load those. If they're any good, I'll put them on a memory stick and get the camera shop to print them on the correct paper.'

Now was his chance. Good as any. 'Mum, yesterday Molly showed me some photos she'd taken, and her mam. It was weird.'

Suddenly, Mum was alert. 'How weird, Andy? Knowing what we know now, they'd be little black and white ones, yes? Like your Gran's ones.'

'That's just it, Mum. Not just *like* Gran's, they *were* Gran's, Mum. I clearly remember seeing some of 'em back home in Adelaide. Like the one of the Tree she took, that tree I climbed first day here. I know that photo's with Gran.'

She shook her head. 'I've overcooked these eggs… This is all getting too hard, Andy. All the puzzle pieces seem to be falling into place but in a crazy way. Andy, there's a market in antique photos. And if the photo you saw is of Gran's Tree, sure and why not? There may have been a few prints of it.'

'Sure, Mum, but…

'Andy, that's enough for now, eh. We're learning to believe what's happened here, but we don't know how. Okay? Just accept it. What you don't need to do is imagine ghosts, Andy.'

Oops. Mum losing her cool like that – not done it for ages. 'Mum. I was just gonna say I emailed Gran about the photos last night. She has to know this family, has to. Remember ages ago I said she'd mentioned a Billy. Anyway, I told her about the photos like hers that Mo showed me, so I'll wait to see if she can sort it out for me, Mum. Okay?'

His mother expelled a long, slow breath. 'Okay, Andy. Sorry. It's all getting to me, too. That was sensible, emailing Granny.' She took the camera. 'You know, I think your grandmother knew exactly what she was doing when she gave you that little marble. Keepsake? Huh. And it was she who waxed lyrical about our rental with Mrs Reeves and pointed me in the Lakeland direction. It didn't seem significant before, just a lovely coincidence. Now…'

She turned away. 'I'll check these shots then load them onto the computer with the others. If they're good enough, we'll take them to the camera shop for printing too. They have better fluids for the job than the little inkjet. You have your day with the lads. It'll be different, being Saturday. You managed to eat all those tough scrambled eggs. Wish I had your teenage tum. Hey, have you shown the lads your DS yet? It could do with more fresh air, that thing. You were once never off it, now you're never on it.'

Andy shrugged. 'Well, I don't get much time, Mum. We always seem to be doing things when I'm up at the Big House.' He swallowed the last bit of eggy toast. 'It's funny, really, when I think of it. We sit on the swings, talk and stuff, and there's a lot of doing what you'd call nothing. Anyway, today they're not allowed to go to the movies because of that Nebby thing…'

'Andy? What Nebby thing?'

'Erm, a sort of an incident, Mum. I'll explain tonight. Mr O is home today but he'll be in his garden mainly. So Molly said. Okay, I'll take my DS with me. Be interesting to see what they think of it. They haven't even got TV and yet I've got two little screens that are pocket-size.' He stood, looking thoughtful. 'At least if the battery stays good, I don't need wifi for the DS.'

His mum leaned over and gave him a big hug. He reckoned she was in a weird mood.

Andy picked up Mrs Reeves's little marble bag with Aggie and the other winnings in and started off up the drive. Pickles wanted to come but he locked him in the garden. Even though it started to drizzle, with the threat of heavier rain, he didn't quicken his stroll. He had a lot to think about – not least about going to that new school next week. *Not really looking forward to that.*

The lads were at the swings and he ran to join them.

Jimmy bounced to a stop and sat on an old crate nearby. ''Ave a go, Ando. It's wet inside, though, so watch it on yer keks.'

Too late, as Andy felt the rain caught in the tyre run gently through to his legs. 'Yuk.'

They all moved off slowly to the old stables, where it would be dry.

It wasn't only the rain that was dampening their spirits. Today was Saturday.

Jimbo was moaning that only Monday was left of holidays.

'Next week, Ando, we'll not see you much. School gets in the bleddy way. Me an' Billy won't get home till nearly six, will us, Billy, and you, Ando, you're going to a different school from us.'

The three lads sat together on the old mounting block under the stable eaves, swinging their legs and complaining about having to go to school. Andy knew that schools didn't finish till four o'clock. And in winter it'd be dark before they could expect to arrive home. Summer was now well over and autumn had come in wet, as Mrs Reeves was frequently grumbling.

'Needn't be so bad, Jimbo. We'll see if we can catch up at weekends. Trouble is, my mum's book is now with some publisher in Manchester so she has to drive down there some days. Like now and again. She says we can stay there with the other old rellies.' He moaned – all that awful cup and saucer stuff. 'If she goes during the week, Mrs Reeves says she'll keep an eye on me if I promise to stay home after school. As if I needed babysitting. It sucks.'

'Eh? Suck what? Never heard that one before, eh, Billy? Listen, we don't have to go to the pictures every Saturday. What say me and Billy come down to yours one weekend when your mum's in Manchester? Or will you have to go with her?'

Billy chimed in. 'Yeah, that's if Andy's there when we come. He wasn't last time.'

Andy pricked his ears. 'When wasn't I there? You didn't say you'd been down to our place.'

'Coupla weeks ago, eh, Jim? An' course we come down the drive – well, sometimes.' Billy stopped. 'We like it best at our place and up Top Drive and stuff. But we looked around back of Mrs Reeves's old place and saw tatty old shed and couldn't work out where you lived.'

Jimmy joined in. 'Yeah, so I knocked on t' front door and old Mrs Reeves came out and telt me off fer frighting her cat, mangy old thing.'

'D'yer mean Mrs Reeves or t' cat,' giggled Billy, 'and you mean frightened, not frighted, you clot. Talk proper.'

Jimmy dived at him from the mounting block and the two wrestled on the wet stable floor.

Andy realised one matter was settled and he hadn't even had to ask the question. *It's definite now: the lads cannot cross over the time warp. They've tried. The Barn was an old shed once, but now it's our unit and they did it up a few years back. Crossing time zones – no can do. An' that's why the photos I took at the Big House a while ago didn't show up. An' Mum blamed me. Now she knows they didn't turn out because they were photos of people who hadn't been born yet.* Another thought rolled around the back of his mind. *Oh, crikey. Mum's putting pics on the computer today and they won't work either. They can't. And I can never explain to the lads about the little green marble. Now they're arguing about whether to play marbles or not...*

'Hey, you two. Stop arguing a sec. What day was it you came to see me? Mebbe I was in the town that day with my mum. Sorry I missed you, though. Would've been good.'

A sudden thought. *Is there a remote chance they might be able to cross the time warp if they had the little green marble? Whatever, I can't risk lending it to them because if they can't get it back to me, and I can't ever get back to them without it – not worth even thinking about. What if I went and called for them and brought them down to the rental and then escorted them back? Yeah, think about it, Andrew.*

'Ando, you dreaming again? Let's get under cover. The rain's pelting down.'

Jimmy gave him a friendly thump. 'Let's have a threesome game of Boss. You're getting real fast at that now, Ando – for an Aussie, that is.'

Andy grinned. 'It's raining cats and dogs, sure, certain and f'r a fact. But before we start, got something to show you.' He took his DS out of his pack and flipped it open. 'I brought my DS. Meant to bring it before. Needs no signal as long as it's charged. Thought we could have a game – this one you're animals and I'm the person. Or one of you can… We can connect to each other.'

The lads had gone quiet, Billy peering over one shoulder and Jimmy the other.

He selected *Animal Crossing*. He clicked over to a submenu screen. Neither of the lads made a comment.

Then Billy took it out of his hands. 'By 'eck, Andy, I've never seen owt like this.'

As Andy leaned over and pressed the start, little figures came alive on the screen. Billy threw his hands in the air, letting the DS drop to the concrete floor. Jimmy rushed to pick it up. Billy stared at Andy, eyes and mouth open wide.

Jimmy turned it over. 'Okay, Andy. Look, it's still working. Only a scratch there, see?' He had a quick look at the screen, closed it up and handed it back to Andy with the tips of his fingers. 'Too much electric for me, Ando. Risky, that. No insulation. Dangerous.' He'd gone pale. 'Never seen the like before. Best not let me dad see it. And 'e's 'ome today. Put it away, eh?'

Andy couldn't believe it. 'You dork. 'Course it's not live electric. Me and my friends in the…in Australia, have all got these. They're great. Interactive.'

He replaced it carefully in his backpack, telling himself to say no more. *Just put it away. Sure it's diff'rent, yeah. But to panic, electric shocks and stuff? What's with these lads?*

Billy decided to take control of the situation. 'Hey, you two, we wanted a game of Boss, okay?'

37

But something had changed. The lads were slow to regain their usual good humour. Andy thought they played the next game with a fierce determination. There were no jokes, no laughs at Billy farting. Andy commented they were both so serious.

Jimbo got up from his knees and looked at Andy. Not his usual devil-may-care expression. 'Okay, Ando. Let's get serious. These hols you've taken most o' my good steelies with that aggie o' yours. Now, t' holidays are nearly over and I'm gonna win that aggie off you.'

Whoohoo. Open challenge. Andy looked at Jimmy curiously. This was a different situation. *This lad is real mad. Well, if he really thinks I've been telling porkies, I'll flamin' well show 'im.*

'Okay, so it's war on the stable floor, eh? Right, Jimbo, we'll play, but the aggie's mine.'

The two lads picked their spot, eyeing each other like two farm dogs circling round sheep. Or so thought Billy. He decided to leave them to it. He'd show Andy his crystal set later. Beat his electric whatsit into a cocked hat, so it did. Hands in pockets, he walked homewards, whistling.

First game in the stables, Andy won two of Jimmy's steelies. This Boss was a tough game and Jimmy had his dander up. Andy needed to concentrate like crazy. Every move had to count.

The rain had stopped drumming on the stable roof. Molly came out to see what was going on. Billy had told Molly the boys were getting serious. David came with her and wanted to join in but Jimmy angrily gestured him away.

Molly decided it was diplomatic to stay out of the line of fire but she still wanted to stay and make sure it didn't break into open warfare. She sat on an old towel on the mounting block with Davo, watching. Davo grew bored when he couldn't play and went off on his bike. The rain stopped. Molly stayed. This game required supervision.

'You've come on grand, Andy.'

Andy grinned and lost his concentration – big mistake. He missed the hole and had to yield his turn. *Yoh. Bad move.*

Jimmy scored against Aggie. 'She's mine. Ando, she's mine.'

'No, she's not.' His aggie was not going to be lost to anyone. *Can't happen. Aggie is my mascot. Aggie is England, and Gran, and Singleton Park and everything that really matters, all wrapped up in a scraggy green marble.* His mum had warned him, too…

'C'mon, Jimmy, another game and I'll get her back.'

Jimmy was determined. 'Warning yer: you'll not win her back, Aussie.' He was fed up with being called a 'dork' by this Aussie kid with all the whiz-bang gadgets – wristwatches that telephoned, telephones that took photos, now a DS thing that was better than going to the pictures. Mebbes he was a good pal, but…

Andy realised Jimmy was going to play tough. Game after game, Aggie stayed in Jimmy's pile. Jimmy could see his myte was upset and trying not to show it. But he'd won her fair and square and she was a good 'un. However, he felt he could afford to be generous.

'Ooohhhhhkaaaaaay, Ando. Come back Monday and I might let you win her back. Prob'ly.' Jimmy grinned. That was fair.

Andy pulled a face at Jimmy. 'She's my mascot, Jimmy. I have to get her back. I have to – sure, certain and f'r a fact.' No way could he leave Aggie behind. 'Give me Aggie, Jimbo and I'll play you for her again Monday, even tomorrow. Eh?'

'No way, Andy. Fair an' square, eh?'

'Jimbo, I promise, you'll have it tomorrow but just let me

take it home tonight, eh? Tell you what, you can have a lend of my DS tonight, instead of the aggie. Swap you back tomorrow, okay?'

Ando was all mixed up. How could he explain he *had* to have Aggie back? Jimmy'd call him a sore loser if he insisted. He – and Mo – wouldn't believe him if he told them the real reason. No way could he say they were in a different time warp and stuff like that. Same kerfuffle as the crisps and the photos…

Jimbo was shaking his head. 'That DS thing was hot on my fingers, Andy. Dangerous electric and no earthing, I could see. I wouldn't hold it and my dad wouldn't want me to, anyway.'

Nothing was gonna work. A last appeal. 'Jimbo, you don't know what you keeping the aggie will do…'

Molly shook her head. 'Cheer up, Andy. I'll win the aggie off him for you.'

Jimbo gave him a wink. He ran off, laughing now. 'Going for me tea. Fair and square, Ando. See you next time.'

Andy shrugged and turned to slouch off down the drive. He gave a reluctant wave. 'Famous last words, Jimbo.'

***

When Andy arrived home, his mother needed only one look at his face. 'Oh no. I bet you've lost Aggie.'

'Yep. Not happy, Mum. Jimmy seemed really determined to win, and sort of angry. The DS didn't go down well, either.' He emptied his pockets. 'I've scored a crooky and five alleys and three steelies, Mum, but how can I get back there without Aggie? Mum, what'll I do? I wanted to take the photos up to them, too.'

Mum didn't smile. She'd been puzzling about this time warp, time zone thing all day. It was too improbable to be real and yet it just had to be. She didn't believe in magic, yet how else to explain things?

'Andy, I've something to ask you. You know those photos? Did you have them on a wrong setting?'

'Eh? Oh, not again, Mum. I've been thinking about them but no, nada, negative, nay, Mum. Took 'em on auto. Same as always.' He noticed Mum's face. 'I suppose we *were* jumping about a bit but… Hey, Mum, they worked. They did. I showed them to the lads. Mum, Molly said you showed her the ones you took when you went up there – she said she was tickled pink. And today, again, they were gobsmacked they were in colour.' He gave a wry grin. 'Sorry, Mum. I mean they were flummoxed.'

He went to talk, then noticed the expression on his mother's face. 'Mum, they didn't print, did they?'

'Andy, not only did they not print, I couldn't bring anything up on the computer that I could recognise. They're the cloudiest, haziest, blobbiest snaps I ever did see. Even playing back on the camera, nothing there I can make head nor tail of. Looks more like a cloud of dust.' She held out the camera to show him and clicked back through the bunch he'd taken in the orchard. 'See, Andy. Look, mate, I'm back to those of the river in the town. That was more than a week ago. Nothing to see 'tween now and then. Mine of the Os in the kitchen – I showed them off to them right away and they were good – and yours of the lads are all a complete failure.'

'No, can't be. We looked at them. The lads saw what I'd taken – they were great. The photos you took of Mrs O and them all were still on the screen when I backtracked to show the lads the ones of them in the orchard. They really liked seeing them again and I could see them all clearly. I could see them clearly: nice sharp pics. They weren't faded or spoilt and yet. Mum, those pics had been here and then back again, yet we can't see them here, only there. There has to be an explanation.'

'Those I took when I had Aggie with me, you mean?'

'Yes. Didn't they…? Not at all?'

'They didn't. Not here. They did there and then, because I showed them to Mrs O and promised her a print. And you showed them to the lads today and they enjoyed seeing them in colour. Oh, Andy, it's so very sad. Obviously, we can't bring things back. Not from then, that is – your earlier time. Though we are able to take things there. It's a one-way street, Andy.'

Andy knew what she meant. The paper those notes had been written on had gone yellowy and the pencil faded. Even the badger's hair he'd collected was stiff and not as smooth as he remembered.

Then he had a thought. 'Mum, what about the mushrooms. They came, didn't they? And how do all my steelies and alleys that I've won come through then?'

'Andy, I just don't know, but mushrooms are fungi and fungus is a weird, persisting fact of nature. Your other marbles, glass and steel lasts forever… Oh, enough's enough, Andy. Let's forget about it all for now. Tea and TV, okay?'

***

Andy lay awake late that night. Hardly anything made any sense any more.

Next morning, he agreed with Mum it might be a good idea to see if he could get back to the lads' nineteen fifties time zone, even though it was Sunday. He was worried, and sensed his Mum was too. They had quite a debate over their Weetabix and toast.

'There is a rational explanation for every situation, Andy, and magic is not an explanation. It's a series of coincidences: fairy tale happenstance at best.'

They were going round in circles, both of them. This time zone stuff had his Mum confused? Yeah, well, him too.

As he trundled off up the drive, worrying at the back of his mind what he'd find up there, he thought about his photos taken in the orchard. They looked good after he took them. He'd shown them to the lads. He'd seen them himself. Young Davo had been gobsmacked at seeing his face, and in colour. And yet, when Mum played them back on the camera, there was nothing on the screen where Davo's pink sweaty face had been. The way they hadn't turned out was not only weird, it was creepy.

Mo's photos in the album really are – were – the same ones Gran has in Australia. Not copies, the real originals. Freaky. It'll be tonight, earliest, before I can get a reply from her. But Mum says the lads can come to our place next Saturday. 'Not before time,' she said. So that's okay, but only if they can get to us. What if they came with the aggie? I know I thought one day I could ask them to come down the drive with me in the arvo, but I never did. That might have worked… Now they have the aggie, so I wonder if they could, after all, break through? Mum says it seems to be a one-way street, this time travel. She's prob'ly right.

38

Andy was so lost in his thoughts he came up to the big gate without recognising how far he'd walked. He was used to seeing it closed, guarding the Big House. Not today. The big gate was wide open. He'd seen it like this twice before. He ran over and ran his fingers along the top. No mould, no tatty old paintwork. There was no old chain, nothing rusty to be seen.

He felt tears well up in his eyes. This told the whole story. He'd seen this smart open gate only twice before. Both times he hadn't had Aggie with him. One day it had been a test with Aggie waiting safely at home. Now Aggie was locked in 1953 or whenever and he would never see the green marble again, nor Jimbo, Billy, Davo, Mo and the others. Tears of angry disappointment rolled down his cheeks. He didn't bother to wipe them.

He hunkered down on the drive, his back against the big white – open – gate. No question: it's Aggie. She's the catalyst bridging two worlds like Mum said; the world of sixty or more years ago and the now of the twenty-first century. Well, she can't work for me any more. Because I betrayed her, losing her.

He got to his feet and blew his nose, then realised, *She's not lost. She's back when and where she came from.*

His mum said only that morning that if all of this marble stuff was true, it was a huge privilege to see how someone else had lived here, so long ago. And what she called 'marble stuff' *was* true, and he knew, deep down, she knew it too. What's more it was true when his grandmother had lived here; Gran, who owned the aggie, had kept it for years and then asked him to bring it back to where it belonged. Gran was the clue. She believed in magic, he knew she did. She knew Aggie had a special power.

He looked over the fence, up the hill to the Tree. Surely it looked taller than that day he and Billy had teased the bull. It looked now like it had been that first day, majestic.

I'll go to the Big House for a look around, to the stables, just to make sure…

He was certain now that his only chance, and it was remote, of seeing Billy and Jimmy again was next Saturday. If they came down to Mrs Reeves's house. If they were able to break the barriers. If they could cross from one time to another with Aggie. He'd kept Aggie's powers secret. There was no way the lads would know they'd need Aggie with them.

He stumbled up the slope to the house. He ran round to its backyard. The bumpy cobbled backyard was the same he and the lads had run over every day but their house door was now painted a bright red. Like Mum described after the first time she walked up. Without Aggie. He looked at the big shiny brass number 2 that served as a knocker.

He turned and ran up to see the tractor tyre swings. They were gone. There was a rock garden, all fancy plants. So many of the old trees were gone that only yesterday had been noisy with big black rooks nesting in them. Andy was shocked to his very insides.

This is the same place but I don't belong here any more. I'm an outsider. This is what Ma Lee knew; what she was telling me and tried to show me, when she pressed her hands on my shoulders and her eyes seemed to go deep into mine.

He turned towards the old stables. *Our marbles place, me and Jimbo's. There's no sign of us and not of Mr Russell's fantastic Morris Oxford either. They're just fancy flats like Mrs Reeves told me about.*

He tripped over a large potted succulent. One of those

aloe vera things like in our garden at home, fat and green. He rubbed his shin where he'd hit the brightly glazed pot. The old mounting block was still there and with the three steps up the side as before. Now it had another big potted plant on the top and others on the steps. He rubbed his fingers along the top. It was just as mossy and grey as it was only yesterday when they'd sat on it, as had Mo with Davo as they watched that last game of marbles.

Yesterday and more than sixty years ago.

Worst of all, I never said a proper goodbye. 'Billy. Jimmy. Anybody – where are you, *all of you?*' he yelled, not caring but wanting them to answer. Angry tears poured down his face. *Huh – tears are no use. Bit stupid for a fourteen-year-old. That's what Mum would say.* He sniffed and wiped across his face with his sleeve. Seemed like his tears had washed his eyes and he could see what was what.

This is no strange future. It's real and this is how it is now. *And without Aggie, I'll never see the lads again.*

Suddenly, a mountain bike came haring down the Top Drive. Its helmeted rider in blue jeans and sneakers looked about fourteen or fifteen too. He yelled out, 'Hey, you. Who are you shoutin' for?'

Andy just muttered something about staying down at South Lodge for the holidays as the rider ripped a wheelie and scattered dust over his hairy legs.

'Yer don't look like a school kid. Hols are nearly over anyway.'

Andy just shrugged and turned his back. *So what, I know I'm tall. So, so and bloomin' so.*

He rattled the allies and steelies in their little bag, safely zipped in his pocket. They were evidence; this place was evidence, even proof. *Mum called Scraggy Aggie my mascot. More like my passport into the past.*

He walked down to the big gate; it was still open, so he just walked through. He looked over to the Tree again. With no Aggie, he had climbed the Tree, that day so many weeks ago; the Big House looked then like it did now. When his mum had come up here the first time without Aggie, things had looked like they were now and she refused to believe his stories. The day she had borrowed the little green marble she'd had tea with Mrs O and met the kids. She'd taken photos, pics that faded from the camera because they were of subjects like the lads who didn't exist when she tried to put them onto a twenty-first-century computer.

Aggie had really gone back where she belonged, as Gran had said. She would belong to Jimmy or maybe to Mo-Molly. Mo had threatened to win Aggie back off Jimmy – was that really only yesterday?

Time to leave it all behind and go home. Andy realised that tears were still rolling down his face. He didn't care about wiping them. He walked slowly down the drive, kicking a pebble along the bitumen as he went.

His mother was in the garden with Pickles. She took one look at him and pulled a tissue from her pocket. 'You got dusty track marks from your tears, Andy. Give a blow, son, give a blow.'

Crikey, like when he was a little kid.

He was reminded of Molly and how one day she'd been so surprised to see him blow his nose on a tissue and throw it on their fire. She had produced a hanky, a cloth one, all neatly ironed, but he'd said no. Molly hadn't known about tissues. Andy considered it unhygienic to keep snotty hankies in a pocket.

Mum and Andy sat on the garden seat for a long time, each feeling sad.

Mum even cried a little with Andy. 'I had a genuine connection with Mary, that's Mrs O, and young Molly. I wanted to go and say goodbye before we went home. I'm so sorry not to.'

'Mum, I know the lads the lads weren't my family but they sort of felt like brothers, like having brothers would feel.'

Mum gave Andy a hug.

'Even Billy in some ways seemed younger than me, yet in other ways he was so self-sufficient. Jimbo at times was a giggly kid. And at others, well, he was showing me designs he'd made for wooden furniture. Just like a family, really, like brothers would feel, I guess. It's only been weeks, Mum, I know, but it seemed like always, you know? I fitted in. I didn't feel different. Only a bit on the first day but after that…no. And we could hang out and wrestle and even quarrel a bit but it didn't last. It was stuff I didn't do at home, Mum. Like at home I'd think they were loads younger than me, yet they knew so much detailed history, more than I even knew, and geography – all about the most obscure places. Mum, have you heard of Popocatepetl?'

She laughed. 'I have, but I wouldn't want to pinpoint it on a map.'

'The lads, they didn't have computers. So they didn't know about satellites and space probes and whatever. But you know, lots of other stuff they knew and they made things, more 'n I ever did. Like Billy and his saucepan lid for the crystal set, that was *brilliant* thinking on his part.' He paused. 'I'm really gonna miss 'em, Mum.'

His mother gave his shoulders another squeeze. 'Me too, Andy. You know, I'm not sure how, but we've been given a wonderful chance to know how life was, and it's only a couple of generations ago. You know, son, ideas of magic don't come easily to me, yet if I refuse to believe in things that defy rationality and logic, how can I explain these last few weeks?'

39

They sat quietly for a while, neither with any more to say but lots to think about. Pickles crept up to them, gave their hands a lick and then settled down at their feet. Andy's mum pulled his ears gently, smiling at the dog's obvious wish to comfort his human friends.

She sat up. 'Okay. It's time travel without the science. That's what it is, Andy. The very best kind.' She pursed her mouth in thought. 'You know, Andy, and I'm just being my rational, logical self here, the Big House experience is wonderful material for another book...'

'Oh, Mother. How could you even think about writing about this? It'd be mocking my mates. Besides, how could you explain how it happened? You couldn't. Not unless you wrote it as fiction. No one would believe you.'

'Er... I suppose. Guess now we know, we know why our photos couldn't possibly work. The digital camera and your mobile, they're recent inventions.'

'Mum, my DS worked.'

'Think, Andy. Your DS doesn't need external signals to operate. As long as it's charged up, it works. Wherever. Your mobile has to have a signal and needs those external signals from radio waves that hadn't been identified – well, not used anyway – then, in the fifties. And how can a camera capture images that don't exist?'

She stood, pushing the dog gently off her feet. 'It's not only you, Andy. I couldn't explain to Mrs O that my muffins were baked in a microwave. As for the mushrooms, why they didn't crumble into dust as soon as you climbed over the gate to come home, I can only think it's some mystery of fungus. Fungus is weird stuff. Andy, I am flummoxed.'

She gave a little sigh, then turned and smiled. 'Okay, better news now. My book's ready for an initial print run, according to the publishers. Once they get going, well, it'll be my job done here. I think we can arrange to fly home in time for you to go back to school for term four, to finish the year.'

Andy calculated. 'That's only about four weeks, Mum. Here it'll be their half-term. Surely I can give this other school a miss for that time?'

She smiled and gave him a hug. 'Cheer up, Andy. You know, meeting new kids, twenty-first-century English kids – even if it's for only two or three weeks – will be different, but could be fun. Seeing what their schools are like, for instance.'

Andy doubted that.

Next day, Monday, was the last day of the school holidays. Andy waited with Pickles outside Mrs Reeves's place, watching the dog. He hoped desperately that Pickles would hear something, sense something, like dogs are supposed to do. Such as Billy and Jimmy's footsteps, their smell even. Maybe there was some kind of ethereal curtain between them that allowed them to communicate. Even to just say a proper goodbye. But Pickles's ears didn't even twitch.

***

School on the Tuesday was okay. One of the first kids Andy saw was the one who'd ridden the mountain bike that day at Singleton Park. He recognised Andy and came over and introduced himself as Jonathan. He lived in the house at the top of the Top Drive. Andy remembered sheltering near the wall of that house when he and Billy were running from the bull. *Bet it's all changed there now.* Then he saw Steve from the home and they did a high five.

As Andy explained to his mother that evening, it was all so ordinary, just like Sunbury. 'First was assembly. Another teacher guy announced that mobiles and DSs had to be kept in students' lockers but we could get them at recess. No running in corridors, watch the noticeboards and things like that. Schools the world over must talk the same language, Mum. It's a long day, though, not finishing till four. And some Upper Sixth kids, that's like Year 12, have lessons Saturday mornings as well. The teachers seem okay. My form teacher's a Mrs McMahon and she wears a black university gown. A few of the others do, but the chemistry guy is weird, he's older and he has a beard he ties up with a rubber band during experiments. He made a joke of it when he lit up a Bunsen burner. Pretty cluey, though. They've got the usual interactive whiteboards and other stuff we have at Sunbury. Like I said, schools seem the same wherever you are.'

Andy said he'd been called up as a reserve for the soccer team. 'They love their football and tomorrow there's a try-out and I can borrow shorts and things if I haven't got them with me. Now I'd better do this chemistry homework.'

As it happened, Andy only played in one football fixture before he had to leave the school. His mother was delighted when, on his last day, the pompous principal gave him a scholastic and character reference, saying that even though he'd only been there three weeks, his work and general conduct were exemplary. The principal shook his hand and said it was always good to pass things on. Well, in his case, it really would be. His mother scanned it and sent it off to his dad in Darwin.

'Wait till that silly old Mr Potts sees this, Andy. He'll have to eat his words. It puts the tin lid on his accusations regarding your behaviour. Dah de dah.'

Sure, Andy was pleased. However, more than anything he

wanted to see the lads, just one more time. Each Saturday he waited at home to see if they would, could, come. No such luck. Deep down inside he'd known they couldn't. Not in his time anyway. Couldn't Jimmy have put his marbles – all of them – in his pocket, just once, and ambled down the drive? Then maybe passed through the time warp?

He and Pickles sat outside by the drive most evenings after tea. He remembered the lads saying they didn't get home from their schools till at least six, but Pickles didn't even prick his ears to attention. His mother was busy packing and preparing for them to tour the Lakes – because of that old *Swallows and Amazons* book of hers. Then they were to visit other rellies down south in Suffolk.

He knew he'd never forget the lads. They were more than friends. They'd never been like strangers after that first day. They felt like brothers and he felt like a part of their family. *Families are good, even Molly. Even Joan of the green eyes.*

Then on their last day, as they left Mrs Reeves's for the last time, Pickles started to howl.

Mrs Reeves said he was sad Andy was going. 'Funny, that, Andy. Pickles isn't a howler. Mebbes when strange dogs are round, but not for owt else, much. Nay, lad, calm down, nobody there.'

Mrs Reeves, you just don't know. What if Pickles is sensing Panty? What if Jimbo and Billy've brought him down, hoping to catch up. Oh, I wish. What if they're here and I can't see them, and they can't see me...

'Cmon, Andy, in the car, love.' Mum patted his shoulder. 'We must go.

He gave a big wave from the car window.

Just in case.

40

Still seems a bit odd being back home, really home, chucking stones in Gran's fish pond. My special spot on the tree root under Gran's apple tree – feels good. Worn shiny from me and other kids using it over the years. Like Gran's spot in the big Singleton Park tree. Seems like ages ago since I was there, yet some days it feels I'm still over there. It's a bit over six weeks ago, I think, when I last saw the lads. Hard to get things straight. Mum says it's jet lag – plays with your mind. Like one of those paradoxes Mum goes on about; a time and a place so far away yet I keep expecting to see Jimbo poke his head round the tree.

It's his birthday around now. P'raps that's why I'm thinking of him. Here it's the October Labour Day holiday Saturday. Jimbo'll be thirteen. How old would he be now, really, if he's not dead? Him and Billy gotta both be really old guys like in their seventies. And I'm back in Australia in the twenty-first century, only fourteen and a quarter and a bit an' still fourteen and a quarter. Hard to get my head round. I feel even older, inside.

Shenanigans going on over there nearer to the Grands' house. That was Mo-Molly's word. The Grands've put on a barbecue for me and Mum, an' all the rellies are around somewhere. Mum's book was published, already had a good review apparently, and that's the main reason for this do; that an' our return. Oh, and Gruncle Roger's birthday.

Lunch all cleared away, afternoon tea spread on tables. Scones and meringues, usual stuff. And friends around, talking. Catching up with each other.

Tom came round the day I got back. I told him he was a lousy writer – only two emails all the time I was away. Tom's talk is non-

stop Facebook. Surely he's not taken in by all that? Me, I'm real, but he talks non-stop about Facebook and Twitter. Said he had twenty-seven friends already. I'm gobsmacked. How could he be so daft? That's a Jimbo word. I keep remembering all the little things… Told him friends on Facebook aren't friends.

'You and me, that's friends. Face to face, talking an' all that. An' everyone on the planet gets to know your private business on Facebook.'

'You're a dork, Andy. Come back a real nerd, you have. Gotta catch up, mate. We're all on it.'

But I got all the news from him, soon as we talked: the teams, all of that. But where's he got to? Can't see him, probably in the family room whacking someone at tennis on the Wii.

Mum acts like everything's back to normal. Well, it is, natch, but I really miss the Singleton Park lads, more 'n I ever thought; in fact, everything that we did and made; just hanging out, talking about nothing.

An' that's what Tom called it; said that's all I did. Nothing. 'Cept for London – he likes the thought of going there. Grumbled because I could've bought the new Star Wars releases from over there or downloaded some new songs on my MP3 for swaps, and didn't. Couldn't convince him I just didn't have time. An' he's not at all impressed with my tales of the Singleton Park lads.

'Freaky they'd no telly, Andy. Okay, so maybe iPads, PSs and MP3s and iPods and Nanos an' stuff – not everybody wants 'em, or has 'em – but a telly? Everyone has a TV. Their life must be so boring, mate.'

'Nope. Boring it wasn't, Tom. Terrific fun in the little dinky – we could do huge spins and figure eights, work out ways of making it so it'd steer better and go faster. Even put big wheels on the back and small wheels on the front and swapped 'em round and about. Then started making a new one so the lads could have races, and nobody saying act your age an' all that.

Just good fun, an' the little kids loved it. Best thing, we made it ourselves, me an' Jimbo. I designed the other axle.'

As for badgers, he said they sounded just like wombats with stripes, nothing special. 'Why sit around, just waiting?'

As for Joan, even, girls are just girls as far as he's concerned. Pull 'em if you can, leave 'em alone if you can't, that's Tom for you. As for jigsaws and making chooks' nesting boxes – called me a silly duffer.

'Why not the moulded plastic ones for the chooks? An' why didn't you update your DS and things, take advantage of the duty free an' all that."

How the heck could I explain they didn't know about plastic at the Big House, specially as he went on to tell me I did just a lot of nothing with those English kids and then said I came back a nerd? Laughed at the idea of 'making' stuff. Said his dad's shed was Open Sesame to him, whenever, so why reinvent the bloody wheel? Went on about RipStiks being great for speed, or the go-carts on the raceway. Called them real fun. Laughed like a drain at me playin' marbles an' said I'd lost mine, meaning my brains. Said I gotta grow up.

Made me think, what he said. In a funny way, I do feel older. And Tom seems younger; the one who needs to grow up. Doesn't seem like we're on the same wavelength any more.

Couldn't help think what Tom would have done if he'd been me, going back to the nineteen fifties. Would he have fitted in like I did – eventually? All he talks about is what he has that's new, what he's done. Sort of fidgety, like everything has to happen at once.

Talking to Mum t' other day, I said how he'd changed and she said no it was me who'd changed. Said I used to be like Tom, a 'push-button' kid. Said I was always in a hurry, dashing from one thing to a next, impatient for programs to come up on the screen. Must admit, Ando, she could be right there.

But me an' her decided not to tell anyone except the Grands about time travel or warps or zones or the lads being in the past. Decided we couldn't not talk about them in some ways so we'd call 'em all environmentalists who tried hard to reduce their carbon footprint. Mum reckons, and I had to agree, it's a good description that fits the modern ideal of people who care for the future.

Anyway, old Potts at Sunbury's having me back an' I can start back there for final term – starts next week. It'll be good to be back, an' I haven't fallen behind so I'm happy about that. Those weeks in that Kendal school were tough enough. I think I'll be okay.

Like to hear from Steve – gave him my email address.

Potts surprised me. That counsellor had written him and given me a clean sheet, so said Potts. Great, and I even shook hands with him. Did it without thinking; got in the habit, I guess. His turn to be surprised. He liked what the Kendal principal had written about me, 'exemplary behaviour'. But he gave a few 'ahems' when he read the report.

'Eating his words,' Mum whispered to me as we left, and we both got the giggles.

I'd already fought back the giggles when he was reading it an' that mental picture of him on Tower Green kneeling at the block came into my head.

Told Tom that bit. He said he'd like to go to London. 'Yeh, mate. Reckon London is where I'd've stayed, been you.'

Only last night things kept me awake like when I was puzzling about the Spindle lads, early on. F'r instance, when I'm an old geezer – like my great-uncles over there near the house – would I think everything of now is old-fashioned? Though it'd probably be my own grandkids that'd be asking, wouldn't it? I'd have grown up learning it all as it happened.

Guess that's why Tom is sort of niggling me with his attitude. And that's not fair of me, because Tom is still Tom. I'm still Andy but I guess I've learned to look at things in a different way. Gran said travel broadens the mind. P'raps that's what she meant.

Good to have time to think but I'd better make my way back or someone'll come looking. All those kids. Some beaut meringues over there, all lemony inside. Hmm.

One really excellent thing: Tom told me Fat Rezzo's been expelled for bringing a knife to school. Not just suspended, he was kicked out. Done other things too, including trying it on with Grade 7 girls, dirty beggar. So he's gone. To Sydney, sez Tom. You bewdy.

Can't live in the past, though. Got to think of the future. After this school year, do I want to do the next years at Sunbury or should I go and live with Dad and finish off up there? Tom's off to some special maths school attached one of the unis. A special maths and science place. So we won't see much of each other.

The funny thing is I don't think I'll miss him as much as I did at first over there…

41

Ahah. Seems like some of the oldies are looking for their empty dishes and eskies. All that kissing the air round each other's ears. Yuk. Better show my face.

'Hey, Tom, there y'are. Come and check out the lemon meringues. Been watching young Aaron skimming down that handrail on that skateboard. Good mover.'

'Ando, what a mob of kids. I didn't realise you'd so many cousins, mate – first cousins, second, third. And they're all your family. Don't think I met any of 'em before, did I?'

'Prob'ly not. Didn't see 'em much. Live quite a way apart some of 'em, yet they drove here today just for us. Never really thought about having family, Tom. Changed my mind, being away. Look at 'em all.

Tom headed back to the meringues. 'You've gone weird, Ando.'

Well, his parents live together. Mine don't and Dad follows his job. Hoped to see Jake but he's playing in some charity match. I'll get his email address off Gruncle Pete.

Tom reckons calling great uncles gruncles is naff. Don't care; it's quicker than saying all the greats. Family tradition. And we say granny and grandad, so why not gruncles? Tom has a nana an' a pop. Just same, but different. Never thought of it before, really, but traditions are good to hang onto; friendly somehow.

Couple of blackbirds in that hedge somewhere. Not native to Aussie but a reminder of Tommo Lee. Still don't think you could put a hole in a cherry stone... Two little green parrots in the jacaranda. Yep, this is really home.

Been away eighteen weeks altogether. That right? Seems only yesterday we left Singleton Park and the middle of the twentieth century. Phew.

Mum's standing near the front door over there as Gran's getting hugs an' kisses. Grandad's about somewhere, chatting. Dad couldn't come today but Skyped last night.

Mum thinks I should see more of Dad, do more 'guy stuff'. Sez she doesn't know what it's like being a young man – cool – and he does. Well, I know she's got another book planned. That means she'll monopolise the computer and forget I'm around – again. Yep, good fishing in Darwin. Not much cricket in the tropics, though. Helps make up my mind for next year.

There's Tom, showing off his skateboard tricks to the younger kids. Young Aaron's sitting on the step with his DS.

'Hey, AJ. What game you got? Aah, which Star Wars is this, then?'

He's a good kid and explains the story. Knows every single one of the characters in the whole bloomin' series, does AJ. I got my DS in my pocket but my games aren't for him. Yet. No marbles today. The steelies and alleys came back with me, to Australia and the twenty-first century. They all survived the trip and the time warp but nobody plays a decent marble game any more – well, not here.

The oldies are still into their goodbyes. Gruncle David telling a joke, and the youngest grunc, Mike, all leathered up for his ride home on the Harley. I'll ask him for another ride one day soon; powerful machine. Gruncle Pete's into old cars, but can't drive now, eye probs. Gruncle Roj collects vintage motorbikes; not for him the Harleys and he rides on a Horrox bike in the Bay to Birdwood. Quite a mix of Graunties as well and their kids with little kids. Not bad for a family, all told. An' they all here together because of me and Mum. An' Gruncle Roj's birthday. Family gives a good feeling. Never really thought of it before I went away. Now it feels good, it bloomin' does.

Mum and Gran have woven a crazy conspiracy of theories about the Big House and all that family over there. Beyond being green. So weird. I don't listen any more but I blew my top when she harped on about that.

'Mum, you talk impossible stuff. We went into the past with the aggie, sure. Great people, and I miss 'em like crazy. But for you to think just because Gran came from there that they're related to you – Mum, your imagination is in overdrive.'

I just couldn't hack all that rubbish. Okay, now it's my turn to get real. Another lemon tart on this table too. Yum. Here's Alexander, coming over – one of the older ones, he's okay. Older'n me.

'Hi, Alex – good game of tennis on the Wii earlier. You slayed me.' *He grins.* 'Got one at home, mate. I had the edge on you. And on your mate Tom. Your mum says another guy called Alex might come out here for a holiday. Another cousin or sump'n? I'd like that, meet new rellies from over there. Cheers, now. See ya round.' *He turns.* 'Hey, Andy, come over to ours soon, eh? Planning a paintball session for my next birthday. Be fun.'

'Yo. Will do. Seeya, Alex.'

He grins again and walks off. I think you gotta be sixteen to go to a paintball thing. Huh. I stuff the last meringue in my mouth, turn round…and there's Gruncle Roger.

'Hi, Gruncle Roj. Happy hundredeth birthday.'

He grins at me an' flicks my ear. He's not bad for a gruncle.

'Cheeky tyke. How old d'you expect me to be? Thirteen?'

I step back. Freaky. How does he know I was thinking of thirteen? Okay, of Jimbo, anyway…

He holds his hand out, fingers beckoning. 'Got your DS on you?'

I fish it from my pocket. Typical oldie – techno stuff turns 'em on but give 'em a remote for the TV an' they're lost.

'Ahah. Still got the mark from when Billy dropped it in the old stables, I see.' *He hands it back and slaps his heavy hand on my shoulder.*

'Huh? What? How d'you…?' *I go a bit wobbly; put my DS back into my pocket.*

He bends down a little bit and looks me in the eyes. 'You okay, Ando? Hey, remember who picked it up?'

My mouth's stuck, I'm choking; I cough and his hand holds me steady. And like when Ma Lee held her hands on my shoulder, I'm hearing that hissing noise in my ears. I close my eyes. Not steady on my feet at all.

I'm not believing this… Crazy stuff.

A slight squeeze on my shoulder an' I open my eyes. He's taller but not much and I can look straight into his. They're Jimmy's eyes. Six weeks or six decades, it's Jimbo. Under that mop of grey hair and that chunky, leathery-skin face, it's Jimbo.

Can't get my voice… Feel I'm looking pop-eyed, wobbly on my pins… I'm trying to focus, staring… Gruncle's big smiley face, in front of me and it's dissolving, slowly; like when kids throw a pebble in a pond and make ripples. His smile is pure Jimmy – Jimbo. Like that victory smile when he won Aggie and wouldn't let me try to get it back. Triumphant, that's the word. That last day in the stables. So long ago. Yet not.

My knees are quivering. I blink, trying to swallow to wet my voice. My feet won't move but my heart's hitting me in my throat. I feel tears running down my face, oh shi-vers. Like I'm a kid.

Grunc Jimmy-Roj takes his hand away and laughs his big hearty laugh. 'Got your army keks on, I see. You haven't changed a bit.' *He chucks me under the chin and my teeth clunk together. He throws his head back, laughing, then pulls his hand from his pocket, and with his other, reaches for mine.* 'Okay. Hold out your sticky palm, Ando.'

Like a kid again, I hold my hand out, thinking he'd give me a peppermint – all the oldies have peppermints. No. He unrolls his fingers, drops something into my hand, then rolls my fingers over – whatever. It's hard, it's small, and…

'It's the aggie. *It's the aggie.*'

Then my spit dries up in my mouth. The little green marble. How…? Impossible. Jimmy took it back… But it musta been here all the time, hey. Cool. But how?

Gruncle Roj is smiling at me. A sort of sorry smile, one that slowly widens. He winks. Jimmy's wink. He does a half turn to walk away.

Then he turns back, an' his voice is sad. He doesn't wink this time. 'Like I said, Ando, you haven't changed. But time's caught up with me, eh?'

Dunno what to say, if even I could. I watch him walk to the house an' he turns a last time an' wiggles his fingers at me. My head's still trying to get round it. Gran turns to look at me. She's grinning so wide; I don't believe it.

Mum's running over to me, calling at me. 'Andy. Oh, Andy.'

She's known of course. She's been trying to tell me an' I said it was rubbish. Earlier on I tried to tell her and she told me it was all rubbish. So 'course I believed someone who's always talking stuff about facts and evidence. But now she knows and she knows I know. We both know. Not sure what, exactly.

My spit comes back an' I'm swallowing but words won't come out. I'm choked. Totally. Absolutely.

Little Aggie, my mascot. Called her my passport. She's here in my hand again. Thought I'd lost her for good. For ever. So…yep so… how come Gruncle Roj has had her over here, all the time, at the same time? Weird. Don' get it.

I close my fingers and feel that friendly tingle again; like holding a new-laid egg. I swallow, bite my lip.

Here's Mum, grabbing my hand and opening my fingers.

'Mum. It was…I think…about six weeks ago I lost Aggie… and it's really six decades… Mum, he's Jimmy. Gruncle Roj is Jimmy. Grown-up. He's a grandpa and Mo, oh no. Mo is… Gran's scar… 'nd here's Aggie. The other gruncles…who…?'

She's squeezing me so tight I nearly topple over onto her.

'Okay, love, calm down. I can't explain either, Andy. Let's just accept being – what was that word you used?'

'Gobsmacked, Mum. Sure, certain and f'r a fact. Gobsmacked.'